A Place to Call Home

A Place to Call Home

Ruth Glover

Five Star • Waterville, Maine

Published in 2004 in conjunction with Beacon Hill Press of Kansas City.

The text of this edition is unabridged.

Set in 11 pt. Plantin by Al Chase.

Printed in the United States on permanent paper.

Library of Congress Cataloging-in-Publication Data

Glover, Ruth.
    A place to call home / Ruth Glover.
       p. cm.—(The wild rose series ; bk. 6)
    ISBN 1-59414-054-5 (hc : alk. paper)
     1. Wildrose (Sask.)—Fiction.   2. Women pioneers—
Fiction.   I. Title.
PS3557.L678P58 2004
   813′.54—dc21
                                        2003053919

In loving memory of
Queena Campbell-Morrison Vogt
full Scotswoman and all lady—
my mother and queen of the bush parsonage
where I was born and raised.

1

The afternoon sun glinted on the brilliant mass of hair that tumbled around a face oddly at variance with its brightness. Lolly Dalton's face, in fact, was rebellious, and her lips, as vivid in their way as her hair, were twisted with what seemed at the moment like bitterness. Her eyes, an unusual tawny mix of colors, were fixed on an approaching opening in the bush and a glimpse of an insignificant huddle of buildings.

"I might have known!" Her words were hardly discernible over the wagon's rattle, and her eyes blinked furiously at betraying tears.

Hearing the half-sigh, half-groan, Minnie Dalton swiveled to look at her daughter, whose quickly turned head revealed nothing. But Lolly's stiff shoulders and the hands clasped tensely in her faded calico lap spoke volumes.

"This is the place—at last—I do believe," Minnie said quickly and cheerfully. "And it looks like a real homey place."

Why can't she at least be honest? Lolly thought despairingly. But always and ever, Minnie was supportive of her husband and his plans.

"Yep, this is bound to be it," Hudson Dalton verified and slapped the reins on the dusty backs of the plodding horses. The patient beasts responded halfheartedly, quickening their pace momentarily, perhaps as disheartened by the prospects before them as the girl in the shabby wagon behind them.

But the setting was lovely. The homestead in a remote corner of the Canadian bush was rampantly green with fresh new growth—growth that sprang lavishly from what Lolly knew was rich black soil, soil that had the reputation of great fertility. Gardens and crops grew beyond expectations; hay flourished abundantly in the meadows, standing as high as the cattle fortunate enough to pasture in them.

Lolly Dalton had fallen in love with the bush, or parkland strip, of Saskatchewan as soon as the lumbering wagon had made its slow way into it. She was relieved to leave the windswept prairie and her father's abortive attempt to gouge a living from it. Lolly suspected that the challenge of the undertaking had been more than her parents could accept. Here in the bush the farms were smaller—usually a quarter of a section. But would they offer an easier way?

The necessity to clear their land of its thick trees and bush, where many days the temperature dropped to 40 below, unsuitable for labor, was a monumental and daunting task. If a homestead was not "proved up" in the required three years and a house erected, it was forfeited. Life for pioneers anywhere in the Northwest Territories—whether on prairie, bush, or boreal forest tract—was almost unbearably hard. Tremendous sacrifices had to be made to get a foothold and endure. Winters were long and summers short; mosquitoes and flies drove man and beast alike to distraction. Food, the homegrown variety, was usually available in fair supply, but the fare was monotonous; cash was almost unheard of. This often caused the man of the household to seek work outside of farming, which delayed proving up the land and placed a near-impossible strain on his wife. No doctor was available, most places, in case of accident or illness. And loneliness was a thing to be reckoned with. Only the strong, the determined, the desperate endured.

Would Hudson Dalton endure? *Could* he endure?

Although Lolly loved the big bluff man who was her father, she no longer had any unrealistic expectations of his performance. The prairie had been too formidable for him—

and for Lolly as well! How her heart had plummeted as, day after day, they had trundled across the endless plains a year ago, seeking a home, following a dream as ephemeral as a will-o'-the wisp.

"Yep, this is it," Hud Dalton said, pulling the team to a halt at a spot that looked no different from any other from one horizon to the other. Silently the family gazed at—nothing. Even Minnie had nothing to say.

Rufus, Lolly's older brother, and Tobias, just 19, looked behind and before, left and right, and were wordless. Perhaps it was from awe, for certainly the prairie was beyond description for vastness and emptiness. More likely it was from helplessness. Helplessness on Rufe's part because it would be up to him, largely, to turn the sod if it were to be turned at all; helplessness on young Toby's part because of his own physical weakness in the face of the overwhelming challenge. Toby was ill much of the time and in despair about it.

But the family's initial feelings of helplessness out on the prairie certainly didn't change Hudson Dalton's perspective about the situation, even if he noticed their reaction. With the hot summer sun beating down on the wagonload of the Dalton family's entire worldly goods and the bare prairie stretching around, Hud Dalton climbed down from the wagon and set up the tent. How many of these sorry camps or abandoned shacks the family had inhabited over the years— stove set up out in the open, surrounded by boxes, quilts flung into the tent—Lolly could no longer clearly recall, or cared to for that matter. But the sensitive child had keenly felt the dreariness of it all. Now as a young woman, she found a certain anger was mixed with the despair that threatened.

The problem with Hud Dalton, his daughter finally realized with shame, was that he wanted something for nothing.

And not wanting much, he made little effort to get more.

Hud Dalton could almost certainly be called a "squatter," and in more ways than one. When he located an empty cabin or piece of land, he moved in with perfect equanimity, regardless of who might have prior legal rights, and stayed until one of two things happened: either he was forced to decamp, or sheer hunger and necessity for supplies urged him out and on, so the family moved again.

At times Hud found work, but always he followed another silent beckoning to what he unflaggingly thought of as greener pastures. And when they moved on, Minnie planted a garden and the children foraged for food—not impossible if one knew how to go about it. On the prairies, game had been plentiful. Rufe had become adept at hunting the ubiquitous prairie chicken, and Toby had done his part by trapping the bounding and abounding rabbits. Lolly had eaten quite enough rabbit stew for an entire lifetime.

How long would Rufe, now an adult, put up with it? No doubt about it: Rufus Dalton was disenchanted and not always successful in covering his growing frustration. The year on the prairie had seen his full maturing; Rufe would soon be his own man, and Lolly dreaded the day this pillar of strength would not be nearby.

Having survived the horrors of a winter in a sod house on the prairie, Lolly had been almost desperately relieved to be on the move—again. And this time, northward.

Their destination was Prince Albert, on the banks of the North Saskatchewan River. It was undoubtedly one of the most picturesque settlements in the Dominion. Immigrants were arriving steadily; the trickle would eventually swell to great numbers of land-hungry men and women eager for some of the last "free" land available anywhere, and certainly some of the best. Along with its beauty—a beauty of trees and bush, rivers and lakes, birdsong and big skies—or perhaps because of it, there was a raw exuberance among the prospective landowners. And it would be needed, if they were to persist and survive. Some arrived pitifully poor and ill-equipped; others, more fortunate, arrived comfortably well off and well-equipped to set up productive farms. Prince Albert and the Lands Office were the logical starting places.

In Prince Albert, Lolly, for so long denied even the conventional things of life, saw as opulence what was merely ordinary. The established houses were so different from the Daltons' shifting, disreputable tent; the general stores had a wonderful array of household goods, so unlike the Daltons' makeshift gear; the grocery stores were filled to abundance, so tantalizing when compared to rabbit stew; the clothing stores showed fashions so changed that Lolly blushed at the sight of herself reflected in the store window, her skirt too short, her bodice too tight.

Not having seen for years more than her face in the small mirror available to her, Lolly gasped and clasped her arms over her too-obviously-revealed bosom in her too-tight dress. Now she understood the bold glances and bolder winks that numerous males had bestowed upon her. Now she understood Rufe's rough suggestion that she keep to the tent and away from town.

Before she turned from the tantalizing and revealing store window, Lolly clutched her clothes around her too-slim middle with its mouth-watering cravings but could do little about her heart and its hungers.

Surely Prince Albert offered an opportunity for a willing man to make a living for his family! With its sawmill, flour mill, newspaper, new railway, cheese factory, and creamery, certainly there were jobs for skilled and unskilled labor, not to mention the logging, fishing, and threshing when in season.

Lolly's heart quickened with hope.

But that evening at their campfire on the riverbank, Hudson Dalton made a casual reference to the Klondike, and gold.

"I saw an advertisement today," Lolly almost babbled in her anxiety, "for a wheelwright . . . another for a freightman—"

"Never done any of those things," Hud said. "Now gold— with all of us working at it, we could make our pile in a hurry—"

Uncharacteristically and abruptly, Rufe interrupted. "Forget the Klondike," he said. "It may be for *you. Not* for the family."

In the silence that fell on the group, Hudson Dalton looked at his oldest son with some surprise. Perhaps he hadn't noticed Rufe's growing discontent across the last year they had spent on the prairie. Rufe's square, bronzed face, darkened with something other than wind and weather, may have gone unseen. Perhaps Hud hadn't paid attention to the long silences and the grim lips. Obviously he didn't recognize the signs now, for he pursued the idea of the Klondike and its gold.

"People are going in with homemade sailing sleds," he said admiringly, "even strings of mountain goats hitched up like teams of horses, pulling sleds over the pass."

"Even bicycles, I've heard," Toby offered wistfully.

"And if they make it in," Rufe countered, "they live in tar paper shacks, or holes in the hillsides, like gophers." His words were clipped and cold and conjured up uneasy memories of the soddy.

"So?" his father questioned mildly.

Even Minnie, who was as easygoing as her husband, looked doubtful. "I don't know . . . ," she murmured uncertainly.

"Come on, old girl," Hud said cheerfully, "you wouldn't back out on me now, would you?"

Minnie, as always, warmed to his cajolery and gave her husband a wavering smile.

If only Mum would expect a little more, Lolly thought and not for the first time, *things might be different.*

But they were two of a kind, Minnie and Hudson, and happy in their own way, Lolly supposed.

Rufe put down his plate and rose abruptly, a tall, strong young man, ruggedly attractive in spite of worn clothes and an uncut thatch of brown hair—hair that was tinged in the day's late sun with the same flash of fire that made his sister so immediately eye-catching.

"You're not taking Mum and Lolly to the Klondike," he said in no uncertain terms, "and I'm not going either."

Hud drooped dispiritedly at the very thought that his son would not oblige him in another enterprise.

"Besides," Rufe finished before he walked away, "the Mounties won't let you cross the border without a ton of supplies. And that's per person."

And with this parting sally, Rufe strode away. Hud blinked and rubbed his chin.

Minnie was silent, torn between loyalties. Toby huddled, his arms around his knees beside the fire, his eyes dark in his thin face, his expression startled. Lolly barely restrained a hearty "Hooray!" for her older brother's courage.

In view of this conversation and its alarming possibilities for a split in the family, Lolly was relieved when, the following day, she saw her father standing outside the Dominion Lands Office. About to pass, she caught a snatch of conversation between Hud and one of the men standing in line waiting for his turn to enter.

"I'm just up from a spell of farming on the prairies,

myself," Hudson Dalton was saying. "Wife couldn't take any more of that soddy."

Lolly paused, surprised at this explanation. Not that her mother might have "taken" the soddy without grace, but that her father would blame the move on her.

The soddy—Lolly shuddered just to think about it. Inside, when completed, it had been about 12 feet wide by 22 feet long, with a 10-foot portion curtained off and divided to form two small areas for sleeping. The sod, cut in pieces about 2 feet by 13 inches and about 4 inches thick, had been laid bricklike, with two small openings for windows and another for a rough door. Set as deep as they were, the windows allowed very little light, and in winter the frost gathered more than an inch thick on the panes, increasing the gloom in which they stumbled or sat as close to the stove as possible during the long, nightmarish winter. Poles and sod formed the roof, and mud ran during every rainstorm.

There were no trees to provide protection from the wind; snow blew through cracks in the sod. Many nights the temperature dropped to 50 below and, in spite of rising often from bed to add fuel, they nearly froze; certainly their water pail and any food in the place froze solid. Laundry, not to mention bathing, done in the summer with water hauled from the distant coulee, became almost impossible in winter, and unpleasant odors added to an already miserable existence. Rufe's reference to a gopher was not amiss; he had learned from experience.

Coming to young womanhood in such conditions, Lolly had faced a bleak future. For the first time in her life she found herself praying for a move—one more move.

And now to find herself in this glorious northland! Lolly dared to think there might be something ahead for her after all.

14

And now her father was at the Lands Office. Surely that was a good sign.

In her reflections she had missed some of the conversation. The stranger was saying something about mosquitoes and flies, early frosts, summer storms, and hailstones big enough to kill a man or ruin his crop.

"Plenty of people can't take it," he reported. "Pioneering isn't for everyone—that's for sure. But usually it isn't the land that doesn't measure up—it's people's reactions to everything demanded of them. They can't take the work, the weather, the loneliness, or a dozen other things. Why, you'll find some homesteads just abandoned—"

"Yes?" Hudson Dalton said, perking up his ears.

"And sometimes they're well on their way to being proved up too. Sickness or discouragement drive some people out."

"Don't happen to know of any such place, do you?" Hud asked casually—too casually for the comfort of the listening Lolly.

"I do happen to. Out there—" and a pointed finger indicated an easterly direction, "about 20 miles—Wildrose."

"Wildrose?"

"That's the name of the district. Post office is Meridian. Well, anyway, man named Mellon pulled up stakes. His wife laid down the law. She had had more than enough, so out they went. His place is vacant . . . abandoned. It has a house on it, maybe a barn, some land cleared, of course. Yep, old Mellon turned around and headed back east—"

"Wildrose, you say?"

The line shortened and the men moved up and away from where Lolly half hid, listening. Wildrose! Surely her father would get in line. What an opportunity to get a place of their own!

With hope, that eternal, fragile blossom struggling to take root in her heart, Lolly went her way.

When she finally returned, it was to find her mother dismantling the tent, folding bedding, packing dishes.

"Come help," she called, pointing to boxes and barrels never too far away and now open and into which she was folding bedding, packing dishes, and laying clothes.

"We're going to a place called Wildrose," Minnie explained matter-of-factly. "Sounds good, doesn't it?"

Rufe, when he appeared, had taken a little persuading. He had spent several days at the river, unloading merchandise, cattle, or whatever newcomers were moving by means of the waterway. Rufe obviously wanted to stay in town and balked at the idea of another move, whether or not the place had the enticing name of Wildrose.

"You could help us locate the place, Rufe, and get settled," Hudson urged plaintively. And then, knowing his son, he added, "Your mother would make it better with you along."

What a low blow—and cunning! Looking over at his mother, who was puffing a little from the unusual amount of activity in which she was engaged, hampered by soft rolls of fat and already weary, Rufe breathed deeply a few times, clenched and unclenched his fists, caught a tentative smile from his mother, and capitulated. He knew he could indeed ease her load a little and perhaps bring a little cheer into her days. Silently he began loading the wagon.

Besides Rufe's earnings, Hudson had brought in a bit of money and Toby had worked several days at the livery stable. Minnie took their funds and went to the store, laying in a supply of food that was unusually bountiful for the Dalton family.

Before she left, "Add some nails," Rufe suggested.

"And mosquito netting!" Toby added, scratching.

"Soap, Mum! Get soap!" Lolly urged, remembering last winter and its noxious odors. And no telling how dusty the new house might be. Would it have curtains? A rug? This place might be a joy to fix up.

Busy with the task at hand, Lolly heard Rufe mutter, "The last time! This is the last time!"

"I'll help, Rufe—you'll see," Toby said quickly.

Rufe smiled at his younger, thinner brother. "I know you will. Look how you worked at the livery stable. Maybe life in the bush is just what you need, Toby."

Toby's pale face flushed. "I haven't had a turn for quite a while, have I?"

"You're much better already—see?" And Rufe tussled with his brother briefly. But gently, always gently.

With lighter hearts than they had known for a long time, the Daltons left Prince Albert and wended their way deep into the backwoods. The further they went, the more remote it all seemed, with roads turning into trails, farms farther apart, and much virgin growth. They noted with interest the small clearings, the plowed fields, and the lush meadows. They heard the thwack of grub hoes, the ringing of axes; they smelled the clean odor of wood smoke; they heard the bawl of new calves.

Some of the homes were built of logs, others of frame and more spacious. Everywhere folks were friendly; there was a camaraderie about the whole experience; invisible bonds united these newcomers into one grand purpose—to tame the wilderness, make it productive, and establish permanent homes.

Now, the second day out, following a trail that thrust them deeper and deeper into the bush, the Daltons had finally come across the small clearing, and Hud had decided, "Yep, this is bound to be it."

And Lolly's spirits—so expectant and so hopeful—had sunk. Expecting a place like many they had passed—with fields and pastures, outbuildings and sheds, and a substantial house into which they might drop anchor—she saw instead a weed-filled clearing, a low, lopsided pile of logs that apparently passed for a barn, and a ramshackle shed. In the absence of anything else, this quite obviously was the family abode . . . a shack—again.

Built in the shape of a lean-to, a sort of half room, the small structure was covered with tar paper. Lonely and neglected it stood, as though accepting its destiny of housing the Dalton clan.

"I might have known!" Lolly half moaned, half sobbed under her breath, and never heard the birdsong or noted the fragrance. It was at this moment she made her decision: "I'll just get out of this sort of life, no matter what I have to do or what it takes!"

They came near to being the sorriest words she ever uttered.

 2

"That's it—I quit!"

There was no one to hear the bitter announcement groaned from the grimacing lips of the man who clutched his middle, bent over with pain, his booted feet stumbling in the fresh furrow.

When he was somewhat recovered from the blow to his solar plexus, Donal Cardigan unhitched the team, leaving the offending walking plow with its blade still battered against the rock that had brought it to an abrupt halt and Donal sharply against the handles. Turned toward the farmyard, the horses stepped more lively than they had all day. If they had hit the buried rock at that speed, Donal might have gone tumbling—and not for the first time.

Today it was the last straw. Donal's thoughts, already wrestling with the idea of going west, suddenly firmed to a decision, given the last nudge by the vicious encounter with the rock in the field.

The plow blade, Donal now thought fleetingly, had certainly lived up to the company's warranty to "scour in any soil." The gravelly soil of Leif County, when it wasn't nicking the merciless blade, scoured it quite thoroughly.

The more stones Donal and his brother picked off, the more, it seemed, came up from below. And the call of the west, at first approach just a whisper and a beckon, had changed for Donal to a siren song and an unrelenting tug.

Perhaps it was the same siren song, ever renewed and resung in a man with an ear to hear, that had brought his father from Scotland to settle in Ontario earlier in the century.

The lure of the land—that's what it was. Men everywhere were feeling it. For Moody Cardigan, a dispossessed crofter, the opportunity to be a landowner was an inducement that overcame all obstacles. To such men, land was almost sacred and worth any sacrifice to obtain. And what a sacrifice they made!

For it was a hard land, harder than any settler could imagine. Unbearable heat in summer, winters too cold to be endured. Bush to be cleared, rocks to be hauled. Many a story ended with hailed out! burned out! frozen out! Many caved in; others endured and eventually made a success of it.

Moody Cardigan spent the first few years logging. But when a gravel road went in from Georgetown to Toronto and free land grants were available along that road, he took what he had saved, secured a grant, and wrote home to Margot Walsh, who bravely gave up home and family to join him.

"I never could have made it without a wife," Moody was known to have confessed. "I didn't have to look after the chickens, milk the cow, feed the pigs, tend the garden—"

And Margot would finish for him: "And churn the butter, bake the bread, make the soap, do the wash . . ."

Well, Moody was long gone and now, just a month ago, Margot had joined him in the hillside graves above the farm they had homesteaded and which their two sons continued to work. Moody, Jr., the oldest, had married Esther, and they were expecting their second child. Donal, working with his brother, had become increasingly dissatisfied, his thoughts and dreams turning toward the vast open areas to the west.

The stone, just one more in an endless succession of them, was the catalyst that drove the restless Donal to the final decision, "I quit!"

"Problems?" Moody asked mildly from the open barn door when Donal and the team approached, with the plow quite obviously missing and the field unfinished.

"Wind knocked out of me," Donal answered, beginning to remove the harness from the horses.

"Another rock, I suppose."

"Moody," Donal said almost savagely, "I'll never put another plow into this soil!"

Moody set aside the pitchfork he had been holding and walked to where his brother was doggedly unhitching.

"Easy, Donal. You'll feel better tomorrow—"

"Don't count on it! By working ourselves almost to the nub we manage a bare living, Moody. If it weren't for Esther's egg and butter money, we'd never make it. Seems such hard work ought to have a better reward!"

"Some years aren't all that bad—"

"Even good years, it's not enough for two families. No," he said quickly in response to his brother's raised eyebrow, "I haven't got matrimonial plans—how could I, considering how things are?" And Donal gave a strap a yank.

"Moody," he added, straightening and looking his brother in the eye, "I'm getting out—going west."

"I knew you'd been thinking about it. All those reports coming from the Hager boys, not to mention the flood of pamphlets circulating all around the country."

"You could hardly go if you wanted to," Donal said, and Moody looked uncomfortable, "what with Esther's family here, a new baby coming, and all. And you'll do all right alone. Maybe get a hired man for little or nothing in busy times. There's just not enough here for both of us."

Moody knew he was right. And perhaps, secretly, he envied his brother.

"You sure about this, Donal?" was all he said, however.

"I'm sure, Moody," Donal replied more gently, but without hesitation, and his brother sighed.

"I can't give you what your share in the place is worth," Moody said, and Donal shrugged the idea aside.

"I'll sell the cattle that are mine . . . you can have the horses." And Donal whacked the released pair on the rump and watched them move toward the water trough.

"I won't need much—just a ten dollar filing fee!" Donal's grin was lopsided in his bronzed face. Taller than Moody, standing an inch over six feet, wide shouldered and narrow hipped, with powerful arms and strong hands, Donal's coloring was an inheritance from some long ago and distant dark-visaged Scot highlander. His black hair, damp from his exertions, curled slightly and capped his head neatly. His face, wedge shaped and as strong, in its way, as his body, had long ago lost any boyish softness. His eyes, blue as the Canadian sky in the morning, were deep-set. Donal's decision was a firm one and based on some knowledge of the distant area he had in mind—the homesteads of the Territories.

"You'll need a lot more than a filing fee," Moody, as informed as his brother, said now. "I heard it's almost a necessity to arrive with a thousand dollars. Why, you'll need everything. Unless, that is, you plan to take some of this." Moody's hand took in the scattered machinery, the leaning pitchfork, a nearby shovel, the harness . . .

"You need it all," Donal said. "Besides, I couldn't pay the shipping charges. No, I'll just have to manage some way."

"I can hardly bear to think of you living away out there alone," Esther said at the supper table. "Perhaps in a soddy or shack, far from anyone. You could freeze and no one would know!"

"But the soil, Esther! Think of the rich, black dirt! Men are putting in potatoes as soon as they break sod and getting a crop the first year. And it's free!"

"If they have seed potatoes," Esther responded skepti-

cally, and silence fell momentarily.

Their conversation was interrupted by the sound of a horse's hoofs. Moody rose from the table and opened the door to a neighbor, who called before he turned his horse and went on, "John Hager is home . . . looking for a wife, they say. But it's a good time to ask questions. Some of us are riding on over; come on, if you want to."

"Maybe we'll do that. Thanks, Tom."

Donal was already rising from the table, reaching for his coat.

John Hager set himself in the middle of the room and readily answered the questions of the men gathered in the Hager house. He was dressed dashingly in what he called a "shaganappi" coat that was heavily beaded and fringed on the seams. Though he was wearing leather boots, he showed them moccasins made, he said, by the Indians. The rare items passed around for inspection.

"Nah, there's no Indian trouble," he assured them. "After Riel and his rebellion was put down, a lot of the principal chiefs were taken by train to Winnipeg and cities in the east here, so they could see the almost endless number of white men. Sure quieted them down, I hear, and everything's been peaceful ever since."

His audience looked relieved, at least on that score.

"Once you get to Winnipeg," John explained, "you can just take off in any direction. Joe and Pete and me, we took off north, finally met a man in this tiny village who offered to show us some land, and then we could go and file on it. When he come with his wagon, he said, 'North, south, east, or west?' "

John's listeners just shook their heads, awed into silence.

"After an hour or so, this feller stopped his team, waved

his hand, and said, 'Here it is. Take your pick.' So we all made our selection, just like that.

"First thing," John went on, "was to build us a shelter— just a shack, but it did until we could do better. Now I got me a house—"

"And need a wife, eh, John?" someone asked cannily, and everyone laughed knowingly.

"Not only for me," John confided, "but for my brothers too. Pete and Joe, they need wives too, and only one of us could come."

"You're going to pick all three?" someone scoffed.

"Sure thing! And I'm going right over here next door to get 'em."

"The Wimber girls? Ah, c'mon! What makes you think you can round up them three, just like fillies, and herd 'em back there with you?"

"It's not like that!" John defended quickly. "We been writing for months—"

"And they're willin' to go?"

"Willing? Rarin' to go, more like!" And John Hager blushed happily while his friends and neighbors hooted.

"Yep," the prospective bridegroom continued, "Sal, Mary, Peg—all signed and sealed and soon to be delivered. That leaves Belinda—" John studied the eager faces pressed around him. "I think she'd be willin', given a chance. Any takers?"

Donal decided it was no time to reveal his interest, though he was full of questions; he settled back and listened to the topics raised by the others and, in so doing, had some of his own questions answered.

Listing some of the items necessary for life in the bush, John said, "Three axes, not a one less."

"For Sal, Mary, and Peg?" some wit commented.

24

"Just to be safe," John explained seriously. "You might lose one and break one—then where would you be?"

The very idea of being so isolated as to be without an ax was a sobering thought, especially if one's fuel depended on it, not to mention the vigorous clearing of the brush and trees for proving up.

"What else?" someone piped.

"What not! A team, of course, and a plow. Sometimes, if you're lucky enough to have a neighbor with implements, you can borrow the others—harrow, seeder, and so on. Should have a cow, 'specially if there's kids."

"Or if you like butter on your bread."

"Bannock, more like, if you're a bachelor."

"Well, let's see. Saws, of course. Nails. Oh, everything," John concluded, frustrated. "I'll warn you about this, though: there are billions of gophers! Everywhere, eating constantly, their little bellies fat with our good grain! Neighbor's boy has 300 gopher tails; gov'ment puts a bounty on 'em. The kid'll be rich before any of the rest of us.

"And rabbits," John continued, warmed to his subject. "Millions of rabbits. People mow 'em down with a shotgun, load up a stone-boat, and drag 'em home. Skin 'em out, feed 'em to the chickens, or throw 'em in a big pot and cook 'em and feed 'em to the pigs—if you've got pigs.

"Prairie chicken," John continued, encouraged by his rapt audience, "skillions of those."

"Billions of gophers . . . millions of rabbits . . . skillions of prairie chickens. What next?"

Undisturbed, John went on with the prairie chicken story. "Thick as fleas. Shoot 'em out of the trees, in winter, and skin 'em. Great meat. In the fall, I declare if there isn't a prairie chicken on every stook—"

"Whadd'ya mean, skin 'em? Don't you mean pluck 'em?"

"Nah. Skinning's quicker. Anyways, you can live pretty well right off the land, one way or the other. And then there's always oatmeal. I'm plumb sick of oatmeal, I can tell you."

Wolves . . . coyotes . . . bears . . . deer. John covered them all. Donal's head was swimming when it came time to leave. But the dream endured; it was strengthened.

Walking home together, Moody and Donal discussed the idea, now shaping into reality, of Donal's move.

"It's daunting, to say the least," Moody said thoughtfully. "You could get off, if you go by train, out in the middle of nowhere. North, south, east, west—nothing but bare land."

"That's the prairie, of course. The bush now—that would be much different."

"Which did you have in mind?"

"I don't really know. Actually, this whole venture isn't too clear in my mind, Moody. Maybe I'll just strike out, play it by ear."

"That doesn't sound like a very good idea to me."

"I'm young, strong, willing to work. Something will turn up. I may have to get a job somewhere first, to earn enough money to outfit myself."

"You'll get a fair amount for the cows and your bull. Your mare—you'll take her?"

"I think so. You know how attached I am to her, having raised her from a foal. Anyway, she's a great riding horse, and I imagine a man will do a lot of that before he finds where he'll settle and afterward going here and there, back and forth. I'd hate to plow with her; hopefully I'll be able to do something about a team."

"Oxen, maybe. Slower, but easier to feed. Cheaper to buy too."

"We'll see. I want to get on my way as soon as possible, Moody. There'll be so much to do before snowfall."

"It'll be good-bye for a long time, Donal."

Soberly now the brothers continued their walk, aware that from this time on their paths would be greatly divergent.

Donal saw the lamps of home with a lump in his throat. When next he should have a home with a window, and a lamp in it, he didn't know. And would that light be but a pinprick lost in the endless prairies, or a faint glow reflecting on pressing masses of near-impenetrable bush?

 3

As in that other attempt to set up housekeeping and make a living on the prairie a year or so ago, the Dalton family sat momentarily in silence. Only the harness creaked as a horse twitched.

Lolly, desperately yearning for a decent, perhaps homelike place, gazed dismally on the scene. If she had had ears to hear, she would have caught the steady hum of bees and other insects and the musical trills of numerous birds issuing from the surrounding bush. If she had had eyes to see, she would have observed the wildflowers nodding in the greenery that carpeted the yard. Her straight little nose, rather than wrinkling with distaste, might have caught and relished fragrances never savored before, an introduction to the bush and its clean, woodsy smell.

Rufus, no doubt instantly picturing the amount of work that would be required of him—to build onto the shack, strengthen the lopsided barn, fix the sagging corral, and, more immediately, set up camp and rustle firewood—felt the soft bands of his father's uselessness tighten around his heart like iron chains. If he had done what he felt like doing, he would have thrown his cap onto the ground and stomped on it in impotent rage and disappointment.

Minnie, true to form, squared her rounded shoulders, fixed a smile on her plump features, and never entertained a thought other than that they would, as always, exist here, as in other places, until beckoned further afield. One place was as good as another to Minnie; her placid nature refused to be put in turmoil over so simple a matter as keeping house.

Hudson, if disappointed, didn't show it. After all, rent would be free (until some authority found out about them and ordered them off or to pay up), it was early summer and beautiful, his wife and children were with him, and winter and further decisions were a few months away. He saw green grass for the horses, berry bushes that would bear in season, and, if he wasn't sadly mistaken, a well. It was enough to cause his lips to pucker in a soundless whistle.

Of them all, Toby was the one to feel the peace of the place called Wildrose. He breathed deeply into his narrow chest the good clean air and found it pure perfume, he saw the green arms of the bush as if it welcomed him personally, and he imagined the small clearing as waiting for him. Toby closed his eyes and breathed again and again, and something very like passion warmed his meager heart, the passion of heart for home and hearth and happiness. Like a young and tender shoot in the process of being transplanted, Toby almost felt the roots of his being searching, searching for permanence. That he might find it in the rich, black soil of the parkland seemed entirely reasonable; that the sturdy, warmhearted people of the bush might aid in the cultivation and flourishing of the sprout that was Toby Dalton was a probability that never presented itself. The bush itself was enough for Toby at this moment.

Surprisingly, his first lucid thought was of a dog. Though he had never owned one, it seemed right and proper that he should. He would always think he had the thought first and then the dog appeared, but perhaps he had caught a fleeting glimpse of it before ever the idea entered his mind.

At any rate, the black-and-white creature, tongue lolling and tail wagging, bounded alongside the Dalton wagon and looked up happily.

The entire clan turned their gazes toward the dog to raise

their surprised eyes to watch the cow, also black and white, coming down the road toward them, her udder tossing heavily, her gait sedate but determined. And no wonder; a girl, stick in hand, followed closely behind.

Bossy sidestepped, at the urging of the stick, and lumbered past the wagon. The girl, a surprised look on her round yet pretty face, paused. Her thick, fair hair hung in a braid over one shoulder, her dress, faded but clean, revealed a girlish figure that was sturdy, firm, and richly brown wherever flesh showed. Her rounded arm, strong graceful neck, bare legs, and scratched feet—as well as her healthy, glowing face—all were darker than her wheaten hair.

Though her feet were bare and her gown old, there was no hint of self-consciousness in the eyes—blue and frank—that lifted to the people in the wagon. Her voice, when she spoke, had the faintest suggestion of an accent, as though raised in a home where some language other than English was spoken.

"Hello," she said, and her smile was as friendly as her dog's wag; her teeth were white and as strong and healthy as the rest of her.

"Hello," Hudson Dalton responded and smiled. Who, after all, could help but smile? Country-bred and totally at home in the rural setting, the girl was a picture of composure and contentment. Toby, a stranger, felt his heart fill with some sort of recognition for the way of life she personified, though he had never known it.

"Is this the Mellon place?" Hudson asked.

"Yes. Yes, it is. Are you going to live here? It's been vacant for, oh, for months now. As you can see."

"Won't take long to make it homelike," Hudson said blandly and no doubt thought he was speaking the truth.

"We'll be glad to have neighbors again. The Mellons," the fresh, young face was suddenly touched with sadness, "had to leave because Mrs. Mellon wasn't well. We think perhaps she couldn't take the long winter . . . in that tiny place."

"We?" Hudson asked.

"My mum and dad, my brother Billy and me. Our name is Szarvas. My name's Katrin, but I'm called Kitty."

Not a good name for her, Toby thought. Kittens were soft and cuddly, almost boneless in their pliancy. This girl, from her direct eyes to her bare feet, was a picture of sturdy good health—all vibrant flesh and good humor. One half-expected her to smell like fresh-mown hay. But there was a peace about her, a calmness—perhaps even a placidity, though Toby found himself hoping not. Would there be a spark of fun about this girl, or was she all tranquillity?

Perhaps the first real clue to Katrin Szarvas's nature was revealed at this, their first meeting. A faint cheep caught their attention in the brief moment's silence, and Kitty, her face immediately solicitous, put her square, small hand in her skirt pocket and withdrew, to the interested gaze of the Daltons and the excited interest of the dog, a young bird.

Holding it cupped gently, she raised it to eye level, turned it with care, and studied a wing. Then, still without any explanation, the tiny woodland creature was returned carefully to the pocket.

"It just needs a little care," she finally said, noting the staring faces above her in the wagon. "I'll take it home, with the others."

"There are others?" Toby said, speaking for the first time since their meeting Kitty.

"You'd be surprised how many deaths and injuries there are in the bush. Lots of creatures [*Would that include people?* Toby wondered fleetingly] wouldn't make it without special care. That cow—" she indicated the animal now half-turned in her tracks, as though preparing to return, "her newborn

31

baby is dead back there. Something has eaten on it." Again her face took on that grieved expression. "She keeps trying to go back; that's why I have to have this stick; it's for her own good."

Truly, it looked as if this was one situation when it hurt the switcher more than the switched.

"Too bad," Hudson said, while various members of his family uttered small sounds of sympathy. To lose any farm animal could well be a tragedy. But Kitty, it seemed, was concerned only with the mother cow's tragedy.

"I better get her home," she offered now and turned to go. "We live about half a mile that way. You be sure and let us know if we can help. I'm sure my dad will be over . . . probably my mum." She looked directly at Toby. "You're about the age of my brother . . . 18 or 19?"

Toby could only nod and give this composed young lady a sort of grin.

"Be glad to meet them," Hudson Dalton said, preparing to move on, only to pause and add, "Better introduce ourselves," and the girl waited.

"We're the Daltons. I'm Hudson, this is my wife, Minnie, my sons, Rufus and Tobias," Hud indicated each young man in turn, and each nodded, "and this is my girl, Lolita."

Why does he insist on calling her that? Toby thought, suddenly angry. *He knows she hates it.*

But Kitty only blinked, though Lolly turned crimson.

Hudson finished. "Lolita is some older than you, I expect. She's a year older than Toby."

"And I'm two years younger than my brother." Now that the introductions were completed, Kitty backed away a few steps, turned, and ran lightly toward the cow to tap it ever so gently with the stick and urge it on down the road.

Heads lowered and standing three-legged, the team was

chirruped to activity, and Hudson turned the wagon into the yard and toward the shack. "Haw, Maude!" he chirruped. "Haw, Claude!"

I'm surprised he didn't introduce her to Maude and Claude, Toby thought, still in turmoil for his sister's sake. Her fanciful name, the result of some story Minnie had read before her daughter's birth, had long been a tender spot with Lolly in a day when Abigails, Marys, Hesters, Ethels, and Idas were in vogue. Even "Lolly," the best diminutive she could come up with, didn't please her. "Sounds like some cheap tramp," she had fumed once when the topic was under discussion.

And certainly Lolly's presence, in camp or on the boardwalk, did solicit bold glances far too often. Both Rufe and Toby had bristled, if they were present, and silenced outright whistles more than once.

It's those clothes, Toby thought now, giving his sister a speculative glance, . . . *partly.*

True, Lolly was bursting out of her clothes. But it was more than that. Her brilliant coloring, especially of cheeks and lips, and that vivid hair could never be disguised no matter how concealing her garments might be. Toby sighed. He knew his sister to be modest, unassuming. Toby surmised that it was a diffidence produced by their situation and lack. Lolly, he felt, might have been a young lady of poise and self-assurance, given a chance. He also knew that he might have a better feeling about himself, under better circumstances. Ruefully he noticed the white skin of his bare knee through a hole in his pants and couldn't help comparing it with the sun-touched limbs of the girl Kitty. Just before leaping to the ground, Toby yanked off his boots, hastily turned up his pants' cuffs, and rolled up his shirtsleeves.

"Wildrose, here we come!" he caroled in an exuberance so unlike him that everyone momentarily stopped what they

33

were doing to gaze at the youngest member of the family with surprise.

"Don't get used to it, kid," Rufe muttered. "It can't be for long."

"A dog," Toby announced. "That's the first thing we need!"

 4

Donal helped his brother remove the offending rock that had stopped the plow and rammed him into it and haul it to the edge of the field where it joined others that had been up-thrust throughout the Cardigans' years on the Ontario homestead. But true to his word, he did not plow there again.

He and Moody, when his brother had time, were busy going through various items, selling those they could to make a fund for Donal's great adventure. It was a wrenching decision, but he finally parted with his horse; the cost of shipping her was far too great and would leave him with funds too limited to set up homesteading in the west where he would have everything to buy, household goods as well as farm equipment.

"It'll be pretty skimpy going for a while, I'm afraid," he acknowledged, and dear Esther mourned, regretting that the abundance of goods in the house could not be divided too. But Donal refused to consider carting and shipping—too expensive, too worrisome, he said.

"Someone told me the homesteader's first home is his wagon turned upside down," he said.

"But you don't have a wagon!" Esther reminded him.

"No, but I'll have some money, and after I locate my site I'll get what provisions I can. At least it'll be summer."

"With winter coming fast." Moody, always bringing up all the problems and warning his younger brother about them, was filled with concern.

"I'll have to get a soddy up, first off."

"Oh, so you'll file on the prairie?"

"I'm considering it. Wouldn't you—file on the prairie?"

"Maybe, maybe not," Moody said surprisingly. "I sorta like the bush. There's something, ah, *cozy*, being surrounded like that. I don't know—" Moody looked uncomfortable and a little self-conscious. "It's safer, maybe, than all those open spaces."

"But there's all that clearing to do! The government says you have to clear five acres a year to prove up. John Hager says a good man, with a good axe, would still find that hard to do."

"You could do more than that!" Moody scoffed, "Young and strong as you are! Four . . . five—no problem for you, Donal!"

"It would be chop, chop all day. No, I think it's the prairie for me."

And so the conjecture went while Donal sorted his clothes, both summer's and winter's, and Esther, still mourning, washed, mended, pressed, and packed. In his heavier clothing, not likely to be worn for some months, this loving sister-in-law hid, in various pockets, a bit of her egg and butter money and shed a few tears thinking of Donal's re-action when he should discover this small windfall. She had an idea he would need it more than she and Moody.

At the last, Esther took Margot's small, worn Bible from the mantel, wrapped it carefully in a hankie, and laid it among Donal's things. Wherever he might be when the Bible was un-packed and laid out on shelf or mantel or table, it would be a poignant reminder of home. And Esther felt certain that the effects of his mother's prayers would follow him—whether in a tent all across a vast and strange land, into the bush and a log cabin, or onto the prairie and its soddy—or even under an upturned wagon.

When the time of actual parting came, Esther bravely

prayed the prayer she believed her mother-in-law might have raised, and neither Moody nor Donal denied her the privilege. With Donal committed to the care of the Heavenly Father, the earthly brother and sister-in-law found it somehow easier to say their good-byes.

"You write!" Moody said gruffly. "There are trains now, you know, and letters will reach us in good time."

"I could be miles and miles from a railroad. But I'll let you know my address just as soon as I have one. Until then," Donal warned, "word from me may be scanty. You'll have to allow several weeks, maybe more, for me to get there, locate a site, get moved onto it—"

"Don't pass a post office without dropping something into it."

"Trains, of course!" Esther interrupted. "I'll send along more of your things, Donal, when you get settled. Bedding—sheets, quilts, a pillow. Until then I'll be stitching away on tea towels and the like. And I can stick in various kitchen things, Donal. Oh, this is great! Some of your mother's things can follow you, after all. Dishes—I don't know about dishes—"

These plans cheered Esther considerably so that her tears were stanched and she was able to send Donal off with a smile, albeit a wavery one.

Just before getting into the wagon and heading for the railroad station, Donal hugged his sister-in-law and said, unsteadily, "Now you take care . . . and let me know when the new little one arrives. And take care of my brother, the big galoot! And this *little* galoot—" and Donal swept small Moody up into his arms and hugged him until the young boy squealed and squirmed and struggled to be set down.

Donal climbed up into the wagon beside his brother and, waving, pulled out of the old, familiar yard. If he saw the only home he had ever known slipping away dimly because of tears that would have their way, his turned head hid them well. As for Moody, he had troubles of his own, and if the team made it down the road for a few minutes with an unsteady hand on the reins, they never revealed it.

Although the man at his side was bigger, stronger, and as wise in the ways of manhood as he was himself, Moody still said soberly, "I'll miss you, boy."

"And I, you. And, Moody, thanks for your generosity in regard to the money . . . giving up things you'll just have to re-place sooner or later so that I can have—"

"You should have had more," Moody said instantly. "But I couldn't sell the place, of course. But the crop—this year's crop should be half yours, and I'll see you get that, just like always."

"Even though I quit with the field half plowed?" Donal asked, relieved to be able to laugh again.

"Even so."

They were at the station in plenty of time, but John Hager and the Wimber girls were there before them—and all the Hager tribe, it seemed, not to mention the Wimber clan. It had been decided that the travelers would journey together as far as possible. John and company, of course, would disem-bark at Winnipeg. If all went well and word had reached Pete and Joe, the prospective bridegrooms would be waiting with a wagon, vows would be exchanged before ever they left the town, and the newlyweds would make their ways northward to their homesteads. Donal, whose plans were somewhat vague, planned to continue on to Saskatchewan or Alberta. "I'll know," he had insisted whenever the subject came up. "Somehow I'll know."

Esther wondered, *Could it possibly be a case of 'In all thy ways acknowledge him, and he shall direct thy paths'?* She thought not; if Donal was a committed Christian, it wasn't obvious. And it should be, shouldn't it? Moody, no nearer the Kingdom than his brother but knowing "the way," having been taught it all his life, could only keep silent on the subject and hope there was indeed a Higher Power in charge of his brother as he took off for the wilderness of the Northwest.

The Wimber girls, Sal, Mary, and Peg, were almost scarlet with excitement. Belinda, being left behind, looked reproachfully at Donal, or so he thought, and he hastily busied himself with his pile of goods.

Just which one of the three maidens was John's intended Donal could not immediately determine; he rallied all three, hovered over all three, and seemed to be surrounded in turn by each of them and their clinging relatives. Great heaps of supplies were stacked farther down the platform; evidently the Wimber girls were going to their bridegrooms well-outfitted.

When the huffing, chuffing engine arrived and with it a line of cars, Donal turned to his brother one final time. Their eyes met across the riotous farewells of the Wimbers and Hagers, and more was unspoken between them than said. With a final salute to his only living relative this side of the ocean, Donal stepped up into the train. But it was not to be— yet. Donal would always treasure the sight of Moody thrusting his way through the crowd, not a hand outstretched, but his arms. Donal stepped down into them and then, wordless, fumbled for the step and the entrance to the colonist car.

Later seated, his bags stowed, he turned to the window to see Moody's back, straight and stiff, as he drove the wagon away.

Then six red-rimmed eyes with three sniffling noses took their places around him, and he was happy for the distraction. Of all the travelers, John alone retained his composure.

"You would think they were going to China!" he muttered to Donal, obviously sorely tried.

There was much leaning from the opened windows, additional farewells, scalding tears, and sobbing voices. Then, as the station and the waving relatives faded from view, a marvelous transformation took place: Sal, Mary, and Peg dried their similarly blue eyes, wiped their matched set of noses on identical handkerchiefs, loosened the capes to their outfits—one green, one black, one brown—sat down in a row, drew identical breaths, and looked around with fascinated expressions. Thank goodness the doldrums were done with, and their innate love of life took over.

"It must be Sal," Donal thought as that young miss turned a smile on John and asked, "Did the foodstuff get on with us?"

But it was Peg who solicitously folded John's jacket. And it was Mary who moved over to make a place for him.

"Which one is, ah, yours?" Donal finally asked in an aside.

"Why, the youngest one," John answered with some surprise as he shut the window for Sal.

For the entire trip, Donal was lost in the mystery of which one was John's chosen. Perhaps when the trip was over, in Winnipeg, and Joe and Pete each claimed his own, Donal could conclude which of the sisters was John's intended bride.

Certainly the girls made the trip more endurable. They were invariably cheerful, unendingly interested in anything and everything, and committed to making things as comfortable as possible for dear John as well as his friend Donal.

"Mum really needs Belinda," one of them assured him, and he was left to surmise whether or not he had been expected, after all, to pay suit to this last sister and had come short.

But if so, they all obviously forgave him for his oversight and never mentioned his dereliction again.

5

Once again Maude and Claude, mother and son and both in the employ of the Dalton family for many years, sagged in their traces, though Claude, always the spryest, stretched his neck toward the rich grasses at his feet and chomped gratefully. If horses have coherent thought, his must have been "Looks like good pickin's hereabouts."

For horses, maybe. The absence of any field or even a garden patch was disheartening, or would be to anyone more inclined to discouragement than Hudson and Minnie.

"Looks like Beulah Land to me," Hud, not a churchman, declared.

"Are there rabbits in Beulah Land?" Rufe asked dryly, as a big one leaped from almost under his feet to bound across the clearing and away. "I don't know if I can stomach any more rabbits."

"Milk and honey in Beulah Land," Hud responded.

"Well, there are plenty of bees," Toby said, cocking a listening ear to the sounds of the bush. "No milk, though."

"First thing is to get us a cow," his father said, and Minnie smiled fondly. "That'll take care of butter and cream, maybe even cheese, eh, old girl?"

Minnie was clambering over the wagon wheel, to the ground, turning toward the "house." Perhaps more determined than her mother to see just what their living quarters were like, or perhaps because of her youth and agility, Lolly was first at the door.

It took a hefty shove to push open the weathered door, but when it finally gave, a dusty room about 12 by 15 feet was re-

41

vealed. Two windows, one beside the door and the other in the opposite wall, were blessedly unbroken but needed washing badly. There were no curtains. Neither, of course, was there a rug. But there was flooring, an improvement over the dirt-packed floor of the prairie soddy.

Lolly gave a sigh of relief at sight of the range—dusty, rusty, but otherwise in good condition. And there were stovepipes. Thank goodness! Without them the entire contraption would be useless, and it would have been campfire cooking again.

"There's a stove, Mum," Lolly said to Minnie as her buxom figure filled the doorway and she paused to accustom her eyes to the dimness of the room after the brilliance of the afternoon sun.

"Only think!" the daughter continued. "We can bake again." Missing a bed and a bath, not to mention a pantry and a cellar, without any wallpaper on the board walls or linoleum on the rough floors, the sight of something so rudimentary as an oven almost brought the young woman to tears.

"Probably not today," Minnie said practically. "Everything will need a lot of cleaning first."

And so it was back to a campfire for the Daltons for the evening.

But first came the unloading. They were practiced at this, and each knew his or her job. Rufe and Toby handed out the boxes and tussled out a couple of barrels, some battered trunks, and, at last, the tent; Hudson unhitched and led the team toward the back of the clearing to be unharnessed and staked out to graze.

The barn door hung open and revealed a small but well-built space with three stalls on each side and a walkway in the center. The unsteady appearance was because of the sagging of the hay that had been piled on the roof, probably of sod over poles. A practical, serviceable log building. Mellon, after all, had built sturdily, well aware that anything slipshod would be deadly to beast as well as man during the bitter weather of the winter season.

"Not bad," Toby observed, studying the structure, having completed the unloading and slipped away to reconnoiter a bit. His brother would excuse him, he knew, from the heavy work, and Toby took advantage of this now, although he ordinarily extended himself doggedly to the end of his strength, half-ashamed when his brow beaded and his breath grew ragged and his limbs shook.

Hudson leaned over the open mouth of the well; his voice echoed hollowly as he reported, "I can see water—looks good, smells all right. Probably should clean it out, though, when we get around to it. Go fetch a pail and a rope, son."

"Looks like the well's going to be just fine," Toby reported, back at the wagon. This was verified a few minutes later when he appeared again with a brimming pail of sparkling water. Minnie produced a dipper, and they all drank, pronouncing it excellent.

"Gimme another pail," Toby asked, "so Dad can water the horses."

The trough leaked a bit, but the horses, in their way, seemed as satisfied with the water as the rest of the menage and went back to their supper better off than they had been for a long time, maybe ever.

Accustomed to the procedure, Rufe set up the tent with Lolly's help. Personal items and bedding were set inside. Crates and wooden boxes were left around the fire for seating purposes. Fuel was no problem; it was as near as the edge of the clearing, where a fair-sized woodpile was discovered. Mellon, poor man, had obviously hoped to the last that they could make a go of it; Mellon's wife, just as obviously, had

43

her own way. But who could subject a woman to the hardships of the homestead unless she was willing? Plenty of people, the Daltons knew, found themselves hopelessly committed, with no means of escape. Some died; some went insane; most aged cruelly. But if they ended up with their own place, it was worth it all, or so they consoled themselves. Mellon was not to be one of the survivors. Would the Daltons do any better?

Certainly Hud had himself a compliant, uncomplaining woman for a wife. His daughter—now that could be a different story. Hud was beginning to have an idea that Lolly might not be as contented as she could be. She was of a marriageable age—had been for a few years, Hud thought—and men flocked around. But Lolly would have none of them. Maybe that would change, here in Wildrose.

While the fire crackled healthily, Minnie and Lolly engaged in going through boxes to search out the old familiar pots and pans and with satisfaction dug into the fresh supply of provisions they had purchased in Prince Albert. Rufe took off to survey the quarter section that had been the Mellon homestead and now lay abandoned.

Small openings in the bush surrounding the farmyard clearing obviously led somewhere; choosing the widest and best, Rufe followed it, often fending off fresh growth that had burgeoned with spring. Pin cherry blossoms hung like snowballs and promised a crimson crop shortly. His worn shoes scuffed through bluebells and dandelions indiscriminately and over all wafted a scent beyond human description.

He broke from the cool, shadowed trail into sunshine; a clearing lay before him, perhaps a five-acre plot. A good man, Rufe had been told, might clear that much in a year. The stumps needed to be pulled, but the limbs and cleared brush had been burned. Perhaps a plow could get around the

stumps and a crop of some sort planted yet—probably potatoes; he had heard they grew like melons here. Not only
would they need them for winter's supply but also could undoubtedly find a sale for them in Prince Albert.

Of the trees that had been cut, some—irregular in shape or
too small for building purposes—had been piled at one side of
the clearing. Another lot was quite obviously being prepared
for a cabin and piled together, a few of them peeled and
squared neatly. Rufe studied them thoughtfully, counted
them, and felt his spirits lift. If the Daltons settled down, and
he earnestly hoped they would, a house was absolutely necessary.

There was so much to do before winter set in. Frost could
come as early as August, although that was a rarity. A reader
and a rememberer and full of quotations, Hudson had been
known to say incongruously—for he was a slow mover—
"What thou doest, do quickly." Never would it be more ap-
ropos.

Whether Hudson would feel it or not, Rufe did; there was
an urgency on bush homesteaders. Deep snows, blizzards, ice
storms, and bitter temperatures breathed coldly on the back
of their necks, sunburnt or not.

Back in the farmyard clearing the table had been set up,
potatoes were baking in the campfire ashes, coffee was
brewing, and Minnie was opening a can of tomatoes and
adding it to a kettle of macaroni. When Rufe returned, Lolly
was slicing a loaf of Prince Albert bakery bread, and supper
was ready—better than they had enjoyed for a long time.

"There are logs back there ready for a cabin," Rufe announced. "If we're to stay—" he paused to look at his father.

"Why, of course—never had any other idea," Hud assured
him, apparently surprised at the very suggestion.

"If we're to stay, we'll need more room than that—" and

Rufe's nod indicated the tar paper shack. "And something warmer too."

Lolly looked hopeful. It was hard not to, with new life springing almost magically to beauty and bounty all around them. What would it be like in the deadness of winter? *No worse than the prairies,* she thought with a shudder. Anything, anything would be better than last winter in a soddy—crowded, often hungry, unwashed much of the time, isolated, and always cold.

Yes, this had to be better. But knowing her father—and her mother, she admitted to herself rather shamefacedly—it was not good enough. Not nearly good enough.

No idea of how to remedy her circumstances had occurred to Lolly as yet. But a glimmer of an idea presented itself when Rufe next spoke.

"Everyone, at least all the men—unless they arrive here with money to set themselves up and keep themselves until their crops pay off—have to work out at something. We've got to be thinking of that." And Rufe's glance touched Toby only briefly and settled on his father.

Work! Would it be possible for a girl—a woman? Could she, by her own ambition and effort, be enabled to purchase decent garments? Just thinking of it brought Lolly's arms up over her chest after an ineffectual tweak to cover her ankles with her skimpy skirt. Just thinking of her exposure brought the warm blood surging up into her cheeks.

Rufe saw it all and suspected the reason, and he sighed. He would do what was necessary, for Mum and Lolly, if it killed him! And then . . . and then . . . and then . . . futility mixed with anger wiped out any dim dream of a future of his own. He stared down at his broken boots, as near helpless as a man can be.

Wildrose—such a lovely name! Could it hold any promise

of a better life for any of them? Lolly—flowering, eye-catching, innocent. Toby—a big soul cramped into a weak body. Mum—settling where she was put, no gumption, no demands. Dad—pleased with other men's leavings, satisfied with today if he had food, fire, and a bed; no worries. Would anything change for any of them? If one man's efforts could bring it about, Rufe vowed—in the flickering of the campfire and serenaded by the relentlessly vocal spring peeper—that if it were possible, he would be the one to bring it about. It helped him go off to the tent and the bed spread there near Hudson and Toby as he mentally prepared himself for the workload of tomorrow . . . and tomorrow . . . and tomorrow . . .

Leaving the fire and its welcome smoke, Lolly and Minnie made their way to the swept and dusted shack, glad they had thought to purchase netting and that they had cut and tacked it to the window frames and now draped a length of it over the open door. Mosquitoes were fiercest at night; with the morning, the blackfly would be an ever-present nuisance. Once again Lolly regretted that so much of her was exposed all day long and renewed her speculation in regard to work.

The first thing to do, she supposed, after settling in, was to get acquainted with the district. Hopefully they were not too far from several farms. She knew the Szarvases were close and wished she had thought to question the girl, Kitty, more fully. She would go there soon and would then know how to proceed.

That many of the district's people might be as poor and needy as the Daltons was a sobering thought. In such a case, she would work for yard goods—flour sacking. Many people made clothes from flour sacks, coming as they did in various patterns and colors; she would even settle for that! Anything, anything to be decent. Lovely, pretty, attractive, becoming—

47

these were effects she had come not to expect.

"We'll clean the stove tomorrow," Minnie said as she donned her threadbare nightie and tucked the netting around the doorway. "We'll have to get Dad, or maybe Rufe to tack this netting around that frame that's lying out there in the grass," she added wisely. "It'll do fine, just fine."

So saying, Minnie, as always, as long as Lolly could remember, got awkwardly to her knees, bowed her head, folded her hands, and apparently prayed. Lolly supposed it was the little rhyme—the one and only prayer—that Minnie had taught her children when they were little.

Meaningless then as now, her offspring had discarded it. Minnie persisted in its recitation. Again tonight Lolly concluded it was the same prayer; it lasted just about the same length of time. Every once in a while, just to test it out, Lolly repeated the phrases to herself, finishing just when Minnie solemnly announced the "Amen."

In no mood for the uselessness of prayer, still the pointless plea unsound itself now in her mind in cadence with Minnie's:

> *Day is gone and night is come;*
> *Jesus, guard my humble home.*
> *Watch above my bed tonight;*
> *Wake me with the morning light.*
> *If I die before the day,*
> *Angels, bear my soul away. Amen.*

If it gave Mum some small comfort, so be it. After all, Lolly supposed, it was a prayer that was answered. They *had* survived each night; they *had* wakened each morning. Wouldn't it be nice if other prayers, for other needs, could be as faithfully answered?

As for angels bearing one's soul away, that hadn't been tested. Thinking about it always gave Lolly an uneasy feeling.

Yawning, she turned over on her hard little cot. Her last thought, perhaps quickened by the small prayer, was *Say! Church could be the answer! Good people go there. That might be where to get acquainted fast . . . to see if anyone has work.*

 6

The colonist car was packed as tight as a homemade sausage and was almost as odorous. The smell of garlic vied with the milder perfume of castile soap; aging cheese competed with faithful dabs of Queen Victoria White Heliotrope Perfume. Carbolic blended with camphor, cigar smoke with peppermint. The rankness of clothes too long unwashed overcame such negligible bathing of the human body as was possible in the crowded conditions and lack of privacy.

Wet diapers and sour milk accounted for some of the fretfulness of the babies; lack of space for frolic exacerbated the crankiness of small children already distressed over strange surroundings, no proper meals, and naps on lumpy seats.

People of all degree, nationality, and belief were crowded together for a single purpose—acquiring land of their own. Foreign languages, like water over rapids, gushed and spurted as mothers called to rambunctious children, women chattered, and men, though perhaps more grave, shared their dreams and plans, their fears and anxieties, with one another.

Canada was experiencing the beginning of what would turn out to be an explosion of settlers in its present vast, empty spaces.

The Dominion of Canada came into being on July 1, 1867, with the uniting of four provinces—Nova Scotia, New Brunswick, and the "two Canadas," which were named Ontario and Quebec. In 1870 the Manitoba Act had set up the first prairie province, and two years later Prince Edward Island came in as another province. In the center lay the area known as Rupert's Land, established by the charter of the

Hudson's Bay Company in 1670 and eventually known as a colony in a state of arrested development.

It was clear that the Hudson's Bay Company could not continue to hold the privileges of trade and government first granted to it; new settlers were dissatisfied with company rule. Finally the necessary terms were agreed upon, and Rupert's Land and the Northwest Territory beyond, where the company had held the monopoly on trade, could be transferred to Canada. Before too long, it was hoped, that vast wilderness in the middle of it all would become the provinces of Alberta and Saskatchewan, the second and third prairie provinces. But now empty . . . so empty.

And how they beckoned! Landless people came, suppressed people, people without hope and often without money. Their dreams carried them along until it became as a surging sea for intent and purpose and as unstoppable. When one pioneer caved in, another took his place and the phenomenon rolled on.

"Why mon, I couldna walk doon the street in Glasgow withoot someone handing me a pamphlet," a thin man with a thick accent was saying now. "Told in glowing terms how I coot make a fortune here, in no time at all, at all." The Scot looked out the window at the empty spaces with a doubtful expression on his face.

Wilderness. It was all wilderness, broken now and again with small hamlets through which the railroad ran, stopping at each one. The fortunate—the early arriver—had obtained land near the railroad, and it was prized land.

"The land companies are getting all the tracts from the railroads," someone said, and it was a well-known complaint. "And payin' only two or three dollars an acre, then sellin' to settlers for double that amount." Several heads nodded gloomy agreement.

"There's still plenty . . . plenty for everyone," another said, more cheerful than his companions. "True, you may have to go farther back, making it harder to get your crops to the cars."

"Not only the crops! How many women are going to want to drive half a day or more to sell butter and eggs?"

In his corner Donal Cardigan listened. He still had not had the nudge or felt the response that he trusted would give him his own personal sense of direction.

Across the aisle an Englishman, perhaps a remittance man and thus assured funds from home, held a dainty cup and saucer in one hand and what he called a "biscuit" in the other. Neatly dressed, even fashionably, the Britisher's shiny shoes swung beneath good old English tweeds. At his side his wife, equally the picture of money, good breeding, and satisfaction, sipped daintily at the fragrant concoction. It was teatime.

"Biscuit?" John Hager, at Donal's side, muttered. "Looks like a plain cookie to me." John was clearly as taken with the civilized little drama unfolding just across the narrow aisle as Donal and several others who watched in open curiosity, perhaps envy.

As worn and weary as the general crowd, a little English maid scurried back and forth from the stove at the end of the car to her master and mistress. Occasionally she upended herself to search through one of the numerous bags and boxes with which the couple surrounded themselves, to dig out a fan, fresh gloves, another tin of biscuits, a novel . . .

Not far from the aristocratic pair, a cowboy hat covered the shaggy head of a lean man in jeans and a pair of sharp-toed boots, "goin' to Alberta to a cattle ranch." Saskatchewan was the chosen destination of a roughly dressed group, with kerchiefed women and whiskered men heading for a Romanian settlement near Regina.

Following the 1885 Riel Rebellion, a pattern of settlement evolved with a slow but steady influx of arrivals coming family by family, singly, or in groups: German and Danish family settlers took up land near Ebenezer; French families settled near Duck Lake; Icelanders chose land near Tantallon. But the majority of settlers before the turn of the century were Anglo-Saxon. And many of these were from Ontario, as were Donal and John Hager and his entourage.

And with a coming of the rails, travel was speeded and simplified. Now it was rare for the noisy Red River carts to creak and squawk their way across the plains. But when long lines of them did snake across the country from time to time, accompanied by Indians, they drew a crowd to the train windows and elicited nervous shudders from women who were hastily assured that the Indian trouble was past and gone.

The English couple were not the only ones today to have tea. The Wimber girls, bored and restless, fished around in their baskets and produced the necessary makings. Flourishing the pot and the tea triumphantly, Sal proceeded gamely down the corridor that ran the length of the coach, toward the stove set up at one end. There, also, was a cistern of water for the convenience of the passengers as they cooked for their families or, as now, made tea.

The seats were arranged into sections, two seats facing each other. Each seat, narrow and hard, accommodated two adults. Their section was filled by John and his three companions, making it necessary for Donal to find a spot elsewhere. For eating purposes, however, or occasional visits, the girls good-naturedly crowded up with much arranging of their wide skirts and wider shoulders so that as a group they could all eat, talk, laugh, and, at times, complain together.

The seats were converted into beds at night. Overhead

stretched a sort of "tea tray" affair that could be closed up into the roof or used for baggage. At night the baggage was stowed under the seats and the "tea tray" became a bed for two. Somehow the three Wimber girls managed to sleep on the seats and there was much huffing and puffing as they settled themselves "spoon fashion" in order to fit into an area designed for no more than two.

More than once Donal, above, with John breathing into his ear, heard one of the girls mutter, "Turn! I've got a stay plaguing me!" And there would be a great rustling and muttering of instructions, invariably rousing their neighboring bedfellows until, like a restless sea the entire coach billowed with shifting passengers.

Now as the teapot and cups were set on a box between their almost touching knees, John called for the biscuits. The Englishman across the aisle turned a frosty gaze their way and John subsided, looking apologetic. The great raisin concoctions Mary produced from the food basket were a touch and a taste of home and, for a moment, the thoughts of all five turned somberly to the loved ones becoming farther and farther from them with each turn of the wheels.

Not that they turned all that fast, Donal thought with a sigh. It was possible, when weary of sitting, to climb down and run alongside, to the cheers and waves of boys leaning from the windows.

Sal, perhaps missing the warmth of the cookstove, shivered. "Don't you think it's getting cold?" she asked, drawing her shawl up and around her shoulders.

Others were doing the same thing; mothers were wrapping babies more snugly, men were donning sweaters, all open windows were closed—even though it meant the intensity of the smells increased.

"It looks like it could snow," someone said, and a great

groan began at one end of the coach and swelled the full length.

"*In April?*" more than one person gasped.

But they all knew it could happen—by experience or warning. And all of them had timed their departure in order to arrive at their new destination with as much good weather ahead as possible. Sites would need to be located, shelter built, *something* planted, and fuel stockpiled for the next long winter season.

Now it appeared they had miscalculated. Not far from Winnipeg, snow swirled down and the temperature dropped alarmingly. Those nearest the stove retained their favored spots firmly. Having roasted earlier when the stove was stoked regularly to allow each family a turn at cooking, they now benefited from the heat, though it seemed meager indeed when one considered the length of the car.

The day was still short, and as the early darkness fell it was increased by the thickening blanket of snow. Soon the train was laboring; eventually it groaned to a stop.

"All able-bodied men out!" shouted the official who stepped into the coach with a swirl of snow and a blast of icy air. Donal and John were already half-prepared and were soon leaping from the car into a blinding snowstorm. Even the Englishman exhibited the Britisher's pluck and not only put on a handsome wool Macintosh with its plaid lining and velvet collar but also, at the urging of his wife, allowed the little maid to fasten around his shoulders the detachable cape. Patent leather lace boots and all, he shouldered a shovel with the rest of them and plowed his way to the front of the train and the drifts that had brought them to a halt.

With much cheering the train moved forward, slowly, and the snow-covered men clambered aboard, the snow from their heads and shoulders and boots flying everywhere as they were removed, causing shrieks and complaints from the already shivering travelers.

Twice more the scene was repeated. Finally the conductor announced that they might as well make themselves as comfortable as possible; they might be stalled for hours—even days.

No sooner were they wrapped and cuddled together for warmth than the word came: we're going through, after all. At midnight—a cold, snowy, dark midnight—they pulled into Winnipeg.

"No use looking," John advised the girls trying vainly to look through the snow-plastered windows. "We're days late. Joe and Pete won't be here. Goodness knows when we'll make connections."

With much shivering and more shuddering the girls were helped down onto the snowy platform by Donal and John and made their way quickly along to the soon-overflowing waiting room.

Scarves were unwrapped and capes and coats loosened; seats were eventually found, and with their baggage stacked until called for, Donal and John ventured out to see about rooms for the night.

None were available. Back they trudged to suggest the girls settle down patiently and get some rest. Still game, Sal, Mary, and Peg, now more than a little hollow-eyed and mussed, leaned one on the next with the third leaning on John's shoulder—who looked harried and happy at the same time. Like three plump partridges in a row, the girls dozed the rest of the night away.

Donal jerked awake from his own uncomfortable sleep to the sound of shrieks of joy. Two big men in fur coats, caps, and mitts were gathering two of the sisters to their bulky bosoms. Tears flowed as cheeks as hairy as the coats crushed the girls' rosy faces, which grew the rosier with blushing. There was much fussing with tumbled hair, straightening of rumpled clothes, and a cacophony of messages relayed, explanations, questions, and perhaps a few answers.

To the side of the happy scene, John and his intended watched, holding hands and smiling. But whether she was Sal, Mary, or Peg, Donal still did not know.

After the excited couples gathered the many boxes and bags the arrivals had brought with them and made ready their departure—first to a minister and the repeating of their vows and then to parts north and unknown to the brides—Donal was left standing on a windswept platform, facing parts west—and unknown.

7

Lolly awoke to breathtaking beauty. The world outside the tar paper shack when she pulled aside the netting and stepped outside was as pure, she thought, as it must have been when it was new. The dewy grasses shimmered blindingly from a trillion and more sun-touched diamonds. The aspen leaves quivered with a syncopation not unlike that of her own heart. Birdsong, as pure and sweet as the day itself, poured from tree and bush, reed and post.

And the fragrance! The prairie, to Lolly, had been strangely empty of aromas much of the time. She supposed it was because of the wind, the drying wind. Lolly touched a hand to her cheek and found it satisfyingly soft. Her hair, red-gold and so alive it seemed almost to have a life of its own, had also responded to the different climate, perhaps the different water, and it too, though she didn't know it, was lustrous in the sunlight.

This was the place and time for life to change for Lolly Dalton. Just how, she wasn't quite sure. But that she had to be in charge of her own destiny was clear; otherwise she was doomed to a life as meaningless as her mother's.

Lolly lifted her face to the day and closed her eyes, her head filled with dreams and plans, her lungs filled with the bush's perfume and, full of life and the possibility of a better way, flung out her arms, lifted onto her bare toes, and twirled. Her hair, loose from sleep, swung freely in its glowing arc.

"Ahem!" That sound startled Lolly from her impromptu dance to an abrupt halt. Someone—a man on horseback—

had cleared his throat, and the sound had carried clearly in the crystal air. It was not a sound of disapproval but rather an announcement of sharp awareness. Lolly was to conclude thoughtfully later that it was more like an *"Aha!"*

It was not the vocalization alone that brought Lolly's arms up automatically to wrap her body, once again, in modesty. The sun shone clearly onto the man's face, and the eyes . . . the eyes were fixed, absorbed and staring, filled with something Lolly had yet to put a name to but which she was beginning to recognize.

And what a temptation she presented, all unknowing of it! The bright sun behind her outlined her womanliness through the worn nightgown, as skimpy in length as her dress and as outgrown in the bodice. The same sun that so obviously etched her body also ringed her head of tossed hair with a scintillating aura. Her face, shadowed somewhat to the man with the brilliance of the morning sun in his eyes, was yet to be discovered.

But what he did see seemed to have startled the rider into immobility. His horse, approaching over the morning-damped sand of the trail, had not been heard above the birdsong, the beating of her own heart, and the blood rushing in her ears with the exertion of her dance.

Embarrassed past words, Lolly stood, clasping herself with a secrecy that was more tantalizing than revelation would have been. At that moment there was a sound behind her and the stranger's eyes, perhaps with an effort, turned and his head gave a slight shake as if to clear his vision and his thoughts, and he nodded to Hudson Dalton, who had stepped from the doorway of the nearby tent.

"Good morning!" Hud said with great geniality.

"Ah, good morning," the man replied. "I think I saw you go by my place yesterday," and his gaze passed over and dismissed the Dalton wagon and its contents now scattered, Dalton fashion, around the clearing. Thoughtfully they returned to the girl who so recently had thrown herself with abandon into the day *and* his line of vision but was now shrinking away, backing a few steps, then whirling to disappear into the shack and drawing the concealing net into place behind her.

Certainly it was the man, not the horse, who was mesmerized into moving toward the Dalton camp.

"Get down," Hudson invited, "and join us in a cup of coffee."

"I've had mine, thank you." The tone seemed to indicate that coffee time was better being earlier and that any dallying was a matter to be disapproved of. Besides, the gaze, fixed on the cold ashes of last night's fire, revealed the invitation was a formality.

Nothing daunting him, Hudson Dalton indicated Rufe and Toby coming rapidly from the bush. "Get a fire going, boys. We've got company."

The "boys" nodded and set to work. The visitor's horse shifted its feet, the saddle creaked, and the man remained seated. One had a feeling that his hesitancy in departing was as unnerving to him as it was to those watching and awaiting his decision.

"Might as well get acquainted," the stranger said and dismounted, throwing the reins of the beautiful horse around the nearby wagon wheel.

Rufe looked up from his squatted position at the side of the campfire. "Nice horse," he said. His voice was noncommittal in its tone; only the hunger in his eyes would have betrayed his longing if he had cared to lift them toward the man who was turning to hold out a hand to Hudson Dalton.

"Kingston Plummer," he said. "People call me King."

Perhaps it was something in his voice; perhaps it was a re-action against the name in a land where no man was truly king and each man was free. (Minnie always rigorously defended the sovereignty of good Queen Victoria, however, and her influence was felt even in remote corners, on isolated prairie, and in the backwoods of the bush country. But no local king held sway and each man reveled in the freedom to be his own master.)

Affably, Hud Dalton shook the hand proffered and identified himself and his sons.

"Hudson Dalton, recently of points south, by way of Prince Albert. These are my sons, Rufus and Tobias."

Both young men stood, extending a hand soiled from the smut and ashes of the fire pit. Kingston Plummer's hand, nails well-groomed and shirt cuff spotless, hesitated only a moment before reaching across the first flickering flame.

"And this," Hud continued, "is my wife, Minerva."

Minnie, having heard the voices, had not only dressed herself but had managed to comb and pile her hair. Her plump features were creased in a cordial smile as she acknowledged the introduction. Hudson's gaze flickered to the door of the shack, and he hesitated. When Lolly wasn't forthcoming and no sound emerged from the small building, he turned back to his guest and waved him to a seat on a box.

"Yes sir, we just arrived yesterday afternoon, late. Haven't had much of a chance to look around. Unless you boys have been doing that this morning." Hud looked questioningly toward his sons.

"We did a little more, soon as we woke up," Rufe said. "Seems like we have a slough back there. I guess that's good."

"Certainly," Kingston Plummer affirmed. "For several reasons. The water is important, of course, for watering stock and for cutting ice in the winter, if it hasn't dried up. But there's usually hay around it, as there is around yours. Saves a lot of grubbing, having a sort of meadow like that, and it will give you food for your animals. You have animals—"

"Ah, horses, at the present time. We'll have to see right off about a cow."

"And chickens," Minnie reminded, her face red from the heat of the fire as she leaned over it, settling a fire-blackened pot in position to boil water for oatmeal—though where milk for it would come from, no one knew. Once again it would be served with a spoonful of syrup only.

"Now Mr. Plummer, you say we passed your place yesterday? Would it be just across the line from our place? The next quarter-section maybe? With that two-story house?"

"I have a half-section," Kingston Plummer informed them. "I've been here almost five years."

"Land all proved up, then."

"Yes, yes, of course. It can be done, with a lot of hard work and perseverance." Not mentioned were the money, the supply of farm equipment, the men hired to help in the tree-felling, the stump-grubbing, the fall stooking, and so on. Mr. Plummer, from his well-fitted clothes to his highbred horse to his half section, imposing house and farm, and, last but not at all least, his very demeanor, spoke of success and satisfaction.

"Can't offer you eggs, I'm afraid, Mr. Plummer," Minnie said regretfully, adding pointedly. "No hens, you see. Can't do a decent job of housekeeping without them—no cakes—"

Oh, Mum, how can you? Lolly, listening, agonized.

"Eggs?" Kingston Plummer said thoughtfully into the silence that fell following Minnie's remark. "I'll be happy to give you some eggs . . . better yet, a few hens. Perhaps you have someone—I wouldn't want to take the menfolk away from more important work—who would be free to come on over and get them. It's not more than half a mile, through the woods. You'll find trails run from most farms in all directions, cutting down the distance it would be to follow the roads. You wouldn't want to attempt the walk yourself, ma'am, of course. But," he concluded temptingly, "some of those hens are laying. A good strong, er, young person could carry a sack of them easily, and you could have eggs from your own hens tomorrow."

"Why, Lolly could go! And while she goes, Rufe could throw a shelter together—"

"There's a small coop back of the barn," Rufe said, rather shortly, "and a wire run. It would just need to be straightened up a bit."

"Lolly?" Mr. Plummer said, and it sounded like a dirty word.

Lolly, usually despising her name and its diminutive, heard the distaste in the man's voice and for the first time in her life felt like defending the unlikely and disliked name.

Minnie was about to serve up the oatmeal and kept casting impatient glances toward the shack. "Now where did she put those bowls?" she muttered.

"Yes, that's the name of our daughter," Minnie said in answer to the man's question, if a question it was. "Lolita, really. I was reading something, I forget what, before she was born, and the heroine had that name. I've never met anyone else who was called that—that's one thing you can say about it."

"Lolita," the man seemed to mutter, unbelievingly. Then, with a deep breath and a glance at the shack, stood to go. "I really must get about the day's tasks. I'm on my way to town—"

"That would be Meridian? Heard it was the nearest post office."

"Yes, Meridian—a hamlet only, but it's where we all do

business aside from going to Prince Albert."

He turned toward his horse. He was a man of medium height but with imperious posture and erectly held head that made him appear imposing. Approaching 50 years of age, the face was smooth, the hair thinning but still brown, the eyes devoid of any hint of humor, the mouth a slash with no touch of laughter. Money and high breeding breathed from every movement. Polished boots gleamed as he swung his leg over the saddle; capable, clean hands gripped the reins; the eyes held no hint of pleasure while the stern mouth said the right words: "Pleased to have met you. I trust you'll make a success of the Mellon place. Mellon was a fool." Kingston Plummer, obviously, was not a man to suffer fools lightly and added, "He let that woman dominate him."

If his gaze flickered toward the shack when he spoke again, Lolly, watching from the window, could only surmise. The handsome fawn-colored felt hat he had removed when he met Minnie and which Lolly remembered seeing in a Prince Albert store window described as "used by wheelmen, tourists, hunters, horsemen, and for general wear," quite adequately disguised his glance when he put it back on.

"Be glad to give—Lolly, is it?—a few hens if you care to send her over."

Minnie breathed her thanks, Hudson nodded agreeably, and Rufe, who had followed the new neighbor to his horse, looked up into the man's set face and hesitated. Then, as though gathering his nerve, Rufe asked, "Mr. Plummer, do you ever hire help? As you know, it's often necessary to find work somewhere until a place starts producing—"

The thin lips curled ever so slightly.

"Well," Rufe finished, "I just wanted to mention it. I'm available, and I'll be looking for work."

This time the watching Lolly felt quite certain the head

lifted and the eyes, under the "sportsman's hat," glanced briefly at the shack.

"As a matter of fact, that's what I was going to town about. Yes—Rufe, is it?—I do need help. The place is too big for one man. Or even—" his voice raised, to carry clear and strong to the shanty, "for one woman."

Looking down at Rufe, he said, "Come on over tomorrow morning, and I'll put you to work."

"I'd be happy to meet Mrs. Plummer," Minnie offered. "Tell her I'll drop by as soon as I get a bit settled here. And, of course, she'd be welcome here anytime."

Giving the reins a tweak and nudging the horse with his boot heels, Kingston Plummer—just before he cantered back to his two quarter sections of good parkland soil, proved up and producing with a handsome two-story house and a well-equipped farm—said, "I'm a widower. I have no wife."

8

With the splendid mount cantering down the road, Kingston Plummer astride, and both disappearing into the quickly enveloping bush, Lolly pulled aside the netting and stepped out of the shack. She had removed the shift that she slept in and dressed herself. Going to the tin basin that had been placed on an upended chunk of wood, she splashed her face with the chilled water of the Mellon well, dried on a bit of sacking laid out for that purpose, and with her hands and a broken piece of comb tried to corral her luxuriant hair into some semblance of modesty. Her exuberant, spontaneous dance had not helped its natural tendency to spring in riotous abandon around her head.

Minnie had returned to her breakfast preparations, having located the bowls and the pail of syrup, and stirred the oatmeal one final time as the family gathered around on boxes, a couple of chairs, and a stump. The coffee was bubbling on the fire, and its aroma filled the clearing delectably.

"Looks like I'll have work," Rufe said, referring to his brief conversation with their new neighbor. There was relief in the sound of his voice.

"Now," Toby said thoughtfully, "if there is just something *I* can find to do—"

"There'll be plenty around here, Toby," Rufe said, encouraging his younger brother to feel his worth.

"It's not the same," Toby began, when once again the attention of the entire family was drawn to yesterday's black-and-white dog. The creature made straight for Toby, who turned quickly to fondle the flopping ears, thus setting the tail in motion in an ecstatic wave over the dog's back.

Already suspecting that where the dog was, so would be the girl, they weren't surprised to see Kitty Szarvas, as bright and calm as the morning, approaching. In her hand she carried a lard pail.

"Good morning," she said cheerily, and the Daltons responded one and all.

"My mum thought you might like some milk," the girl said and removed the lid to reveal this particular treasure.

"How nice!" Minnie exclaimed.

"We have lots of milk," Kitty explained, "more than we need. The pigs get all they want."

Toby, with his weak chest and thin limbs, came under Kitty's kind scrutiny.

"They look healthier than you," she said quite seriously.

Toby's slender face flushed. "They're probably better fed," he replied lightly.

"Well, until you get a cow of your own, my folks say you can have milk every day. I can probably run over with it—"

"No need," Toby said firmly. "I'll come get it . . . perhaps I can help with the milking. We'd want to do something."

"Well—"

Toby was firm. "It's the least we can do."

"We have a large family," Kitty explained, "but I'm the youngest—most of the others are married and gone. There's just Billy and me now to help. Billy wrenched his knee last week when he had a tumble off of a horse he's trying to break for riding, and he's hobbling about, not a lot of help right now."

"So Toby could be a help," Minnie concluded, and looked pleased with the arrangement. Milk and eggs arranged for, the first day—this Wildrose place was indeed promising. If Minnie looked a little wistful, no one recognized that there might be a tiny bit of longing, on her part, for something more than she had. If they had so much as suspected it, they would have scoffed. "What? Mum dissatisfied? C'mon!"

Perhaps it was just the need to continually feed her family that spurred her to this small feeling of relief . . . or was it more than that? Could Minnie Dalton be reacting positively to this small sign of something on which she could depend?

The moment passed, but it sent Minnie into her day with a lift of spirits, almost as though the tiniest of seeds—like a carrot seed small, insignificant, yet full of life—was threatening to germinate and—and what? The idea, if it had occurred to any one of them, including Minnie, would have been dismissed as entirely out of character, even ludicrous. Something dependable indeed!

When the girl had departed, the dog at her heels, the Daltons added the fresh creamy milk to their porridge and a foamy spoonful to their coffee, a treat they hadn't enjoyed in a long time.

"Just think," Minnie marveled, "we can have cream now, and butter. Hud, you'll have to keep us in flour for baking."

"Of course, old girl!"

"We'll have to put the rest of this down the well, to keep it from souring. Days are getting warm."

Minnie seemed to be uncharacteristically full of plans. Hud looked a little surprised.

"Rufe," Minnie continued with more animation than they had remembered seeing in her for as long as they could recall, and now not only her husband looked surprised, "could you spade up a garden spot first thing?" Mum, laying plans?

"Glad to, Mum. It shouldn't be too much work while the ground still has some of the spring dampness to it. Looks like wonderful soil, just like we heard. You locate your seeds, and before the day is half over you and Sis can be planting to your hearts' content."

"If I'm back," Lolly said, eyes on her porridge bowl.

"Back? Oh, you mean from going over to that Plummer place for hens. That shouldn't take all day."

"Maybe," she said, looking up half defiantly into the eyes of her family, "I'll talk to Mr. Plummer about work too."

Minnie blinked; Toby frowned; Rufe's face darkened; Hudson shook his head. "No daughter of mine is going to work," he said.

Lolly, if she weren't so serious, might have laughed at the foolishness of this ultimatum.

I won't be tarred with his brush! was her rebellious thought. *Someone has to have a little ambition in this family!*

"Work?" Lolly asked, with control. "I work *here!*"

"Work *out*, I mean," Hudson explained patiently. "Outside of home."

"It isn't the working out," Rufe said now, somewhat tautly. "It's that man—that *King* Plummer."

"Why, *you're* going to work for him," Lolly said.

"That's different." Rufe's words were clipped, and Lolly frowned, feigning ignorance of his meaning.

"I don't understand—"

"The man isn't married."

"That's the whole idea! How can a widower run that house—that big house?"

"He must already have help," Minnie suggested.

"Probably has a houseful of children," Toby added.

Lolly looked nonplused momentarily. "Well, if so, that's all the more reason he needs help. Anyway," she said with stubbornness that caused her family to look at her with raised eyebrows, "I'm going to see about it. I need—" Instinctively Lolly's arms crossed themselves over her body, and her eyes had an awareness that made Rufe half sick to see. So she *did* understand, after all. So she wasn't as entirely innocent of the ways of men—some men—as he had supposed. In a way he was glad; it would be a protection to her. "I need . . . things," she finished.

"Let her try," Rufe said now quietly, and Hud shrugged. A little extra money would help a lot.

When the dishes were done and the camp tidied, Lolly located the small sewing box that traveled everywhere with them; darning was a way of life with the Daltons. Turning her two dresses inside out, Lolly inspected their seams. One was hopelessly worn and would not stand any changing of the seams; they would simply have torn loose from the thin material. The other looked more promising.

Carefully Lolly picked the seams of the dress's bodice, heated an iron, and laying a sheet on the table pressed the seams open. Pinning the material into place, she began the hand stitching that would give her a little more room in her clothes. The hem had already been lowered, and nothing could be done to lengthen it further. But, she felt, a show of leg, although not fashionable, was surely not as objectionable as a show of—of a far more feminine part of her anatomy. Until recently she was perfectly at ease with her femininity and accepted her body's changes matter-of-factly. It was only the gleam in the eyes of certain males as they brashly surveyed her curves that had put her cheeks to burning, her gaze to dropping, and her arms to crossing themselves in a foolish—and perfectly useless—attempt at concealment.

The sewing completed, Lolly rinsed out the garment and draped it over a bush to dry.

"I can help now, Mum," she announced, picking up the rag and preparing to blacken the stove that Minnie had thoroughly scrubbed. She hesitated.

"Let me do that," Minnie said gently. "No need to go over to the Plummers' grand place with blacking under your fingernails."

Lolly relinquished the job to her mother. "I'll start putting things on the shelves," she said, and called to Toby to help carry boxes into the shack. "Before the day's over, we'll be cooking our meals like real people," she laughed, and neither she nor Toby saw the momentary flash of pain in their mother's eyes.

Rufe, true to his word, was spading a garden spot, obviously one the Mellons had used. The dirt, black and rich, turned easily and seemed to invite planting. Toby followed his brother with a rake, removing grass and weeds and smoothing the area.

Hudson, thinking of the eggs that would soon be available for his breakfast table, set about cleaning out the chicken coop and straightening the fence of chicken wire that had fallen over in places. But with the lack of feed, the gate would have to be left open, beginning tomorrow after the hens had become more or less accustomed to the place, so that they could forage for themselves until grain might be obtained. There were grasshoppers, bugs, insects of all sorts, and wild seeds to be had for the picking. They would survive—and hopefully lay! With luck, one or more might become broody and so increase the flock. Chicken dinner would be a rare change from the wild meat to which the Daltons were accustomed.

Hudson cleaned the small wooden trough Mellon had made and filled it with fresh water. "Praise God from whom all blessings flow!" Hud quoted with no gratitude whatsoever.

Early afternoon, with Hudson up from his rest and Minnie and her sons well into the making of rows, planting of seeds, and watering the garden with pailsful from the well, Lolly sprinkled the clean dress, spread it again on the tabletop, and ironed it.

Her hair, freshly washed and still damp, permitted itself to be tamed, to a degree, and fastened at her neck with a ribbon. Then, taking a gunnysack she found in the small shed that passed for a granary—and which, to the satisfaction of the family, held all sorts of surprises in the way of useful household and farm equipment—she headed off toward the general direction of the Plummer place.

"Take the shortcut through the bush," Kingston Plummer had said before departing, pointing to one of the faint trails leading out of the Mellon clearing.

Pushing her way at times through the abundance of growth that marked the area, Lolly walked a historic route, though she didn't realize it. Despite the fact that the farmers were new, the land was already rich in history.

This was the land of the Cree. Here, their legend said, Wee-sack-ka-chak built a raft and saved all the animals and birds from a great flood. Sending out a muskrat to find land, he created the land of today from a scrap of earth in the muskrat's paws. Here the buffalo roamed in great numbers; here the white man came to barter until the Indian gradually became dependent on the trader for guns, shot, powder, axes, knives, foolish and meaningless trinkets, tobacco, and liquor.

Not far from here Louis Riel and his dissatisfied followers had rebelled. At Batoche they had been finally routed and forever defeated.

Not far from where Lolly walked flowed the North Saskatchewan River; not too far away, the South Saskatchewan; the parkland nestled between, a productive strip greenly splitting the forest from the plains. The river had become a great highway for the fur trade and the collection of pemmican and northern furs.

Not far from here Poundmaker had surrendered; Big Bear, wily chief of the Plains and Forest Cree, also turned himself in to the Northwest Mounted Police.

Now the railroad reached its long finger up the center of the territory that was Saskatchewan, as far as Prince Albert. Now settlers, no longer afraid of the Indians, were trickling in. Now some of them, like Kingston Plummer, were developing small kingdoms of their own, claiming and holding land with a death grip. And for some it was to the death. But their sons and daughters would survive—and the land would be theirs.

Knowing some of this and feeling more of it, dimly, Lolly was more concerned with her own private plans. No sooner had she made up her mind to change her own destiny, regardless of the cost, than this door had opened to her. And not just the job and the money. There was the Plummer place itself—infinitely attractive to one tired of poverty and humiliation. And the owner was unmarried.

Wiser than she had known, Lolly had recognized the gleam in the eyes of Kingston Plummer. Sophisticated he might be and a man of some importance, but the expression on his face and the look in his eyes had been no different from that of the crude and lusty boys who had followed her with their eyes, if not their feet, when she walked down the streets of Prince Albert.

Just when she was wondering if she had taken the wrong trail, she came out of the bush into the Plummer yard; she recognized it from the drive past it the day before. Moreover, the horse—that black beauty—was grazing in a meadow nearby, along with others of almost equal quality.

Walking over the lush grass toward the house—large,

gingerbreaded, gleaming white in a land where most were a weathered gray—Lolly had a feeling of destiny. It served to firm her step, lift her head and, hardest of all and yet important, straighten her shoulders.

It served to keep her eyes level with his when Kingston Plummer, perhaps awaiting her, opened the great front door to which she had determinedly gone. It also served to quiet her rapid heartbeat when, head still high and posture erect, she stepped inside.

"Good afternoon, Miss Dalton," Kingston Plummer said, formally.

Equally formally, "Good afternoon," she responded, hoping the quaver in her voice would go unnoticed.

To a girl of lesser determination, her courage would have flagged when she was ushered into the parlor. Lolly didn't know when, if ever, she had been in an actual parlor before. But no other word suited.

Having wandered, awed, through furniture stores in Prince Albert and studying the various selections now available, Lolly had no trouble identifying the wood on the parlor suit as curly birch, the upholstery as a fine grade of brocaline crushed plush, and very expensive. Six pieces—sofa, divan, large easy rocker, arm chair, and two parlor chairs—were ranged effectively on a Tapestry Brussels Carpet, magnificent in its scrolled oak leaves on a background of yellow, wine, and tan colors. Several small tables held lamps and numerous gewgaws and knickknacks typical of the parlors of the day.

On one wall, by a braided cord, hung a massive painting of a girl in a white garment with long, flowing golden hair. Seas billowed below, but the girl clung tightly to a cross set in a rock. Several additional paintings, mostly dark and somewhat forbidding, graced other walls.

The curtains on the bay windows fell from near the ceiling to the floor and were, Lolly felt sure, made of Nottingham lace. Through an arch she could see heavy dining room furniture and more lace curtains. Across the entrance hall half-opened doors revealed other equally luxurious rooms.

Lolly supposed, from the silence, that they were alone. But once, from some distant part of the house, a small thump issued. Kingston Plummer frowned slightly, his narrow eyes flickering upward momentarily.

"Sit down, Miss Dalton," he invited.

"No, thank you. I've come, as you so kindly offered, for the hens."

"But we could take the time to get acquainted first." Kingston Plummer allowed his eyes once again to do their not-so-secret work. If he was disappointed to find her dress not as revealing as the day before when the Dalton wagon crossed in front of his property, he gave no indication. Standing as close as he did, Lolly was glad she had washed her hair. His breathing seemed to indicate that he was taking her in with more than just his eyes.

Lolly, as though born to the drama, stood her ground quietly with dignity and just enough reserve. Seeing his dress, his taste in furniture, she had correctly surmised that Kingston Plummer was not a man to count as precious anything that was cheap or too easily obtained.

But he tried. Oh, yes, he tried. Only her grim determination brought her through the next few moments the winner.

His opinion of her was revealed when he put his hand on her bare arm, urging her toward the sofa. "Surely, my dear, you can take a few minutes to—"

"Yes, Mr. Plummer?"

For the moment the distinguished squire of Plummer's place was at a loss for words. This snip of a girl—was she different than he had supposed? Different from what her near-squalid home situation had suggested?

"Well, get acquainted," Kingston said, doing some quick backpedaling until he was more certain of his ground.

"I think, Mr. Plummer, that it would be wise to get about the business for which I came." But Lolly did not remove her arm from the man's touch, further roiling the waters as far as Kingston was concerned.

He seemed to have trouble with his breathing, Lolly thought. And when she delicately put her hand on his and removed his touch from her arm, looking levelly into his eyes, it was almost to Kingston Plummer's undoing. His breathing increased alarmingly, and Lolly had an idea that he restrained himself from additional contact—just what, she was too untaught in this new endeavor to know. But he was unsure of her, and that was all to the good; she recognized the uncertainty in his hesitation. Should he? *Could* he?

At last Lolly stepped back and turned to the door. "I think it would be wise to see about the hens," she said gently.

"Certainly," Kingston Plummer responded quickly.

Just before the door shut behind them and they proceeded to pick up the sack Lolly had dropped over the porch railing, one last glance inside revealed a face—big-eyed, childish, curiously lonely—leaning over the banister.

"Do you have a family, Mr. Plummer?" she asked.

"A daughter," he said, leading the way down the steps and around the side of the house.

"And does she keep house for you?" (Silly question—the girl was a child. But an important question, a leading question.)

"She's just 13."

"Well, then, Mr. Plummer," Lolly was making an effort to

keep up with her companion who, having finished one scenario, was going at a good clip toward the hen house, "how do you manage? Keeping that big house, and all?" *Not to mention the care and companionship of the child,* she thought.

"It's been a problem. Especially at certain times, like spring cleaning . . . putting up garden stuff . . . making jams, and so on."

"Have you and your daughter been alone for long?" she asked, delicately, she hoped.

"Eight months," the man said, and it sounded like eight *long* months.

"And you've had no help all that time?"

"Oh, occasionally Lyddy Grimes has been available to help. But she has her own home and things to take care of."

Having reached their objective, Kingston Plummer raised his voice and called, "Hey, Arnie!"

A gangly youth appeared around the corner of the barn. "Will you sack up a half dozen of these hens?" Kingston asked and handed over the gunnysack.

To escape the hubbub of the chase, Kingston took, chastely enough, Lolly's elbow and turned her toward a bench near the garden. There, in the shade of a crabapple tree, he turned to look at her again.

"Miss Dalton—Lolita, is it?" Again a certain distaste was obvious in the tone of his voice.

"Lolly," she said. "I'm called Lolly."

"If we're to be on a first-name basis . . . and I trust we may be . . . how about—" Kingston hesitated only a moment, "how about Lita?"

"If you wish," she managed to answer lightly, stilling the aggravation that threatened. *Easy, Lolly, easy!*

"It occurs to me," Kingston said, as thoughtfully as if his words at the Daltons' camp earlier that morning hadn't hinted at this very thing, "you might be persuaded to take on the job."

"Why, Mr. Plummer—"

"King, please."

"Why, King, I'd be happy to help. What an excellent idea! There certainly isn't much for two women to do over at our place, at least not until the men get a house up. I think you may count on my help. Shall I come every day?"

"Good idea," Kingston said heartily, his color mounting with his enthusiasm—and his breathing also.

With the chickens successfully bagged, the hired man, Arnie, brought the sack over, having tied it closed securely. As Lolly reached for it, Kingston decided, "That's too heavy for you to lug all that way. If you can wait, I'll drive you home in about an hour in the buggy."

"Oh, thank you! That's very kind of you. But I think I'll walk. I enjoy the bush and need to time myself. That's the way I'll come and go, I'm sure." And Lolly reached again for the sack.

"Leave it, my . . . dear." Lolly had an idea such expression would come forth more readily in the future.

"Well, then—I'll be on my way. I'll see you later?"

With an unaccustomed swing of her hips, Lolly—Lita— turned and walked across the grass toward the trail and the bush. Not looking back, she was as certain as certain could be that Kingston Plummer's narrow eyes, probably with that glitter in them, were fixed on her. Still she managed to keep her head up and her shoulders back, tight dress and all.

Gaining the privacy of the bush, she paused, aware that she was trembling.

"Round one," she muttered and felt, in spite of a sense of having come off the victor, a sense of shame.

 9

Kingston Plummer personally delivered the half-dozen hens
Arnie had bagged up and added a generous supply of feed. At
Minnie's invitation, he had settled himself gingerly on an unsteady chair in the shade of a tree and accepted the cup of
coffee she offered. If he had hoped for further conversation
with "Lita," he was disappointed. Lolly was quietly showing
previously uncalled-for wisdom. Though not coy, she was
demure. It was a trait so unlike her usual forthrightness that
Rufe, passing through from the house site to the logs he was already considering for building purposes, paused, surprised,
and went on his way with suspicion in his eyes. *Lolly was up to
something.*

That his sister was contemplating earning money for
decent clothing, he knew. Perhaps his earnings could go for
some basic things for Lolly, and she would have no need for
further contact with the neighbor—the unwed neighbor—
with the big house, the handsome homestead, and the absorbed gaze turned, Rufe recognized uneasily, too often
toward his sister.

Tired of Minnie's chatter and apparently resigned to no
further possibility today of any intimacy with Lolly, Kingston
soon said his good-byes, adding, "I'll see you in the morning,
then, Miss Dalton. And Rufe too, if you'll kindly remind him
of our agreement."

"Oh, he'll remember, Mr. Plummer," Minnie assured
him, with another expression of appreciation for the
chickens.

"I'll send along a rooster," King Plummer said, turning to

mount his light wagon. "Should have thought of it sooner. Hens are no good without a rooster, eh?" His tone was heavily jocular.

If his veiled glance in her direction caught Lolly in a surprised flush—not having missed the inflection in his words—it only served to please him. *Aha! She wasn't as missish as she might let on!* Strong on the proprieties (at least on the surface), Kingston found himself titillated by what he interpreted as a secret revelation: *A little dallying might be in the offing after all!*

Watching him go in his expensive clothes and his excellent wagon—the hubs of oak and black birch, wheel rims of the finest white oak, axles of young hickory, box of clear yellow poplar, and the paint applied by brush with "positively no dripping" (she had heard his recitation in response to Rufe's admiration of the rig)—Lolly closed her mind deliberately to the shame that had swept over her earlier and firmed her scheme, if scheme it was. In her own defense she thought, *A woman has to use the means at her disposal,* and placated her uneasy conscience.

The following morning before Rufe and Lolly were up and thinking of their day's work at the Plummer place, Toby slipped out of the tent, picked up the now-empty lard pail, and turned toward the Szarvas place. Swinging the pail, Toby found himself whistling, reveling in the glorious day and its early-morning promise.

I do believe I'm feeling better than I have in a long time, maybe ever, was his joyous thought. *And this milk will help, and the walk, and the work.*

The girl had spoken truly—the Szarvas place lay just about a half-mile beyond the Mellon place. Approaching it, Toby paused, not knowing he had an artist's soul, and almost drank in the *rightness* of the homestead. Nestled with trees in the background, the buildings were so well constructed, sturdy, and strong, the fences so straight, the fields so perfect. It was all a picture of industry and order and careful attention to every detail, and the drab soul of the watching boy—young man—responded with a surge of emotion foreign to him. That one could be attached to one's home, never desiring to leave, was a new thought. For Toby it was a transforming moment. Life for him would never be the same again.

Early as he was, there was activity in the big barn, and Toby hastened in that direction. His first greeting was from the dog, and it was a friendly one. The rumpus brought a man to the doorway.

"Down, Spot!" the man commanded, but with a smile in Toby's direction.

What a common name for such a superior dog! Toby thought. But then the girl Kitty was inappropriately named too, in his opinion. As inappropriately as their Lolly, although he never equated "Lolly" with a woman of light morals, as his sister seemed to. As for Kitty, nothing was farther from a young cat's frolicsome ways than Katrin's down-to-earth, matter-of-fact manner. He doubted that she had an imaginative bone in her body, healthy and strong and magnificent, in a way, as it was. Toby looked at his own weedy limbs and narrow waist and sighed. *Now with more of this rich milk—*

"You be da boy from Mellon's place," the man—short, square, strong, and as healthy as his daughter—said and held out a callused hand.

"Toby Dalton, sir."

"I'm Szarvas, fadder of Katrin . . . and about a dozen odders." The man's good-natured face split in a hearty laugh. "Ya, ve got much milk here, plenty for us, da pigs, da cats—" There was a great twining of these creatures around Szarvas's overalled leg, "and you too. Yust a minute and I'll haff one of dese cows emdied out." And again came that infectious laugh.

"I came early, so I could help," Toby said, and so earnestly that Lazlo Szarvas was immediately convinced and offered no argument.

"I tink you mean it," he said and drew out another three-legged stool and plopped it beside a full-uddered cow, who turned her head and studied the milker fumbling so ineptly at her turgid milk-giving apparatus.

But she was patient, and so was the man, and in due time Toby stripped the teats of their milk. Standing to his feet, he felt his head swimming momentarily from having been lowered for such a length of time, and he leaned on the side of the stall.

Oh no! Not now . . . not here! And though the man looked at him keenly, and Kitty, who had been watching for the last few minutes, took a quick step in his direction, her face concerned, they both stepped back and said nothing when Toby straightened himself and carried his pail to be set with the others.

"Ve take dese to da house to be sebarated," Szarvas said, picking two of them up and starting for the house. Toby and Kitty followed, each with a brimming pail.

Never had Toby been in such a house. The outside, of log, had been added on and added on until it made a good-sized home, low and deep-eaved with heavy, handmade doors and windows recessed in the walls. Inside was equally warming. They stepped directly into what was obviously the living area, with full kitchen at one end, table and stools and chairs in the middle, and old and comfortable chairs grouped around a tin-bellied heater at the other end.

"My vife, Marta," the man who called himself Szarvas said, and a kind-faced, well-padded woman bustled toward him, plump hand outstretched, her lips smiling her welcome.

Introduced as "our Billy," the son rose from one of the chairs at the side of the table and hobbled forward. Taller than his father, still he was sturdy and healthy. Like his sister, Billy had thick, fair hair; unlike her, his first words disclosed a more impatient, volatile temperament.

"I can hardly stand it, being laid up! You, Kitty, are doing my work!"

Billy dropped back into his chair; Kitty lifted his foot up onto a stool and smiled amiably. With a tutting sound for his activity, she began rearranging the cloths with which the young man's knee was bound. "Take it easy, Billy. You'll soon be free of this and back to work—but not with that horse until you're fully healed."

Billy smiled at the bent head of his sister. "Two years younger," according to her report to the Daltons. "If anyone can get me well, you can," he said tolerantly, explaining to Toby, "Kitty has a heart as soft as butter. Anything sick or hurt gets her attention right away. Should have been a doctor, our Kitty."

"Not really," the girl said. "I'm happy being a farm girl." And Toby could see it was so. Never had he known such a contented, satisfied person as Katrin Szarvas. Taken away, living anywhere else, she would fade away, he thought, like a fish taken from water. Did she never long for anything different? He felt she did not and had an unusual ache at the thought of such stability, such contentment.

Marta was filling a platter with great slices of ham and a dozen or more fried eggs.

"Kiddy, pud on anudder plate for dis young man," she instructed.

"Oh, no, thank you!" Toby said quickly. "I have to get back, before my own family has breakfast." And though they were persuasive, he resisted. But the temptation was great to share not only the food that had, he knew, put the color in their cheeks and the strength in their muscles, but also the compelling warmth of their circle.

"Well, den, Kiddy, figs his milk," Marta instructed, and her daughter strained one pail of milk and filled the lard pail. Marta handed Toby another pail in which she had placed a pound of butter and a jar of brilliant-colored jelly.

Toby tried, stumblingly, to express his appreciation. "I'll come and help," he insisted. "There must be many things I can do—maybe in the garden, or cleaning out the barns—now that Billy is laid up."

"Vell, vell—" both mother and father tushed, but Toby had meant what he said, and they recognized it.

Ready to take his leave, his two pails in his hands, Toby's attention was drawn to a box beside the range. A kitten's head lifted over the edge, and it mewed piteously.

"Don't vorry aboud id," Marta said, "id's almost vell by now. Our Katrin iss feeding id, and id can soon ged along by idself."

From another box a scrabbling sound emanated, and Toby peered in, not surprised to see a dozen baby chicks.

"A coyote, or something, got the mother," Kitty explained, picking up one ball of fluff and cuddling it to her.

"If you zo much as step on a tack," Szarvas said fondly, "look oudt—our Kiddy vill luff you and make you vell."

And with that, Toby, weak and thin, given to "turns" at unexpected times, walked homeward.

 10

Donal was glad to be free, momentarily, from the crowded colonist car. The hard, slatted seats, the "tea tray" sleeping, the wretched facilities for personal hygiene—all had been a trial; he could only imagine how it had felt to the women who had the care of the children, the meals, and slept in such disordered publicity.

He paused on the platform, at a loss. Just when the next train across the prairies would be in, he hadn't inquired. Having just quit the noisome coach much as a fish is slithered from a barrel, he had no desire to resume the wearing journey.

It would help if he knew for sure where he was going. Without a definite goal, Donal hesitated, welcoming a breather.

And a "breather" it was as he relished the pure air under a very blue sky. Cold, but the snow had stopped and, in April, was sure to melt quickly, given a chance. Already the platform was clear and the street growing muddier with every passing rig—so muddy, in fact, that Donal thought twice about plunging his best boots into its morass.

But he was hungry for a decent meal, and a wide, busy thoroughfare promised grocery stores and restaurants. He shrank from locating a "transient hotel," where stranger would bunk with stranger—worse than the crowded conditions of the colonist car.

This spot, where the Assiniboine met the Red River, the Cree had named *Win-nipiy*, or "murky water," because of the reddish-brown silt churned up by the swell of the confluence.

From the first, the colony lay across the main Northwest trade routes to the west, in the heart of the buffalo country where the Hudson's Bay Company secured the pemmican supplies that were essential for the feeding of its western posts. With the eventual completion of the transcontinental railway system, Winnipeg rose out of Fort Garry as the chief prairie center. And the land seekers began to come.

For years men had been slow to take advantage of the offer of 160 free acres. Though the west was indeed fertile, it took people of vigorous strength, along with a certain brashness—perhaps even a desperation—to claim it and keep it. From 1881 to 1896, between Lake of the Woods and the Rocky Mountains, a vast stretch, settlers took up only 56,000 homesteads and abandoned some 16,000 of them, a sure sign of the harshness of the land and the hardness of the task. Ships, packed with immigrants, were almost as full on the return trip.

But things were changing. The serious depression was at an end; a far-reaching and persistent campaign for immigrants was strongly underway; land-hungry people everywhere were hearing and reading about the wonderful opportunities of the Canadian West. "A man can earn . . . the price of an acre of land a day," the Russians were told. It was heart-catching and appealing.

But warnings went out too. "No man should emigrate to the northwest who will not live and work hard," an early report warned. In an attempt to stem the flow of its people who were responding to the enticing bait the Canadian government dangled before them, Germany lodged an official protest against the "attempt to lure our countrymen to this desolate, subarctic region." And still they came.

In the line of Donal's vision was a chattering, eager but anxious-eyed group of "servant girls" from Scotland, come in answer to an ad that said they could "command 8-12 dollars a month." Bunched together, a roughly dressed family group—perhaps an extended family group with uncles and aunts and grandparents—fit the description of what Donal had heard referred to as "Sifton's Sheepskins," perhaps Doukhobors, those religious zealots from Russia who held their property in common. The "man in the sheepskin coat with the big, broad wife," was sponsored by Leo Tolstoy and the English Quakers and would rate a paragraph and more in every history book to follow.

But with all of them—the Galicians, Ruthenians, Hungarians, Magyars, Russians, Americans, eastern Canadians, and French, as well as those few from China and India—there was room, much more room for more.

Making up his mind at last, Donal struck out, down the street to a hotel and a dining room. From his scanty, hoarded store he ordered "real" food—roast beef, potatoes, peas, a slab of raisin pie and, with all of it, cups and cups of hot coffee. Donal had had enough tea to last him for some time, thanks to the Wimber (by now Hager, he supposed) girls.

Next to him and as alone as he was, another young man dug into his food with as much energy as Donal, and, catching each other's eye, they lifted their steaming cups in a salute, and grinned—quite apparently akin in purpose.

"May I?" the stranger said, and, coffee cup in hand, joined Donal.

"Glad to have you," Donal said sincerely and suddenly didn't feel quite so far from home and brother.

"Name's Jenner Coy," the newcomer said with another infectious grin.

Here's one of a kind, Donal thought. Jenner Coy, probably a little younger than Donal, was slight of build but wiry. His square face was freckled and a mop of curly red hair competed in brilliance with a handsome mustache. Donal had a feeling that when he put on his cap it would be at a rakish angle. His eyes sparkled with good humor and an interest in life.

"Donal Cardigan," Donal answered, and the young men shook hands heartily, grinning again.

"Where are you bound?" Jenner Coy asked.

"Now, that's a good question—I really can't say at the moment. West, of course."

"West—and north, for me."

"Oh, yeah?" Donal's curiosity was piqued. "How far west? How far north?"

"Just far enough west to get me into Saskatchewan. Then on up to the end of the line—Prince Albert."

"Traveling by train, are you?"

"I was—came from Ontario. You too?"

The men took a moment to compare notes, relating a little about family and the situation back "home."

"From here," Jenner Coy explained, "I'm going by team and wagon."

"Oh, yeah?" Donal said again. "How come?"

"Well, it's this way—I'm only on this . . . excursion . . . because of my great-uncle Willoughby."

"Sounds interesting," Donal said with a laugh, preparing himself to settle down, enjoy his coffee, and hear more. It sounded as if Jenner's tale were much more interesting than his own.

"Let's hear about Uncle Willoughby."

"My mum's uncle. He has no family of his own; was married, but she died young and there were no children. Uncle Willoughby sort of took to me, I guess. Anyway, a number of years ago he pulled out . . . sold out his quarry business and made this strange decision to homestead. He's made a good start, I hear, and wants me to join him. I suppose," Jenner said thoughtfully, "I'm his heir, in a way. Truth to tell, I'd rather have inherited the quarry than a raw homestead. I don't know if I'm cut out for farming."

"That's all I've known, of course. And that's where I'm heading, for a homestead of my own. That rocky farm back home—you can have it, I told my brother."

"Well, I'm going to give it a try. The reason I'm here in Winnipeg is to latch onto a wagonload of goods Uncle Willoughby wants—"

"From here? Why not get things right there in Prince Albert? I hear it's becoming quite a thriving town, now that the railway has reached it."

"For one thing, Uncle stopped here for a while, looking around. He decided to go on farther, but while he was here he bought some things he seems to treasure—I don't know what all. It's packed and pretty-well loaded on the wagon. Probably books, for one thing; maybe some treasures of his wife's; it looks like there's some furniture on board. A small load, really, but select. Of course, right now I'm loading up on grub and a tent and stuff like that. I'm waiting for the weather to clear before starting out."

"I hated to go on with such miserable conditions too," Donal said. "Sort of takes the enthusiasm out of everything. Land hunting wouldn't be the most pleasant experience when it's like this."

Donal and Jenner Coy settled their bills, clapped their hats on their heads, and went outside together. The sun was well out, eaves were dripping, and the late-season snow was quickly disappearing under the wheels and hoofs of passing rigs.

Donal glanced up and down the street, still undecided. Where to go? What to do next? What direction?

Jenner Coy started up the street and, with only a moment's hesitation, Donal fell into step with him.

"Uncle Willoughby has a man here who handled some of his affairs for him," Jenner explained. "They keep in touch, and this gent had things pretty well organized when I got here. I think he'll be glad to get Uncle's things off his hands. One good thing—there's plenty of funds. But, funds or no, camping is camping, and roughing it is the same for paupers or millionaires. Can't say I look forward to it. Frankly, Donal, I'm a city fella. This trek across the wilderness has me worried."

"You'll make it fine, I'm sure. There are plenty men more green than you heading out for the unknown. At least you know where you're headed."

"Wildrose—that's the name of the place. Uncle Willoughby's homestead is in a place called Wildrose . . . can't seem to say enough good things about it."

"If names mean anything, it could be great. Now Great Slave—that's enough to chill anyone's enthusiasm."

"You bet! They do pick descriptive names, if you've noticed—Reindeer Lake, Swift Current, Moose Jaw, Maple Creek . . ."

"Wildrose, eh? I like the sound of it. And not nearly as far, nor as cold, as Great Slave country, right?"

"Right out of Prince Albert, Uncle says, in the parkland. Parkland sounds better, somehow, than bush."

"I've thought about the bush country . . . either it, or the prairie."

"Big difference, man!"

The men had been walking down the boardwalk, Donal knew not where. But Jenner Coy seemed to know and took a straight path toward a livery stable.

"The wagon is parked here, and the team of horses too, of

course. Everything is ready except to put in fresh food, like bread and butter, bacon—that sort of thing. I wish I felt better, easier, about this. Say—" Jenner Coy stopped in his tracks and looked at Donal out of his brilliant blue eyes, "why don't you come with me, at least until we get into Saskatchewan Territory? Then you could make up your mind—keep going west, or turn north. How about it, man?"

Somehow it seemed so right. Though unexpected, it rang the bell Donal had been instinctively listening for. Margot, his mother, would have said, "This is the way, walk ye in it" (Isa. 30:21).

"It would get me off that miserable colonist car," Donal said with an immediately favorable reaction.

"You can share my digs for a night or two, Donal, and we'll be on our way with the first meadowlark. That is," the exuberant Jenner said, less poetically, "as soon as this rotten weather passes and the roads dry out a bit."

Wildrose. Somewhere that same bell rang, distantly echoing in Donal's heart, but insistently . . . fetchingly.

11

It was breakfast time at the Dalton-Mellon place. Today, because of Toby's early-morning trip to the Szarvas farm, there was milk again, and not only for the everlasting porridge. Minnie had made pancakes, a special treat made possible not only because of the milk, but also the eggs. The hens had laid! Five eggs had been found at first dawning, a dawning yet unbroken by rooster call. But soon they would have a rooster to crow, if Kingston Plummer was a man of his word. And somehow he seemed like a man who was used to arranging matters.

"Now, Toby," Minnie said, filling her son's cup with milk, "I'm going to insist that you drink milk every day. And with these eggs—why, we'll have you strong and healthy in no time!"

Toby was willing and drank gladly and ate happily.

"Soon," Minnie continued, equally happy, "we'll have green stuff from the garden. Things have a way of just springing to life here, I'm told. We'll be having lettuce and radishes and such before you know it."

"No dandelion greens, please," Toby begged, heartily sick of this prairie fixture.

"That shed out back is a godsend," Rufe said now. "For one thing, there are lots of jars out there. We'll be able to put up any extra vegetables. And what's more—"

The entire family stopped their chewing, eating, buttering, and cutting to look up at the tone that seemed to sing in Rufe's voice.

"And what's more—we should be able to store things

92

away in a cellar. There are almost enough logs prepared for building! Poor Mellon—he really had a dream here and had to give it all up."

"Well," Minnie said lightly, and no one caught the pathos in what she said, "perhaps we can carry the dream on for him."

"So we can, old girl," Hudson said heartily.

Rufe, wise son, followed up this positive declaration from his father by suggesting, "Dad, you could begin digging out the cellar while I'm over at Plummer's today."

Hudson was a trifle taken aback by the firm voice, but at the chorus of approval and encouragement that emanated from his family, he cleared his throat and nodded.

"Sounds like a good idea. The sooner the better—don't put off till tomorrow what you can do today, eh?"

Minnie looked at her husband proudly; it would have energized that distant South American mammal, the sloth, to action.

"Now, let me see," Hud said, frowning into the early-morning sunlight, "where should we build?"

"Right here, in front of the shack," Rufe suggested, having given the project considerable thought. "We'll connect the shack onto the back, keeping it as the kitchen. It's big enough to eat in, if we want, and to keep a bed at one end for Toby and me. That way Mum and Dad can have a room, and Sis one too, as well as a—we won't call it a parlor, but it will be a sort of front room, I guess you'd say."

"Just like real people!" Toby chortled, quoting his sister's words of yesterday. Again the small flicker of—was it pain or hurt?—crossed Minnie's usually composed features.

This time it was seen, and misunderstood, by her husband.

"What's the matter, old girl? Got a touch of dyspepsia?"

"No, no, I'm fine." And Minnie buried her telltale face in her cup.

"What'll you do today, Toby?" Rufe pursued, with the thought of winter nagging at his mind and an urgency to see that they were better prepared this year than last.

"I'll help Mum with whatever she needs to get straightened around here," Toby said, and Minnie smiled on him fondly, "and then—then I think I'll go back to the Szarvas farm, see if I can help there. Who knows? Maybe I can earn something too."

Toby hadn't had a thought of earning any money until that moment. Rather, he felt an undeniable tug toward that place of comfort, goodwill, and contentment. He had been so accustomed to failure and impotency that now to him the Szarvas place spoke of purpose and accomplishment and gave an aura of personal satisfaction that seemed to spread itself over the home, the faces of the people, the very fields. It was nothing Toby could put into words, but it called to his heart and begged for recognition.

"Won't hurt to find out," Hudson said hopefully. "They'll need help, I think, as long as that boy of theirs is laid up with that bad knee."

"But he can't take wages," protested Minnie. "Think of how kind they've been to us. You go on over, Son, and see if you can't repay them a little."

"*If* they want to give you something for your work, *if* you work," Hud said thoughtfully, "a little pig or two—"

"A dog," Toby said promptly.

"You know," Lolly said as she and Rufe were making their way through the thickets and trees toward the Plummer place, "I could get to like this Wildrose."

"Maybe you better not get too attached, Sis," Rufe

warned. "You know how it's been."

Lolly was silent as she stopped to see if pin cherry blossoms had any fragrance. "I'm through moving, Rufe . . . through moving on at the slightest whim of Dad's. I'm an adult now . . . well, I *am* . . . and I've got something to say about my own future!"

"Don't count on this job as it. Hired girl is no permanent future. If Dad decides to move, you'll have no choice."

"I'm not moving on again, Rufe. I've got some ideas on the subject."

"Well, decent clothes will be a good beginning," Rufe said, casting a look at his sister, slim and lovely in the dappled light through the poplars, but—too much of her loveliness showed.

Lolly had put on the second dress for working today, and it was too skimpy by far.

"Sis," Rufe said seriously, "keep out of that man's way."

"Rufe! What a thing to suggest! I know what you mean, and it isn't nice!"

"You're a young woman now . . . a *pretty* young woman. And that dress *is too tight!*"

Lolly flushed, overcome by her brother's remark. But whether it was because he was so frank or it was a backhanded compliment, she wasn't sure. Certainly Rufe had never indicated she might have grown into an attractive woman; brothers didn't do that.

Rufe had been catapulted into his complimentary remark because of his need to warn his sister. There was much more he could have said in warning and also about his sister's attractions, but he felt he had overspoken as it was.

So he finished gruffly, "Just wise up a little, OK?"

Pulling out of the greenery into the farmyard, Lolly looked at the clear indications of prosperity and said thoughtfully, "I know what I'm doing. You'll see—"

Sure enough, Toby was put to work in the garden. Weeds responded to the bright sun and brisk rains as well as vegetables, and, at the Szarvas place, weeds were not countenanced. Unwelcome interlopers, they were dispatched as soon as they dared show themselves.

"Why, Toby, how nize off you," Szarvas himself had said, and instructed Kitty to find the hoe for "the poy," and went off to his own day's work.

Hilling the potatoes, already displaying their fat green leaves, Toby worked down one row and up another, as contented as he had ever been in all his life. A call from the barn door brought his work to a halt. Leaning on the hoe, he turned to see Kitty in the doorway, something in her hands.

"Come on over for a minute," she called, and Toby jumped over the rows toward her.

"Oh, wow!" Toby took the small, wriggling pup in his dirt-grimed hands and put the little creature to his cheek in as loving a gesture as it is possible for a man of 19 to do, with the blue eyes and pink cheeks of a 16-year-old girl not three feet away.

"Want him?" Kitty asked, sure of the answer.

"*Want him?* What a question!"

"We have four more."

"He looks just like—" Embarrassed, Toby paused.

"His father," Kitty finished matter-of-factly. Paternity and reproduction were no matter for false modesty here on the farm.

"His mother," Kitty continued, "is Floppsie, and she's right in here with the rest of them."

"Floppsie"! As common as "Spot"!

"It's because of her ears, you see," Kitty explained,

kneeling beside the mother dog and lifting a large ear and letting it drop.

"And what's this little feller's name?" Toby asked, cuddling the warm bundle to his thin chest.

"Hasn't been named—you can do that."

Well, it won't be "Rover" or "Fido" or "Pal"—that's for sure! Toby decided on the spot. Something descriptive, with some imagination. And again Toby studied the serene face of the girl Kitty and found it lacking in animation and excitement.

Having played with the tumbling pups for a while and noting the passing of the morning, Toby reluctantly put his dog with the family, for the time being, and returned to his task. Nearby Kitty was erecting stakes for the day the pole beans would be ready for climbing.

The rattle of buggy wheels drew their attention to a rig driving into the yard.

"It's the widow Fanchon," Kitty said.

"Widow?" Toby had never remained in one location long enough to become acquainted with a real widow.

"And a widow she'll remain, no doubt," Kitty said, not too loudly. "But you'll see why."

"Morning, Kitty."

"Good morning, Miz Fanchon." Kitty laid aside her stakes and walked over to the buggy.

In it sat, or more aptly reigned, a large, prepossessing woman of about 60 years of age. Her bonnet was old-fashioned, as were her voluminous clothes. In fact, Toby thought, she looked like a large Queen Victoria. And something about her called for a respect not unlike that which the good queen commanded.

Miz Fanchon's gaze fixed on Toby, and Kitty said, "This is our new neighbor, Toby Dalton. Toby, Miz Fanchon."

Widow Fanchon greeted Toby kindly, and Toby removed

his hat and nodded, managing a polite "Miz Fanchon," though the manner of this assuming female was strange to him.

"I've come to see your mother," the widow informed them and drove on to the house.

Watching, Toby saw her alight heavily and greet Marta Szarvas with a kiss when she came from the house to welcome her guest. The pair disappeared inside, and Toby and Kitty resumed their work.

"She lives just on down the road, not too far," Kitty explained. "Her land is across from ours—just next to yours, in fact. She's on one side of you, Kingston Plummer on the other."

"What happened to Mr. Fanchon?"

"I never knew him; he died a long time ago. Widow Fanchon manages with a hired man. She's quite wealthy, you know. Nobody knows why she stays on here. She has family in the east that are in trade in a big way; I think a brother has something to do with the government too. In spite of that, she lives in the same log house her husband built for her; it's been added onto, of course, and is as convenient as any home can be, for a homestead. They were here even before we were. She and Mum are great friends."

When the visitor had clambered back into her rig and turned to leave, she stopped the buggy again at the side of the garden plot.

"Say, there—Toby Dalton!"

"Yes?" Toby looked up and in response to her imperious beckon went to the side of the buggy, looking up into her small, keen eyes. With cap in hand he exposed, if he had but known it, a face too pale and too thin but with frank eyes and a straight look.

"Yes, ma'am?" he said.

"I need help at my place, Toby Dalton," the lady said (and probably she was the first true lady Toby had ever known).

"How may I help, ma'am?" he asked now, respectfully.

"I see you're doing a nice job on this garden. Mine is fast going to weeds. I have a little trouble sashaying around sufficiently to weed properly." A small smile softened her otherwise rather stern countenance.

"Yes, ma'am," Toby said and, because of the smile, added, with one of his own, "I sashay quite well."

"You'll do, Toby Dalton," the widow said, and her smile widened. "Could you give me half a day, say, starting tomorrow? I could pay cash, if you wish, or you might want to take a piglet, maybe a calf, things your family may want for getting started."

Now Toby's smile widened into a true grin. "It's a deal! I'll see you tomorrow!"

Almost giddy with pleasure and satisfaction, Toby returned to the potatoes. A job! Working as surely as his bigger, stronger brother. The sun climbed higher in the sky, the day grew progressively hotter, and still Toby worked doggedly on, stopping from time to time to draw a bandanna from his hip pocket to mop his brow.

The giddiness, which he had accepted as a natural reaction to his pleasure in Widow Fanchon's offer, increased. Toby's heart increased its beat, his breath shortened in a well-remembered pattern, his brow beaded and, with a gasp and a faint "Oh, no!" he staggered, reeled, and fell into the soft dirt of the garden.

It seemed the worst thing that had ever happened to him but was perhaps the best.

12

Behind a pair of matched bays—an excellent team, Donal thought—the rig rolled across the prairie with Winnipeg far behind.

Donal had seen many an immigrant and his family heading out for their homestead, goods piled a dozen feet and more above the wagon with mattresses balancing on top of the precarious load. At times there was little or no room for the family and they trudged behind or alongside.

First you had to locate your land. If you had filed, you had a legal description of your homestead, a series of numbers that told you exactly where it was. Everything was set off from the first meridian, which was about 10 miles from Winnipeg, Donal had been told, when in a deep conversation about such matters with a crowd of immigrants rooming at the place where Jenner Coy had taken temporary quarters.

After the meridians, the land was marked off in ranges; then you looked for your township, then your section. Townships numbered their sections on the map from bottom right to left, 1 through 6; then up one step above 6 and that was 7 and so on until all 36 were numbered.

The meridian located your area largely, the range brought you closer to your destination, and then it was a matter of finding your section in your township.

You could measure distances pretty well, Donal learned, by the "buggy-wheel method." If you knew the circumference of your wheel and tied a tag to its rim, you simply counted every time it came around, did a little mathematics, and then had a fair estimation of how far you were from town or wherever.

Just now Donal and Jenner, having made a good 20 miles since morning, were tired and looking for a camping spot. The snow was gone and the day had been a pleasant one, but evening promised to be cold. A fire would feel good. Moreover, it would be cheerful, and Donal, growing more dubious about the prairie by the minute, welcomed a little cheer.

Not that Jenner wasn't good company. His grin greeted the day and his laugh punctuated most experiences, good or bad. Rarely had Donal met a more happy-go-lucky individual than Jenner Coy. Nothing was too serious to elicit a joke or a disclaimer; at times Donal felt a little thoughtfulness would be a wiser way to go. But he shrugged it off; Uncle Willoughby's plans and their fulfilling were none of his business. Soon enough he would leave the small wagon train that had assembled around them as they journeyed and take off on his own. But where? Donal couldn't forget the scene just a few days ago when one of the families had pulled off the trail, checking stakes, and the man had announced, "This is it, Mamie."

Mamie's face, as she gazed out over the bald prairie, was a picture frozen in Donal's mind. Obviously a lady of some refinement, she had paled, drawn in her breath, looked right and left, back and forth and, outside of the accompanying wagons, saw absolutely nothing but sky and land.

Even as she stood, a desolate figure, her man was unloading. Donal and the others had helped, stacking a pitifully small store of equipment in a mound at Mamie's feet.

Now Donal saw the reason for the "buffalo chips" the children had picked up along the way, dropping them into a sack hung below the wagon. Not buffalo offal, of course, but nowadays cow chips. And even these were scarce. They would travel many miles for fuel; even the grass was too green for use this early in the year.

Donal hoped that when the homesteader had sunk his off-loaded hand plow into his land, turned his sod for half a mile or more, and stopped to look back at the first furrow ever to rupture this virgin soil, it would be worth it all.

Not one wagon had been capable of shoving on. As one person they disembarked and set to work. Four thousand sod "bricks," give or take a few, were what they would need for a house 16 feet by 24—an impossible and overwhelming task for a man alone. Before the wagon train went on they had cut and stacked most of it, piling walls up and up with a small slant inward. Then Jenner, checking his timetable, moved out. "Uncle Willoughby will be wondering where in the world I am. After all, he has a crop to get in too." Farther north, planting would be a little later. Still, there was need to press on; for one thing, supplies would run out.

Now pulling into a rather shallow but tree-lined coulee, the three wagons still together drew to a grateful halt.

"Honest-to-goodness wood!" Jenner exclaimed, sick to death of gathering buffalo chips and perhaps finding it hard work to be good-natured about cooking over them.

Of the Falza and Bumberg families, Leona Falza prepared the prairie chickens her son had shot that day; Alma Bumberg made a bannock in the mouth of a flour sack. Their older children unloaded what was necessary for the evening meal and the night's rest—bedding, frying pans, pots, foodstuff, wash basin, chairs, table. The men unhitched and led the horses to the small tricklet of water, then went farther upstream to fill empty water containers and fetch clean water for coffee and bathing later.

Donal stretched, weary of the day's incessant jiggling and rocking, though he had interspersed it with long walks beside the rig.

"I'll set up camp," he offered and lowered the tailgate for

easy access to the items they constantly used.

"Hand me the axe," Jenner suggested. "As I water the horses, I'll take a look-see for wood, and we'll have a fire going in jig time."

Uncle Willoughby's money had provided well for his great-nephew; there was no lack of food. Looking over the supplies, Donal decided to bake a couple of potatoes as soon as the coals might be ready, then fry some bacon and pour the grease over the piping hot potatoes. He determined to ask Mrs. Falza for her recipe for bannock; tonight they would have the hardtack Jenner had made a couple of days ago. Soaked in an opened can of peaches, it would finish off their meal satisfactorily. And, of course, coffee.

The early-evening air was rent by a hoarse cry. There was in it such a tone of anguish that every head in camp rose, every foot turned to run toward the sound emanating from the depths of the coulee.

Farther from the spot than the others, Donal reached the streambed to find a tight group of people bunched around a figure on the ground and heard continued groans. Pushing his way through, Donal saw Jenner in a crouch, his arms wrapped around a leg from which blood poured, saturating the pants leg and already spreading in a stain on the ground. His face, as pale as death itself, lifted to the circle of startled and frightened eyes ringed around him.

"Help me!" he croaked. At his side lay the axe, its blade red.

Quick hands lifted and carried the injured man up the bank, into camp. Someone brought scissors and slit the pant leg to the thigh. There, above the knee, wide and gaping and exposing the bone, the full damage was revealed. Blood continued to flow, almost to spurt.

Donal's first thought was "Thank God we weren't alone!"

The two ladies of the group, shocked almost speechless, did what they could.

"Hold that wound together!"

"Get some rags!"

"Salve! No—that wouldn't be any earthly good! Oh, what can we put on it?"

Eventually flour was packed into the wound, but a doctor's expertise was what was needed, and there was no such help available.

Finally, with the terrible gash bound up as tightly as possible, still seeping red, the shaken company, for the most part, turned to their own camps and the need to feed their families.

Donal, with shaking hands, managed a fire and put coffee to boil. Jenner, teeth fixed and eyes closed, tried a few swallows when it was ready but refused food.

Before bedtime the ladies crept back with fresh bandages, throwing the saturated cloths into the fire with a shudder. The wound gaped fleshily while Jenner's lifeblood, not a lot brighter than his flamboyant head, soaked steadily into the prairie's dryness.

By morning, Jenner was so white, so still, that Donal despaired, thinking him dead. But a pulse beat faintly in his neck, though his breath, when discerned, grew more and more ragged. Sitting on the ground beside his new friend, Donal felt such an impotency, such a frustration, that it threatened to choke him. The sound that escaped him—part groan, part cry—reached the injured man as nothing else had. Opening his eyes in the early-morning paleness, Jenner tried to focus his eyes, finally fixing them on Donal, and he made a faint sound. Donal leaned toward him, covering him in a protective gesture, though Jenner had remained so still all night the blanket had barely moved.

"Donal—" the word was a whisper.

"I'm here, man."

"Uncle Willoughby—he won't know what happened . . . his treasures are all in that wagon—"

"Don't worry about it," Donal urged hoarsely.

"Donal—"

"Jenner? Jenner?" For a moment Donal thought his friend was gone.

Finally, as though struggling, as though thought and speech were too much, Jenner whispered, "Donal—"

"I'm here, man."

"Please go on . . . to Prince Albert. Tell Uncle Willoughby—" Words failed momentarily. "Tell Uncle Willoughby . . . I tried—"

Donal couldn't help it; tears flowed.

"I will, Jenner! I will!"

More silence. Finally, a small smile, a ghost of the old smile, touched Jenner's colorless face.

The hand, once so brown and firm and strong, had reached for . . . for someone, long ago. Groping across the sand, it had touched Donal's knee in the dark of the night. Instinctively Donal had grasped it, wishing his own pulsing blood could transfuse into the collapsing veins of the young man losing his into the thirsty prairie.

Now Donal felt that hand go limp. Gently he laid it on Jenner's chest, and gently he pulled the blanket over the face now relaxed in death.

It was here the gathering women and men of the other wagons found them. Kind voices urged Donal back, and caring hands, hands of strangers but tied to one another because of common need, prepared the body for burial.

Upon the lip of the coulee they laid him. "Face him north," Donal said roughly, and they did.

What rocks could be found were piled over the grave; no wood was available for a marker, so a piece of cardboard box was fastened to a stick and thrust into the ground and read, JENNER COY, PIONEER. Soon it would blow away on the prairie wind; someone would find it caught in the grasses and would rejoice that they had something for their supper fire, and all trace of the man that had been Jenner Coy would be erased from the face of the earth. The prairie would be as blank and as empty as ever—emptier—because one man would walk it no more.

13

Toby came to consciousness to find his head cradled in the lap of Katrin Szarvas. Her solid youthfulness kept the sun from his eyes. As she bent over him, her braid swung toward him and her face leaned close as she stroked his hair back from his sweat-beaded forehead. The smell of her, he discerned hazily, was one of earth, sun, and soap. Earth, sun, soap—it seemed to typify what he knew of her and what would forevermore in his thinking be associated with Kitty Szarvas.

Embarrassed and humiliated, Toby wished he had never to open his eyes. But Kitty had obviously seen his lids flicker.

"There, now," she crooned tenderly. "You're fine . . . just fine." Gritting his teeth, Toby sat up and Kitty leaned back on her heels, looking at him compassionately.

Dazed as he was, Toby thought of the little bird Kitty had pulled from her pocket the first time he met her. "It just needs a little care" she had said then and put it comfortably and sensibly into her pocket.

It would be, he thought groggily, a good place to be. But he was too big and, besides that, supposed to be a man. Again a wave of the familiar shame swept over him.

Kitty, watching calmly, said, "Take it easy. Sunstroke is no fun."

"It wasn't the sun," Toby managed, determined to reveal the truth, miserable as it was. "I have these—turns, I guess you'd call them. I've had them ever since I hit my teens."

"You'll outgrow them," Kitty offered, rising to her feet and offering him her hand.

That hand, that plain square hand, accustomed to hard

work and devoted to kind deeds, was extended for the first time to one who very much needed it. Toby found himself relying on its strength without hesitation, without embarrassment.

On his feet again, he looked around for the hoe.

"Forget it, Toby, for today," Kitty said reasonably. "It's getting too hot for work in the garden, anyway."

About to turn homeward, Toby found himself herded houseward. Inside in the cool, refreshing atmosphere without any word concerning his "problem," Kitty brought him a cold glass of water and had one herself. The condensation ran down the outside of the glass, and Toby's finger played with it casually.

"Say, thanks a lot for—helping me out there."

Kitty looked up, almost blankly, as if the matter he referred to had already been forgotten. "Oh . . . don't mention it," she said, and Toby felt there was no need to.

Still, as he left the shelter of the house and made his way down the lane toward the road and home, he was aware of Kitty's eyes, alert and aware, on his back. It was a good feeling.

Turning around, Toby waved a good-bye.

"I'll call him Faithful," he called back.

Kitty placed a hand behind her ear, an indication that she hadn't heard or, hearing, hadn't understood.

"Faithful," he shouted. "The pup—I'll call him Faithful!"

At home, announcing that he now had a dog and had decided to call it Faithful, Minnie smiled her approval.

Hud raised his eyebrows a bit. "Isn't that rather a fanciful name, for a dog?" he wanted to know.

Toby supposed that it was. It'd also be a fanciful name for a girl who, of all things, was as far removed from anything capricious or frivolous, as a worker bee devoted to its task.

"And I've got work too," he said proudly.

"You shouldn't take money from those folks," Minnie said reproachfully. "They've been too kind."

"Not them, Mum. This is for the widow Fanchon. If you keep going rather than turning into the Szarvas place," he explained, "you'll come to the Fanchon place, except it's on the other side of the road. The same side as this place. Widow Fanchon is our neighbor on the east. Plummer, *King* Plummer, that is, is to the west of us."

Toby couldn't explain why he emphasized King in that way. But he knew he was grateful that he would be working for the keen but kind-eyed Widow Fanchon rather than the narrow, too-keen-eyed Kingston Plummer.

Rufe and Lolly had reached the Plummer place to find a slick-haired, freshly shaven, sweet-smelling Kingston Plummer ready for them. He sent Rufe to the big barn to clean the stalls, the first thorough cleaning since the long winter, he said. Arnie, the "hired boy," was planting corn. "We're a little late on that," Kingston said with a slight frown, "just not enough hands to go around. You see," he said, turning to Lolly, "I've had the care of the housework since the wife—er—passed on, and my daughter's care too."

"I look forward to meeting her," Lolly said politely.

The young girl—though at 13 she looked very much a child—was standing at the table, her hands in a dishpan of water, when Lolly followed Kingston indoors. She looked up shyly.

"Anna-Rose," the man spoke more sharply, Lolly thought, than the occasion demanded, "this is Miss, ah, Dalton—"

"Call me Lolly," Lolly said quickly and sympathetically

and felt rewarded by the light that came into the soft gray eyes.

"I'll need to show you about," the man said, "and outline some things that need to be done. Anna-Rose should be able to do it, but—"

Anna-Rose looked properly humbled by the criticism, more implied than spoken. But perhaps Anna-Rose already knew her father's opinion of her.

"The house has been sadly neglected since my wife's— er—demise." King Plummer seemed to have trouble saying death. But it was inferred at every turn: he was a widower; he was in need of—

This was where Kingston Plummer's motives were unclear. That he had "eyes" for her, Lolly knew. She suspected, too, that her appearance—bright, easily tumbled hair, too-tight clothes, and red mouth—conspired to brand her a woman of easy virtue.

Kingston Plummer, Lolly was determined, would find her a woman who, though desirable, was attainable only through the legal rite of marriage.

To accomplish this would take all the skill and artifices Lolly could muster, and she was totally unskilled. Presenting herself as virtuous was no problem; she was that, through and through. But representing everything that was desirable was another, touchier, matter. It must be done with restraint yet with a veiled suggestion: touch-me-not versus I-dare-you.

One part of Lolly was appalled at what she was contemplating. Another part, the desperate, poverty-weary part, goaded her on like a burr under a saddle blanket. She herself was her only commodity of barter. Put that baldly, Lolly was scandalized. Thinking of the scheme as "something for something" made it entirely reasonable, however. Anyway, what other option did she have? In an isolated corner of the bush, poor and deprived, what was her future? More poverty and deprivation? Never!

So with quaking heart but determined feet Lolly followed Kingston Plummer around his house. It was decided that the windows and curtains, showing the effects of the winter's smoke and grime, should have first attention.

"Anna-Rose can show you where cleaning materials are. I'll get Arnie to bring in a ladder."

"Anna-Rose," Lolly said, truly concerned, "is there something I can do for her?"

"Anna-Rose has her own duties. No doubt she will be pleased to have company. Life has been lonely for her—as for me."

"You've both managed very well, I'm sure," Lolly offered.

"Perhaps. We're ready to get on with our lives now—"

Again there was the hint of Kingston's need and the possibility that she might fill it.

With sympathy only half feigned, Lolly put her hand on the man's arm. "Anything I can do to help—"

Instantly his own hand covered hers. Again, as he looked down on her upturned face, his breathing quickened and his gaze seemed to burn into hers. *Easy, Lolly, easy!*

When the moment had passed and Kingston had left the house for duties elsewhere, Lolly had a brief feeling of panic. But catching sight of herself in her washed-out, outgrown, out-of-style dress in the buffet mirror, she firmed her resolve. Anything—*anything* was better than this!

Back in the kitchen, Anna-Rose had finished washing and wiping the dishes and was contemplating a large pot around which she had assembled various items indicating she was in the process of cooking something.

"Dinner," Anna-Rose said simply.

"Can I help?"

"Oh, would you?" There was relief in Anna-Rose's voice. "I never know what to fix."

"What have you got here—some leftover roast beef?"

At Anna-Rose's nod, Lolly continued, "How about beef barley soup? Let's see—do you have barley?"

On being assured barley was a staple in the pantry, Lolly worked with Anna-Rose to assemble the remaining ingredients. Anna-Rose made a trip to the cellar for a panful of last year's carrots, now withered almost past use, an onion, and a couple of potatoes, as withered as the carrots.

Paring and slicing, the girls progressed speedily toward getting the soup on to boil, then simmer, in plenty of time for the noon meal.

"It really should simmer all day," Lolly said, "but it will just have to do. Is there bread? No? We'll make biscuits, right at the last. You do have flour? Baking powder?" Lolly listed the ingredients needed, and Anna-Rose's head bobbed in response. What a delight a full pantry was! No bannock here, apparently, and definitely no hardtack.

"I thought you were supposed to do the windows," Anna-Rose said timidly.

"Pooh! They can wait—but not too long," Lolly added quickly, noting the anxiety in the girl's eyes. "I'll help you, and then you can help me. How's that?"

It seemed fine to Anna-Rose.

"Now," Lolly said when the soup was simmering satisfactorily, "let's think about some dessert for those menfolk."

"And us," Anna-Rose insisted.

"I saw some rhubarb when I crossed the yard. You scoot out and get some, and I'll scout around in the pantry and see if we have flour. Sugar? Lard?"

Again Anna-Rose's nod affirmed the availability of these items. When the child was gone with a knife to remove the leaves and ends and with a pan to bring the rhubarb in, Lolly visited the pantry. She was awed at the abundance.

Besides generous supplies of the basic items—flour, sugar, butter, baking powder, salt, soda, yeast, and a basket of eggs—there were unusual items such as rice and tapioca, honey, a keg of syrup, bacon, dried apples, and a shelf of cans of chopped beef, mackerel and salmon, potted ham, condensed milk, mincemeat, horseradish, even California raisins. Besides the barley there was, of course, the ubiquitous oatmeal, but much more—Cerealine Flakes, popcorn, arrowroot, sago, and something called granola. Lolly's head was awhirl with the extravagance displayed here. His pantry was more compelling than was Mr. Plummer!

When the screen door slammed, Lolly managed to exit the storeroom with some amount of calmness, carrying with her the pail of lard, a bowl of flour, and a cup of sugar.

Anna-Rose prepared the rhubarb while Lolly, with more pleasure for baking than she had ever felt before, put together the crust.

Thrusting her hand into the oven, she deemed the temperature correct and set the pie inside.

"Now help me remember to look at it in about 45 minutes," she said. "And now—to the windows."

Arnie had taken the ladder around to the dining room windows. When Lolly had mixed a pail of ammonia water, she and Anna-Rose took a handful of clean rags and went outside.

"We'll need an old broom," Lolly decided, looking up at the dirt and cobwebs. Dipped in the water, the broom swished off the first layer of the winter's grime. Then, with Anna-Rose holding the ladder, she climbed gingerly up and, with stretching, managed to reach the top of the long windows and wash and dry them.

Inside, the lace curtains were taken down and the windows washed.

"The curtains will have to wait until tomorrow morning," Lolly decided now. "We'll need to get dinner on and, after that, we'll clean up the kitchen, and that will be all for me today. Mum needs me at home. We'll do the curtains bright and early tomorrow, giving them time to dry and put up before the day is over. You do have stretchers, I suppose?"

Dinner was served at the big kitchen table. When Arnie, Rufe, and Kingston sat down to light biscuits with fresh, sweet butter, hearty beef barley soup that had, after all, cooked long enough, and finished off with warm rhubarb pie smothered with dollops of cream, Lolly felt her stock went up considerably.

What was it her father quoted at times? "Kissin' don't last; cookin' do."

Certainly King Plummer looked at the table with a different satisfaction than when he turned his narrow, glinting gaze on her. Even Rufe said, on leaving the table, "Nice going, Sis."

When the dishes were done and the kitchen put into order, Lolly took her departure, though Rufe would stay a few more hours. "See that Dad keeps on with that cellar," he urged his sister.

True, when she reached the homestead, Hud was taking his "rest" but soon decided, in the wake of Lolly's and Minnie's warm comments of approval for the hole thus far, to get back at it.

"Mum, you wouldn't believe that pantry!" Lolly exclaimed to her mother as they gathered from the line the clothes that Minnie had washed that morning. "I never saw so many supplies! Mum, what's sago?"

Minnie didn't answer for a moment, then with an ache at

her heart that her daughter couldn't see, said, "Sago? It's nothing more nor less than a dry granulated or powdered starch. Used for thickening food." To think her daughter had no knowledge of sago!

"Fancy that. Is it any better than cornstarch?"

"Probably not. Maybe more expensive. Supposed to come from Germany, according to what I remember reading on the box. I don't see the advantage of having both kinds—"

"Mum," Lolly asked, "when you were a girl—didn't you have more, that is, different things than we do now?"

"I've told you over and over about all that, Lolly."

True, it had been a fascinating subject to her children when they were small—the stories of Christmas in the Verner family back in Toronto, their birthday parties, tennis games, their bathtub. And now, their sago. Lolly, too big for bedtime stories by far, still thought wistfully of those accounts and the fairyland-like quality with which they had sent her off to sleep.

Sprinkling Rufe's best shirt that, like her dresses, was wash-worn, Lolly thought about her mother's change in social status and wondered about it.

"Mum," she asked hesitantly, "how can you put up with— all this?" Her waved hand took in the shack in which they worked, the rough homestead, the worn shirt, the shelves with their scanty supply, and, yes, the man shoveling dirt out of a hole on what Lolly strongly suspected was not even his own property.

"Why," Minerva Verner Dalton said softly, "I fell in love with your father."

And I suppose, Lolly thought without surprise, my father would quote "Whither thou goest, I will go" (Ruth 1:16) and "Minerva" became, in due time, "Minnie, old girl." It seemed a dreary prospect for the daughter.

Rolling the shirt tightly and thrusting it into a pile with the other dampened clothes being prepared for ironing, Lolly pushed a vagrant tendril out of her eyes and thought, somewhat fiercely for so good-natured a girl, *Not me! If this is what love gets you—forget it!*

On so small a thing as sago, Lolly's resolve fixed. Cut glass, sterling silverware, velocipede, lawn settee, gold-filled chatelaine watch—all those things denied her were epitomized by the lack of so much as one small box of sago.

If one could have sago, one could have anything! Or so she dreamed.

 14

It was with mixed feelings Donal took leave of the two wagons belonging to the Falza and Bumberg families. He would miss the company, and in light of the terrible accident that had taken Jenner Coy's life, he felt a certain insecurity in being alone. Who knew when tragedy might strike again? And to be alone could be disastrous.

But it was with a sense of satisfaction that he turned north. And it was with some excitement he began to move into the tree belt, or parkland. Donal understood that the "bush" was depressing, even threatening, to some people. But he loved it. His spirits, battered by the death of Jenner, began to lift when the prairie grasslands with their loneliness gave way to the aspen groves. This land, he knew, had been the hunting and fishing ground of the Cree and Chipewyan Indians; and bears, wolves, badgers, caribou, and wapiti still roamed here.

As early summer crept over the land, the greenery was dense, dotted here and there with small clearings where some determined homesteader had staked his claim and began the monumental task of clearing away the growth.

The western red lily, one day to become Saskatchewan's floral emblem, highlighted open woodlands and moist meadows with its vivid flame-red flowers. Pink at first but becoming blue or lilac with full opening, brightening shady woods and stream edges with its bell-shaped blossom, the tall bluebell grew thickly. Black-eyed Susans here, as on the prairies, waved dark-brown disks surrounded by 10 to 20 yellow petals. Throughout the aspen groves, Seneca snakeroot lifted its spikes of greenish white blossoms and was used, Donal had heard, by Indians to cure snakebite.

Deep in the forest the olive-brown hermit thrush, with its darkly spotted breast, made up for its plainness by its clear, flutelike song, a long pure note followed by a cluster of notes. The bluebird's song, as near as Donal could make out, was higher pitched than the eastern bluebird. The sleek blackbird, with its bright red epaulets, flitted from perch to perch singing its bubbling song. But the pure, jubilant trill of the meadowlark was Donal's favorite. No one could hear the paeon without equating it with sheer joy.

What Donal would find in Prince Albert, where Jenner's Uncle Willoughby was located, was part of the unknown with which this entire venture was marked. But Donal persisted in feeling a sense of destiny as he made his way steadily northward.

Last night Donal suspected there had been a hint of a change in the weather; the clouds had largely hidden the sun, and a luminous circle around that setting orb was clearly a mark of coming rain.

The day had brought further changes in the sky; the wind was easterly and feathery cirrus clouds spoke of rain within 48 hours. Now the clouds were darkening, and the skittish breeze was lifting the manes and long tails of Dandy and Willie, the team.

Although it was not his usual time to pull off, Donal began to look for a camping spot. Brush pressed close in most places. Finally he drew abreast of an opening made, a season or so ago, by fire. Already beginning to heal itself, small poplars, birches, jack pines, and lodgepole pine were sprouting; fireweed, some of it almost five feet tall, swayed its magenta stalks in the wind and gave the entire clearing a glow as of spreading flames.

Here Donal pulled off, avoiding the half-burned tree

trunks and bumping and swaying over fallen and rotting logs. Even as he pulled back on the reins and commanded "Whoa, boys!" the first drops began spattering down.

The first thing to do, even before unhitching, was to wrestle up the tent and have a dry place to sit out the storm. Reaching under the black oiled tarpaulin that covered the wagon's load, Donal pulled out the "A" or Wedge tent Uncle Willoughby had provided through his Winnipeg businessman, and he could not restrain a groan. Even with Jenner to assist, erecting the tent had not been easy. Now, with the wind whipping freakishly around and the rain beginning an insidious seep inside his coat collar, Donal paused to think over the situation.

"Unroll the tent in the exact position you want it to be when up," the instructions had read when he and Jenner first figured out the procedure. "Place the ridge pole, rounded side up, inside the tent, and on a line with the large eyelet holes, which are in the center of the roof. Then insert the uprights in the holes bored in the ridge pole, and let the pikes in the upright pole come through the top of the tent." Easier read than done!

Even Jenner's good humor had faded before the next sentence: "If a fly is used, let the pikes also go through in precisely the same way as the tent."

"Fly? What fly?" And Jenner, in some grim attempt to restore better feeling toward the job, had added, "Plenty of flies around . . . the trick is to catch one!"

"Secure the corner guys first . . . angle the stakes . . . the tent now being up and the guys adjusted, all should bear equal strain." The only part of the instructions Donal felt certain of was the digging of a "V-shaped trench all around the tent, about three inches deep; this will insure you a dry tent at all times."

The forest floor was even now becoming sopping wet; the folds of the tent were filling with rain while he hesitated.

Finally, turning up his collar and pulling down his cap, Donal turned to the shelter of the trees. It didn't take long to find a windfall—a tree fallen and caught in the branches of other, upright trunks. Limbs, leafy and full, spread a ready-made sort of canopy under which the ground, so far, was dry. Donal laid aside the ridge pole and guy lines and "flies" and dragged the heavy canvas toward the windfall. Under the heavy drift of overhead boughs, Donal laid out the tent, located several broken or partially burned limbs, thrust them under the canvas, and lifted up. It took patience and strength, but slowly the canvas was hefted until it formed a roof of sorts under the boughs that would shortly begin to run with rain.

In the end Donal had a three-sided shelter six feet long and about four feet wide. Unhitching the horses, he led them under one end of the leafy bower and left them fairly well protected.

With rain pelting down now and slicing across his exposed face, Donal dug under the wagon's oiled cover, located by memory several items and a box of food, and ran with them to shelter, first making sure the wagon's load was again secure from the storm.

The farther north he had gone, the more he noted the difference in the time of the sun's rising and setting. Now, using an old woodsman's trick that he and Moody had practiced in childhood, Donal determined the length of time until sunset by extending his arms toward the west with his palm toward his face and placing the edge of one hand on top of the other. Lining the lowest finger with the horizon, he counted the number of fingers between it and the bottom tip of where he thought the sun to be. Each finger represented 15 minutes of daylight.

The little exercise pleased him enormously, bringing a touch of fun into the entire situation. How Jenner would have laughed! Especially so because the position of the sun had to be guessed at. Still, Donal figured he had about two hours of light; enough time to get himself settled comfortably before full dark.

"If Uncle Willoughby had to put this wretched thing up," Donal muttered, grazing his head on the sagging canvas, "he might have bought one more reasonably sized." Donal and Jenner, after the first disastrous attempt to erect the tent, had opted for sleeping under the wagon. Even at that last, long night of Jenner's life the stars had been winking comfort, and Donal would miss them now. But the horses blew and stamped, and the raindrops drummed musically all around, and the canvas flapped accompaniment.

Donal made one last dash from shelter for fuel. Fortunately there was an abundance of wood available, some half burned, some rotting, all aging from the time of the fire. Quickly Donal gathered an armful and dragged other, longer limbs to the shelter. Most of it was wet, at least on the surface, but would dry quickly after he had a fire going.

Donal knew that bark from a dead birch will burn furiously even when wet. Even in the dimming light he could see the white glimmer of birch trees not far away, and, he felt quite sure, nearby would be the remains of any that had fallen to the disaster when it swept through the area.

Feeling quite sure he had misjudged his estimation of daylight left—or perhaps the sky was darkening further from a thickening of the clouds—Donal made a quick foray, found the birch bark just where he had supposed it to be, and returned to build his fire, using the canvas backing of his covert as a reflector.

A large aged log marked one boundary of his sanctuary.

Though wet on the outside, Donal knew he would find fairly dry wood on the inside of it. With his knife he feathered small pieces and eventually had a tiny flame from them that he fed carefully with the birch bark until his fire was burning briskly.

Now Donal removed his coat and hung it from a broken limb to dry. For a few minutes he leaned back from his seat on the log and stretched his feet toward the fire and felt a good self-satisfied warming in his heart. Ah, this was the life! Ontario and Moody and Esther seemed far away.

Hunger pangs brought reality. Donal buried a potato under the coals and over them he set the coffeepot, which soon began to show signs of steaming to a boil.

Donal burrowed into the box he had brought from the wagon, lifting various cans into the firelight, deciding what else to have for his supper, now that he was dry and comparatively warm.

"Hello the camp!"

The sound startled Donal, coming as it did through the shroud of rain pouring off the canvas roof, proceeding as it did from the dark curtain just beyond his small circle of light.

Donal rose abruptly, his head bent to accommodate his height under the sag of the canvas above him. Coming through the mist of rain, a man approached.

Donal reached for the knife in his belt and watched warily. The stranger was a pathetic sight. Rain ran in rivulets from his hat brim; he seemed shrunken inside his coat. A ragged beard ran with rain; his hands were extended, open and somehow questing.

"Are you alone?" Donal asked cautiously.

"No," the man said, and indicated the darkness behind him. "The wife is with me, and our baby. We're wet and cold."

"Come on in," Donal said, stepping to the side of his

shelter and watching carefully.

There could be no harm come to man or beast, he thought sympathetically, from the bedraggled pair who sank wearily beside the fire. Cradled under the woman's outer garment was a baby. Bringing it out, she loosened its wrappings tenderly and laid it on her lap, from which steam was beginning to rise. The eyes of the man and woman went to the coffeepot.

"Have you eaten?" Donal asked, feeling silly as he said it.

"Not since morning," the man said. "Couldn't find a place to stop earlier, and we just kept pressing on, hoping to—" The voice faltered, as though uncertain of its hopes.

"We're about out of food," the woman said softly. "And we couldn't seem to find any game—in the wind and all."

Donal was raking aside the coals and burying two more potatoes. Without needing to ask, he poured two cups of coffee, which the two uninvited guests reached for eagerly.

"I'm so grateful," the woman murmured.

"I'm Dave Smedley," the man said, and Donal extended his hand to the man's wet one.

"I'm Donal Cardigan," he replied simply.

"And this is my wife, Angie." Angie nodded shyly. "And our son, Frankie."

"Homesteaders?" Donal asked.

Dave Smedley smiled, but it was a rueful smile. "Supposed to be. Sure feel like a greenhorn, though. Haven't got a rig near as good as yours, what I could see of it in the rain. We're heading for Prince Albert. Angie here didn't cotton to the prairies—too flat and lonesome, she said."

"I'm heading for Prince Albert myself," Donal said.

The fact that Dave Smedley did not suggest that they tag along with the bigger, stronger, better-equipped rig was Donal's first indication that this couple, though poor, were proud and independent. His second clue was Dave Smedley's outstretched hand of coins offering to pay for their meager supper.

"Please take it," he said. "We can pay."

"I'd be glad to," Donal said, "except that I may need you to help me farther up the road. You see, I'm alone, and I confess it's tough going without a woman to bake and—oh, you know, all those little things they do so well."

Angie managed a smile.

"Eat with me tonight," Donal continued, "and we'll try to work out some arrangement tomorrow. Two rigs are always safer than one."

"Right," the man agreed, and his voice, as well as his lean face, showed relief.

Never did Donal appreciate Uncle Willoughby any more than when he dug around in the box and located a can of marrowfat peas and another of white cherries. Angie's eyes, too old in her young face, sparkled in the firelight.

With an almost festive air three strangers, drawn together by their mutual plight and their shared hopes, ate and drank and went to sleep side by side in a makeshift, canvas-draped corner of that quiet, waiting, beckoning strip of land known as the bush and never counted their loneliness and misery too much if it resulted in the fulfillment of their dreams.

15

Lolly was immersed in the most satisfying undertaking yet to bless her move to the district of Wildrose. It was the making of a shirtwaist and skirt, her first new garments in as long as she could remember. Usually her mother had made something from her own clothes, which she regularly outgrew with her ever-thickening girth. Occasionally something had been given to the child, prompted by pity or concern.

First, for four cents, she had ordered a pattern book, and even before she could afford the patterns themselves—not to mention the materials—she had studied the book and dreamed and planned. If the fulfilling of the dream was some-what less than she had anticipated, she scaled her expecta-tions to size and was satisfied. The material was plain, the pattern simple, and the cost reasonable. But the costume was new, it was suitable, and *it fit*. In it she would be decent.

The actual purchasing of the materials was not done, after all, from the catalog. Though the pictures were appealing, they were in black and white, and Lolly longed to see colors. Neither could quality be determined, and Lolly, so long denied the experience, could picture herself lifting up a corner of the bolt and experimentally rubbing it between her fingers, a rich and satisfying moment.

Cash in hand, she made the trip to Meridian and the gen-eral store, where, though the choice was limited, most every-thing a homesteader might want from pins to pickling spices could be obtained. Prince Albert, with its greater selection, had no appeal for Lolly; Prince Albert held no good memo-ries. As for Wildrose—Lolly looked up from her sewing, glancing through the shanty door at the circling greenery, catching a whiff of farm and flower and fresh, fresh air and felt the memories adding up past counting.

If Kingston Plummer and his attractions—not personal ones, never personal ones—cast a shadow on her day's contentment, Lolly shied from it like a skittish colt from a shadow.

Actually the making of the new outfit firmed her resolve. Without her present work at the Plummer farm and the small wage she earned, she would be right back where she had always been and still was—the dependent daughter of a rootless, happy-go-lucky ne'er-do-well. Just putting this evaluation of her father into words, though unspoken, hurt Lolly incredibly, for she loved her father and appreciated his easygoing, kind nature, aside from the fact that it brought such deprivation to his family. Rufe and Toby, being males, would be free to pursue their own ways and make their own futures what they wanted them to be. But for a single daughter with no alternative but to live at home, the outlook was bleak at best.

Feeling almost desperately trapped, Lolly had grasped at the straw that was Kingston Plummer and what he represented: stability, provision, and even comfort.

What did she have to offer? Not much, she admitted, but she was determined to make the most of her assets.

The skimpy dress had done its eye-opening bit, embarrassing and cheapening as it was. Yes, it had been a come-on. Now it was time to leave that a memory and go on to respectability and maturity. Lolly's pleasure in her new clothes was tainted with the knowledge of her purpose for them, and that knowledge took the shine from what might have been pure enjoyment in the lovely, novel experience.

The shirtwaist would be simple, but it was in style—or so

she supposed. The pictures that reached them in magazines (often long outdated) or the ubiquitous catalog determined style in the backwoods.

The waist's material was of the purest, softest French lawn. The yoke was double-pointed in back, the sleeves were puff-top, and the detachable collar and cuffs were of linen; the bodice was gathered enticingly front and back. Every tiny stitch was a pleasure; every button seemed a gem for beauty.

Lolly had chosen black serge for the skirt. But it had a four-yard sweep, was lined with rustle taffeta, and was bound with velvet. The nipped-in waistline was accentuated by the wide tops of the sleeves, and Lolly felt like a veritable queen when she put on the ensemble.

Yes, life looked good to Lolly at this particular moment; Kingston Plummer was just across the way, Rufe was laying plans for a house-raising, Toby was working, her dad was showing unaccustomed energy to get them prepared for winter, and Mum was humming as she pulled a pan of cinnamon rolls from the range's much-loved oven. What more did she need?

At that moment—was it chance?—the minister came to call.

At the sound of the approaching rig, Lolly glanced out the window thinking it would be a passing neighbor. But the buggy with its two occupants pulled into the yard and came to a stop outside the shanty door.

"Mum, we've got company!"

Minnie turned the cinnamon rolls out onto a platter; the brown sugar and butter ran stickily over the sweet rolls, and the fragrance filled the small room and wafted out the open door.

Minnie stepped to the doorway and out onto the step; two people were clambering down from the buggy, a man and a woman. They turned toward the house, smiling a greeting.

"I'm Gerald Victor," the man said, "and this is my wife, Elva—Ellie, we call her."

"How do you do?" Minerva Verner Dalton said, extending her hand. "Won't you come in? I'm Minnie Dalton."

The gentleman and lady, for such they were, stepped inside.

Gentleman he might be, but he sniffed appreciatively and said with a smile, "Nothing smells better than fresh bread."

"And I'm about to make tea," said Minerva, "and I'd be happy to have you join us."

Lolly had risen, folding her sewing and setting it aside. She was more caught up at the change in her mother than in the presence of the newcomers. The board walls faded away, the linoleum-covered floors might as well have been a Turkish carpet, and the straight wooden chairs to which Minnie ushered her guests might as well have been upholstered in rich tapestry.

"This is my daughter—" Minnie was saying.

Somehow Lolly knew her mother would not say the despised "Lolita."

"—Lolly."

Lolly's hand was gripped in a warm grasp, and the nodded head and smile of Ellie Victor [*Perhaps she hates "Elva,"* Lolly thought fleetingly] were equally warm.

"I may as well confess it," Gerald Victor said as he took the proffered chair at the side of the table. "I'm the minister."

If he had thought it might dull his welcome with Minnie, he was mistaken. Minnie's face wreathed in a genuine smile, and her words were as genuine: "How nice! Just what I've been praying would happen. It seems the next step in our new lives here should be church attendance."

Prayer? Mum? Was there more, after all, to her nighttime

murmur than "Jesus, guard my humble home . . . watch above my bed . . . If I die . . . Angels, bear my soul away"?

As for church attendance—Lolly was in agreement there, although possibly for a different reason. It was, she supposed, highly respectable to go to church.

"We meet in the schoolhouse," the pastor explained, giving the time of services.

Minnie was telling the Victors about the rest of her family. "Hudson, my husband," she said, and Lolly recognized the pride in her voice, "is engaged in digging that big hole you see out there. We're getting ready to build."

"I hope you'll announce it," Ellie Victor encouraged. "It's a time when people enjoy getting together. They bring food, you know, and the whole family comes and everyone has a wonderful time. The work goes quickly, and the house can be pretty well built in a day."

"It just leaves chinking and things like that," Gerald Victor continued, "but perhaps you've been to house-raisings."

"No, we haven't," Minnie said, "but we'll look forward to it. What a friendly thing to do!"

"Bush people are friendly. I had no idea how dependent they all are on each other when I came six years ago. Anything they do for you, you'll have opportunity to return the favor before long."

Minnie was nodding. "I hope so. Already we've had kindness shown us by the Szarvas family and Mr. Plummer. Our son Toby is working for Widow Fanchon—"

"The widow Fanchon. There's no one quite like her. Toby is a blessed young man if she takes him under her wing. I understand her niece is coming again. Miz Fanchon's family is all back east, quite wealthy and important, and this niece—"

"Nannette," Ellie Victor supplied.

"Nannette Fanchon. Quite a little miss. I expect she's grown up since we saw her last. It's always been thought she is Miz Fanchon's heir. I can't quite imagine her living here permanently, however. But then, we trust Miz Fanchon will be with us for many years to come."

"Toby says she's suffering a bit from rheumatism."

The kettle was boiling, and Minnie excused herself politely and turned to make the tea. Lolly found herself explaining that Rufe worked as hired man for Kingston Plummer and that she had also found employment there.

"Little Anna-Rose," the minister said, "needs a friend just now. I'm sure you'll be good for her."

Once again Lolly had a surprising glimpse of the transformed Minerva as her mother placed serviettes before each of her guests, filled her best cups with tea, and offered cream and sugar, which she had quickly put into their one and only creamer and one and only sugar bowl. The cinnamon rolls, served on individual plates, were flaky and delicious, and conversation flourished as the three adults got acquainted. Lolly listened and felt as if she heard three strangers.

It was Minerva Verner who bade her guests farewell graciously, urged a return visit, and assured them she would indeed attend church, perhaps next Sunday.

A few moments later Hudson came striding from the back part of the homestead where he had been squaring logs, and catching sight of the afternoon tea, asked, "How about some for me, old girl?"

It was Minnie Dalton who washed out the creamer, put the sugar bowl back, and resumed her day's activities.

 16

Before many days had passed, Donal Cardigan decided that it was a good wind that blew the Smedleys into his life. The morning following the storm they crawled out of their canvas shelter, Donal explained his predicament in trying to erect the tent alone in the wind and the rain, and with the hearty laughter of his new acquaintances, he was able to laugh too. It had been too long since he had laughed. The night they spent together, before they slept, he had told Dave and Angie about Jenner Coy's death and dying commission to Donal to carry out his obligation to deliver his uncle's treasures to Prince Albert.

"So that's the reason I'm going that far north," Donal explained. "But I had no definite goal in mind when I started out, so—" with a shrug, "—one place is as good as another, I expect."

"Now, Angie here," Dave said fondly, "wouldn't agree with you. She would probably say 'The steps of a good man are ordered of the Lord.' Right, Angie?"

Angie blushed, but her gaze held steady and her chin rose as she answered the gentle teasing.

"And where would we be right now, I'd like to know, if it weren't true? Still out in the storm somewhere, no doubt."

"*You* were praying up a storm, I'll say that," Dave admitted good-naturedly, and then amended his words. "Praying us *out* of a storm, more like."

"That sounds like my mother," Donal said and reflected again momentarily on just how likely it was that a mother's prayers would follow her son down across the years and into strange and distant paths. He had a feeling that if he asked Angie, she would have an answer for him. It was a good and comforting feeling as they journeyed on, to think someone was praying.

The oiled cover had held firmly in place, so Uncle Willoughby's goods were safe and dry. The Smedley wagonload hadn't fared as well. The trip was delayed a day while they unloaded and dried their meager supply of household goods and tools. Dave was a builder, it appeared.

"I may not be fitted for farming," Dave admitted. "It was just an idea. Perhaps I'll settle again for building, if there are such jobs in Prince Albert."

"Sure to be. It's a growing place, I've been told. That's as far as the railway goes, so it's a jumping-off place for lots of people. Must be eating places and hotels and all sorts of stores. You'll find work—never fear. How does Angie feel about it?"

"Angie favors the homestead idea, I think. Though," and Dave grinned again, "she's prayin' up another storm about it. It's bound to turn out for the best, whatever."

It was with such optimism Donal now found himself joined. Not only optimism but also laughter. Dave Smedley almost equaled Jenner Coy for good humor. But where Jenner had been carefree, without definite purpose or plan, Dave Smedley had a serious side to him and a will to work. Perhaps it was having the care and support of a little family. Angie, his partner in all, would stand by her husband, praying; it was a winning team. So, though they were poor and lacking in some things now, they were indeed optimistic. But Angie didn't call it optimism. "Faith," she said.

Another two weeks, and they were passing through the outlying fields and meadows of the various communities and districts that had sprung up around Prince Albert. There was still much virgin growth, and Donal studied it thoughtfully. Civilization was definitely coming to the wilderness, but it had been a long haul and was still in its infancy. Homesteads were still available.

The fur trade dominated the history of the region that, after 1870, was to be known as the Canadian West. The Canadian Indian was a peaceful farmer, fisherman, and hunter, but it was the fur trade that brought him into contact with European culture.

The Cree that inhabited the Prince Albert area were the "Swampy Cree"; they were hunters of the coveted beaver. The Plains Cree, who were more nomadic, hunted buffalo and wolf, were more warlike than their northern brothers, and were often at war with the Assiniboine, Gros Ventres, and Blackfoot. The "Swampees" preferred the woods and lived congenially with the new settlement, working with and for them.

The early settlers learned much from the Indian. Red or wet dog trillium was used to hasten childbirth, laxatives were made from slippery elm, jewel weed was applied to rashes, mashed clover used for bee stings, and bitterroot used for coughs and colds.

Eventually the ponds were emptied of beaver, and the prairies, "once black with buffalo, taking so much as a full day to pass any given point," were empty. Bitterness and discontent culminated in the Riel Rebellion, with its sorry outcome. The Métis and the Indian, from that time on, were more and more assimilated into the lifestyle of the pioneer and homesteader and were, for the most part, accepted.

The last pamphlet Donal had read, admittedly several years old, stated that Prince Albert, even then, had seven general stores on River Street, two hardware stores, and several specialty stores for shoes, furniture, and so on. There was a druggist and a dentist, several lawyers, two bakeries, and three banks. Sawmills and flour mills were operating; the *Prince Albert Times and Saskatchewan Review* was published weekly. There were several elementary schools, and Emmanuel College for boys.

Yes, it was a thriving and bustling little metropolis Donal and the Smedleys approached. Setting up camp just outside town, along the river, they had a strangely satisfied feeling of having dropped anchor.

"The first thing for me," Donal decided after breakfast the next morning, "is to locate Jenner Coy's Uncle Willoughby. Do you know," he went on with some dismay, "I don't even know the old gent's last name."

"You say he's well off—had a business of some sort in Winnipeg," Dave offered thoughtfully. "The banks may be the place to begin."

Donal shaved and changed his clothes, Angie having offered to iron them for him, heating an iron over the campfire and pressing on a tabletop. It had been many weeks since he was in a town of any size—ever since Winnipeg, in fact. Donal looked forward to exploring any possibilities for his future. First though, Uncle Willoughby.

Donal had success in the first bank he entered. Approaching what appeared to be an official, Donal broached the subject hesitantly.

"I'd appreciate your help, sir. I'm looking for a resident of this city, but I have only the first name."

"Be glad to help if I can," the gentleman said doubtfully.

"That one name is Willoughby—"

"Couldn't be but one Willoughby in the entire Territory, could there?" the other replied with a smile. "You could only mean Willoughby Ames."

With the address of Willoughby Ames written on a scrap of paper and directions on locating the very house, a boarding house, Donal set off briskly and soon was knocking on the door of a large, plain, three-story house with a small front yard and what appeared to be a fine and flourishing garden in the backyard.

The girl who answered the door was plain too, and so was the woman she called—her mother, she said—in answer to Donal's request for a Mr. Willoughby Ames.

"Mr. Ames?" the large, no-nonsense woman repeated, almost blankly. "Oh, you mean Willoughby, of course. Mr. Willoughby. Well, you can't see him, sir. Mr. Willoughby is a very sick man."

"I'm sorry to hear that," Donal said in some distress. "You see, I've come a very long way. In fact, I have a wagonload of possessions—"

"Jenner! Willoughby speaks of you all the time! Even in his sickness he keeps rambling on about Jenner. But really, he's out of his mind most of the time."

Donal hesitated, unsure of how to proceed. He had been led to believe the items on the wagon were of importance to Uncle Willoughby. Just to go off and leave them uncared for—

"Come in, young man. Come in!" Mrs. Janeway, the landlady, urged, her full, plain face now a wreath of good-natured wrinkles. "Just sit here," she pointed to a bench in the hallway, "and I'll go see what the situation is now."

Soon the lady of the house returned, her face pink with her importance and her exertions on Donal's behalf.

"It's all right," she reported. "He's bright enough today. I've told him you're here. Just follow me."

In some ways it was a typical boarding house, probably catering to gentlemen only. Donal could see a large dining room; the girl who had let him in was clearing away breakfast dishes. Wide stairs led above, and the downstairs hall was barren with closed doors on each side.

Mrs. Janeway opened a door that led into the front bedroom. It was a large, sunny room, with its own heater that even now had a small fire burning in it. A timid lady rose from a rocking chair and advanced on Donal, a worried look on her face.

"I sit with Mr. Willoughby, daytimes," she half whispered. "He really isn't—"

"Boy! Is the boy here? Has he come?" The voice emanating from the bed was strong enough, but cracked in tone, half a croak, as though it wasn't in the habit of speaking much these days.

Donal went quickly to the bedside. Half propped on numerous pillows, an elderly gentlemen with bushy eyebrows, deep-set eyes, and scanty hair now pointing in all directions stared up at his visitor—rather blankly, Donal thought.

Then recognition seemed to dawn, or understanding. "Jenner!" the old voice quavered.

"I need to explain—"

"I've been waiting for you, boy! Did you bring the wagon and all my things?"

"Yes, I have them, Mr. Willoughby—"

"*Uncle* Willoughby, my boy! Let me hear you say it. Say it, my boy! Uncle Willoughby." The voice continued its plea until Donal, to placate and soothe him, repeated the title to the old man's satisfaction.

"My boy—listen to me. Listen carefully."

"Mr.—Uncle Willoughby, there's something I must tell you—"

Uncle Willoughby seemed to become agitated, plucking at the covers on his bed, opening and shutting his still strong-toothed mouth, and blinking his eyes furiously.

"Don't upset him," the sitter-nurse pleaded, smoothing the white crocheted bed spread nervously. "Listen to him—agree with him. We don't want him to have another spasm!"

Donal held his tongue and listened.

"My boy . . . my boy . . . the homestead—it's just sitting there, waiting for you. If you don't get out there and take hold, I'll lose it! I got a lot done—me and that helper I had, before I got down with this . . . this . . ." Willoughby went into such a mumble of complaints that Donal was at a loss to know just what was wrong. The little nurse made strange gestures, indicating various body parts as the source of her patient's trouble. That was more mystifying than the sick man's attempts.

"Go on, Uncle Willoughby," Donal soothed at last. "I'm listening."

"There's hay to get up. The house needs chinking before winter. My animals—they're at Szarvas's place. Get them, Jenner; the little white heifer should have freshened—"

Donal looked with despair at the babbling old man. "Look here," he began, trying again to explain the situation, "you'll have to find someone else—"

"What? After all this? My plans—they were all for you! You gave me your word—I've been counting on you! What else can I do—a poor old sick man?"

For one brief instant Donal thought he detected a sly gleam in the piercing, deep-set eyes. The next moment the voice continued, however, more quavery than before, pleading for "Jenner" not to let him down—to save the homestead, to prove up the half-section on which he had lived and worked for two years, so close to finalizing the terms of the Lands Act requirements.

"For heaven's sake!" the elderly, shaken nurse burst in from time to time, "why are you arguing with the old gentleman? You can see he can't do a thing in the world about it himself. Give him your word, young man, and set his poor mind at rest!"

Finally, in desperation, Donal managed to insert his promise. "Don't worry, Uncle Willoughby—everything will be taken care of."

"You'll go, Jenner, you'll go on out to the homestead?" Again the old eyes seemed more keen than senile. "Promise! Promise!"

With a sigh, "I promise," Donal said, wondering how in the world he was going to get out of this pickle.

The old man sank back against his pillows with a long sigh, his eyes closed, his wrinkled old lips in a satisfied smile.

"Good boy," he muttered. "You won't be sorry."

But Donal wasn't so sure. He turned away greatly perturbed. Could he write a letter of explanation and slip away? Would the old gentleman be in shape tomorrow to hear him out? About to leave the room, he heard, strong and clear, the voice from the pillows: "You promised."

In the hallway, Mrs. Janeway met him. "I'm glad you've come," she said. "The old gentleman has this room here, has had it for a couple of years, and has come and gone. He pays for Mrs. Prine to help look after him . . . has plenty of money, that's for sure. And he really is very little trouble. Pays his rent on time—"

"I'll come back in the morning," Donal finally managed to interject. "I really need to talk to him when he's, well, more inclined to listen. Tell him, please, or have Mrs. Prine tell him—I'll come see him again tomorrow."

Back at camp, digging into the biscuits Angie had made, sopping up her good chicken gravy with them, Donal said gloomily, "I'm in trouble—*big* trouble. Do promises given under pressure count?"

"A promise is a promise," honest Angie said.

"Then I'm in trouble—*big* trouble."

 17

Toby, on his way to his first day's work at the Widow Fanchon's, stopped at the Szarvas place long enough to help with the milking. Today, however, Billy was back on the job. "The old leg is working just fine," he insisted, though he still moved a bit stiffly. "Besides, you've more than paid for any milk you'll get from here on out."

"Rufe's dickering with Plummer for a cow of our own," Toby said. "She's due to freshen, too, and that'll give us a start on a herd."

"Take time to come look," Kitty interrupted mysteriously, beckoning Toby to follow. "I want to show you something."

Her rounded, brown legs flashed before him as she nimbly climbed the ladder to the hayloft. Still following, Toby began to suspicion the "surprise" as they approached a pile of hay in the far corner. Kitty dropped onto her knees, and he did too. With a little searching, she produced two kittens, one in each sturdy, work-toughened, small hand. Leaning toward her to see them better, perhaps to take one from her, Toby thought, *She smells just like the hay,* but he didn't find that strange.

For a few moments they gently fondled the kittens, Kitty making soft noises in the back of her throat. One kitten in particular claimed Kitty's attention; it was smaller than the others. Its blind eyes seemed to exude a wetness of some kind; its cry was persistent but weak.

With a sort of clucking sound, Kitty carefully put this kitten into her smock pocket. "I can see this one needs a little special care," she said, not to Toby's surprise. "I'll have to take it to the house . . . nurse it a bit. It'll be all right—you'll see." Toby never doubted it.

Only once since that sickening display of weakness in the garden had Toby had further symptoms of his strange "turns." It had been while he and Kitty had been searching the bush for a cow that had failed to come in with the others. That time he caught himself as the wave of weakness swept over him and leaned against a tree until it passed. Even so, Kitty had seen and been immediately at his side, her strong arm around his waist, her sturdy body holding him up as he sagged momentarily.

"There, now—you're ever so much better this time," she had said hardily, and he knew it was true.

Now, leaning over, even with the air thick with dust, Toby felt no vertigo or hint of any weakness. Besides the fresh and plenteous milk, eggs, butter, cream, and new garden vegetables, Kitty had dosed Toby almost daily with a potion the family kept on hand, ordered through the catalog. One day, reading for himself the description of Dr. Rowland's System Builder and Lung Restorer, Toby had decided he needed to get well in self-defense! "As a remedy for torpor of the liver, generally termed Liver Complaint or Biliousness," he read "it has no equal. For loss of appetite, indigestion and dyspepsia, and for general or nervous debility or prostration, in either sex, it has no equal. It is very valuable in all forms of scrofulous and other blood diseases, also for all skin diseases, eruptions, pimples, rashes and blotches, boils, ulcers, sores and swellings arising from impure blood, and cured by the use of a few bottles of this compound."

True, he had been prone to a few pimples and an occasional blotch. But these were fading, and he supposed it was because he was outgrowing childish skin problems.

But whatever the reason, Toby was doing better. Certainly he looked better. His skin was clear, his eyes bright, his color good. He even dared think his shoulders were straighter and his muscles larger.

At times, knowing full well Kitty's penchant for coddling the weak and needy, he half-worried that, in the full bloom of health, her interest might be directed elsewhere. But that was silly! Kitty was, above all, sensible.

Aware of her good sense and practicality, Toby asked Kitty now what she would call the kittens, knowing before she spoke that the names would be prosaic, unimaginative. He was not mistaken. *Is it good to be able to predict what another person will do?* he wondered, a trifle impatient, one step ahead of her in the choice of names.

"This one," Kitty said, holding up a black one, "I'll call Blackie. This one," indicating a gray one, "will be Smokey. And this one—" Kitty fondled a golden-mixed scrap of fur, faintly striped.

Will be Tiger.

"Will be Tiger," she said, and Toby sighed.

"You can have one if you want," Kitty said generously, again so like the dependable, kindly girl he knew, that Toby was restored to good humor. After a lifetime of transient, unpredictable moves, with nothing dependable or enduring, Kitty's permanence—in nature and personality as well as physically—offered a safety and an appeal like "a rock in a weary land," as Hudson would have said.

"Thank you," Toby said now. "We do need a cat. I never saw such a place for mice." He chose the gold-striped one. "I'll name it Tiger," he said kindly.

"It should be ready to leave its mother about the time the pup is weaned," Kitty said. "This sick kitten I'll call Nightingale."

Toby approached the Fanchon homestead with interest.

Here the bush was more fully cut back and restrained. First he passed a good-sized field greening nicely with wheat, bounded, of course, with bush, and truly beautiful in its lush promise of harvest from both the controlled crop and the wild.

The house, a large one, was surprisingly, of log. And also surprisingly, this one had been allowed to weather until it was a silvery gray in color, fitting into its rural setting with grace. Behind it, a small cabin, even more weathered and obviously also lived in—for a feather of smoke rose from the stovepipe—had probably been the original home of the Fanchons when they first homesteaded. The barn was large, the corral beside it sturdy, as were the other buildings—hen house, granary, blacksmith shop . . .

The widow Fanchon met Toby as she stepped from her back door and greeted him with a smile.

"Good morning, young man. Glad to see you're a man of your word. Important! Now, if you'll follow me we'll get you acquainted with my man—hired man, name of Yukon."

Following this powerhouse of a woman—stronger in mind and will than body, Toby suspected—they crossed the farmyard to locate a big, dark-skinned, ragged-headed individual who extended a callused hand when he was introduced.

"Yukon has been with me for eight years," Widow Fanchon explained. "Couldn't make it without him. Lives in that cabin—" She indicated the one with the drifting smoke. "He'll put you to work. Do as he says, and you'll do fine."

The widow returned to her house, and Toby underwent a keen-eyed study from the man, perhaps part Indian. Toby had a feeling he had been weighed in the balances and, thankfully, found satisfactory. And somehow it pleased him immensely that this hired man, in his nondescript clothes, should accept him.

"You stick with Miz Fanchon," the man said in a throaty voice, "and you won't be sorry. Good woman. The best."

It was odd. Toby felt he was hearing an echo of Miz Fanchon herself. And the man's devotion was obvious in other ways. He quoted his mistress often, described her ways and her plans, confirmed her decisions. And always in that clipped voice.

The two men went first to strengthening existing fence posts and stringing barbed wire. Toby learned that hog wire has barbs about three inches apart and cattle wire about six inches apart.

"Don't use 4-point wire now," Yukon explained. "Two-point turns stock just as well. Get a little more length to the pound too."

Yukon, though not talkative, answered questions without making Toby feel ignorant and offered informative comments from time to time. Toby felt it was a day well worthwhile for him.

At noon they sat down to a full meal in Widow Fanchon's spotless kitchen. It was roomy and filled with light. Curtains softened the windows, and scattered rugs brightened the floor.

"Yukon always eats dinner here with me," she explained. "His supper he manages for himself. And, of course, his breakfast. When I bake anything special, I share with him. When he goes hunting and gets partridges or ducks, he shares with me. One or the other of us, or maybe both of us, go to Meridian every week when the weather permits. By the way," she spoke now to her hired man, "I don't think I mentioned that Nannette is coming next week. School is out for her. We'll have her with us all summer, I suppose.

"Nannette is my niece, Toby. Not much younger than you. About the age of Kitty Szarvas. Now—," she turned to the business of the farm, "I'd like you to sashay—" Toby grinned at her remembrance of the word. "—on out to the garden and work your magic there."

Thanking her for dinner, Toby put his old cap on his head and followed Yukon outside. As he loped beside the big man toward the garden and further instructions, Toby asked, "This Nannette—I suppose she and Kitty are friends?"

"I don't believe they have much in common," Yukon said briefly. "Totally different, of course."

Totally different. An unknown quality. Toby found his interest rising in regard to this—this "totally different" girl.

 **18**

As promised, Donal returned to the Janeway boardinghouse the next morning. Hopefully, the bedfast man known as Willoughby, "Uncle" to Jenner and now Donal, would be more lucid and able to grasp the fact that his great-nephew had perished along the way. Donal hated to be the one to thrust this disturbing news on a man already not coping well, physically and mentally.

The four-square Mrs. Janeway—the same today as yesterday except for a fresh apron that, starched stiffly, accompanied her down the hall like a ship in full sail—opened the door with a flourish and departed.

Mrs. Prine rose again from her rocking chair by the window and laid aside a book. Tiptoeing across the room, she greeted Donal with a whisper, both the tiptoeing and the whisper unnecessary because the deep-set eyes of the man on the bed were turned toward Donal with expectation. A bit of something . . . egg, perhaps, was stuck in the well-trimmed beard. With a cluck of disapproval and with neat skill, Mrs. Prine plucked it off and looked at Donal brightly, as though saying, "Ah . . . these nursing responsibilities!"

"Good morning, my boy!"

"Good morning—"

"Uncle Willoughby!"

"Uncle—I need to talk to you, sir—"

"Air! Air!" the old man gasped, and a great waving of fans and fluffing of pillows resulted.

"*I'll* talk, boy—you *listen!* I'm expecting you to go out to the homestead and take charge. Do what needs to be done.

You know something about farms, my boy? Any bumpkin can do what needs to be done out there."

"Now wait just a minute," Donal began, determined to stem the flow of instructions and face the old man with the truth.

"Medicine, Mrs. Prine, medicine!" A great kerfuffle ensued, with the nurse measuring out a spoonful of something called Dr. Echols' Australian Auriclo—a newly discovered cure for heart trouble. During the administration of this draught and the subsequent coughing and snorting, Donal picked up an unopened box of this remedy and scanned its manifesto:

> Weak hearts are as common as weak stomachs, lungs or eyes. Every heart that flutters, palpitates, tires out easily, aches, etc., is weak or diseased, and treatment should not be postponed a single day, and there has never been found a remedy so effectual in healing and strengthening and restoring the heart as the newly discovered cure—Dr. Echols' Australian Auriclo. It is daily curing thousands in every stage of heart disease . . . remember that such simple ailments as cold hands and feet, spots before the eyes, hungry spells, etc., indicate a weak heart or a diseased one . . .

Somewhat dazed and inclined to put a hand—a cold hand, he noted uneasily—to his somewhat whirling head, Donal recalled that he himself often had hungry spells.

Uncle Willoughby seemed to effect a remarkable recovery after downing the amazing Australian Auriclo, and his renewed conversation brought Donal to attention.

"My boy," Uncle Willoughby was saying, "I've made my will, and you're to have the homestead. No, no—don't say anything," he rasped, raising a wonderfully capable-appearing hand to discourage Donal's attempt to interrupt. "Don't argue—it will blow my poor heart into Kingdom come. Now listen—"

Suddenly Donal, half-angry, half-hilarious, and totally at the end of his patience, decided. "So what? What if the old rascal does give me the farm! If he won't listen to reason—so much for him!"

Leaning over the bed, Donal said, sweetly, "You were saying, Uncle Willoughby?"

"What I've been *trying* to say is—" Uncle Willoughby motioned Donal closer until his whiskers almost tickled Donal's cheek. "There's a false bottom in that wagon, boy. All the money you need is there. And it's all for the homestead! You hear me, boy?"

Donal must have shown in his face some of the skepticism he felt, for the old man's grip on his lapel tightened, and he pulled Donal closer.

"I don't have anything else to spend it on, you hear? Get yourself a man to help, if you want. It's a half section, you hear? Not a quarter, like most. You'll have plenty to do to be ready for winter. Hey—you hearing me, boy?"

"I hear, Uncle Willoughby."

"Get yourself through the winter—then come on in and see me. You hear me, boy?"

"I hear, Uncle Willoughby." Donal's back was growing tired, bent as he was over the muttering old man.

"There, in the drawer, is a description of the section . . . it's not too far . . . place called Wildrose. You'll like it, boy. Get him the papers, Mrs. Prine."

Donal straightened, looked grimly into the innocent, wide eyes, turned and took the papers from Mrs. Prine's hands, and moved toward the door. His future, it seemed, had been taken out of his hands—again.

At the door, he turned. Uncle Willoughby's eyes were beady, his lips, like Donal's, fixed in a grim smile. "Goodbye—Jenner. Until spring."

"As you wish, Uncle," Donal said, gave a brisk salute, and walked down the hall, for all intents and purposes—if Uncle Willoughby knew what he was talking about—a man of some substance.

Back at the camp, Donal seated himself, but with such a bemused expression on his face that Angie studied him anxiously and Dave voiced their question. "Everything all right, Donal?"

Donal gave a bark—half laugh, half groan. "You'll never believe it."

"Want to tell us about it?"

"Of course. That old reprobate—Uncle Willoughby—has me lassoed, hog-tied, and thrown! He wouldn't, or couldn't, hear a thing I said. I never saw the likes! I tried over and over to make him understand that I wasn't Jenner. Do you think he'd listen? No, he went into this performance—coughing, spluttering, fainting—and shut me off completely every time. Then he'd start back in on what *he* wanted. His plans, his homestead, his arrangements. Finally—" Donal paused, shaking his head.

"Finally?"

"Finally I just gave in. 'So what?' I said to myself. 'If he thinks I'm Jenner, I'll be Jenner. If he wants to make me his heir, why not?' "

Angie blinked.

"You won't like it, Angie. Maybe my mother wouldn't have, either. But the die is cast; I've made up my mind. I'm looking for a homestead, and here's one dropped in my lap. And what's more—"

"There's more?"

149

"He says—if what he says proves correct, I'll believe him on the rest of it—he says there's a false bottom in the wagon, and there's money, plenty of it, in there."

So saying, Donal got to his feet and strode to the wagon. Dave followed. Angie continued by the fire, the baby on her lap, her face a study of dismay, disapproval, and disbelief.

Donal walked around the rig, Dave behind him. "I've done this dozens of times," Donal grunted, "and never saw anything out of the ordinary."

"Let me crawl underneath," Dave said and suited action to words.

It wasn't long until he said, "There *is* something odd here, Donal. Right below the seat, I'd say."

Climbing up on the tongue, Donal leaned over, peering under the seat. "There's too much stuff under here. We'll have to move a bunch of things."

Dave crawled out and together they lifted and shoved and adjusted until, with the aid of a crowbar the boards were pried loose in one spot. A metal box was revealed. The eyes of the two men met. Reaching in, Donal pulled the box out; it wasn't difficult to open. Two dark heads bent in amazement over its contents.

Dave whistled. "The old gent isn't completely potty."

Rather pale of face, Donal closed the box, replaced it, and battered the board back into place.

"It's not yours, you know." It was Angie, looking over their shoulders.

"He said it's for the homestead," Donal quoted slowly. "There can't be any harm in using it for the homestead. And what's more—"

"There's more?"

"He said to hire someone to help. It's a half-section, Dave. Hire someone, he said."

Donal looked at Dave. Dave looked back. Angie watched them both.

"How about it, Dave? Are you with me?"

"I'm with you, man!"

"Wildrose," Donal exulted, "here we come!"

 19

Like colorful scalloped edging on a lady's fancy clothing, the dainty wild rose traced the edges of every trail, bounded all fields, and graced each forest clearing, spreading its fragrance and lifting its pink, five-petaled flowers heavenward. Fragile in its appearance and sturdy in its performance, it epitomized the tenacity and femininity of the pioneer women who endured unimaginable hardships and persisted in adding those small touches that brought a measure of refinement and comfort. Happy the home with a homemaker. Whether coming from far-away Europe, distant Ontario, the British Isles, or Timbuktu, when she had set out a well-loved picture, carving, bit of lace, set of napkin rings, engraved butter dish, bonbon tray, porcelain figure, or mantel clock, the rude dwelling—whether a soddy or a shack, a cabin or a hillside dugout—became the place toward which feet turned gladly at the end of day. Where wife or mother reigned, there the heart found home.

Curtains hung starched and prim against mud walls; colorful rag rugs brightened rough pine floors; tea cozies covered china teapots set on wobbly handmade tables; sepia prints graced irregular sod walls that had been plastered with newspaper.

Deep in the musty recesses of Minerva Verner Dalton's trunk, brought with her to her husband's house on her wedding day and following her from shanty to shack ever since, wrapped in an ancient piece of flannel, was such a treasure, a memory of better days, a faraway home, and a carefree childhood. Minnie had never found the occasion or the spot suitable for its unwrapping and displaying.

On the day the logs went up and the roof went on the cabin in the bush, Minnie went to her knees beside the trunk to search for and find the tiny silver napkin ring that she had cherished for so many years in silence and in secret.

Just a few inches high it was, and she cradled it in her work-worn hand. Satin finished and chased with exquisite ornamentation, the small ring, like a miniature barrel, was balanced on a delicate cart with wee wheels that turned. Between the silvery shafts a little figure, no taller than a thimble, bent in a perpetual tug on the entrancing conveyance.

"Oh, Mum," whispered her beauty-starved daughter, touching the precious treasure with a fingertip roughened in the employ of someone who could—if she played the game right—enrich her life with just such cherished items.

But what about her hungry heart? Could any amount of worldly possessions satisfy that?

Having been deprived of so many things, Lolly had determined to go after them, fill her life with them, never counting the cost to her young, untouched heart. And although her conscience had troubled ever so slightly a time or two, it had been for Kingston Plummer's sake and the ruthless, heartless manner in which she had been planning his future.

That her own future and feelings might be involved had never really been considered. She had blithely laid her plans and never realized she might be consigning herself to a loveless life. And all for the sake of *things.*

Her awakening had come blindingly clear during her first church attendance.

Happy and confident in her new skirt and shirtwaist, Lolly had prepared herself on Sunday morning with some excitement. Hearing a sermon, or worshiping, was the least of her interest. Meeting new neighbors, enjoying the drive through the summer beauty of Wildrose, perhaps seeing (and being seen by) Kingston Plummer (her "intended," in that she had set her intentions on him), were her chief reasons. Kingston had yet to see the new Lolly; workdays found her wearing her old skimpier-than-ever garments.

The ride, with Toby driving and Mum beside her on the wagon seat, was indeed delightful. The day was gloriously bright, filled with early-morning birdsong and heavy with summer's distinctive aromas, most of which she had yet to recognize and identify. Toby had cleaned the wagon and curried Maude and Claude within an inch of their long-suffering lives; even they seemed to respond to the challenge and stepped out more briskly than usual. Numerous buggies and wagons were ahead of them, behind them, or pulling from farmyards to join the stream of good folk who had gladly laid the week's toil behind them and willingly obeyed the Bible's injunction, "Remember the sabbath day, to keep it holy. Six days shalt thou labor, and do all thy work."

Callused hands gripped reins shiny with use; farm boots, scraped of barnyard muck, dangled below springy wagon seats. Ancient hats perched on freshly washed heads. Tired shoulders lifted beneath calico gowns from which the colors were often faded—but they were freshly washed and starched. The children riding in the wagon behind them were scrubbed from their Saturday night encounter with the galvanized tub, and their feet, without exception, rebelled at being stuffed into boots after some weeks of running blissfully free.

Friendly, outstretched hands and genuine smiles greeted the Daltons—Minnie, Lolly, and Toby. Pastor Gerald Victor, remembering his visit, asked about Hudson and Rufe and was assured by Minnie that they would soon join the circle of the faithful. Lolly was silently skeptical; Minnie, ever hopeful, always trusting her man's good intentions, made the promise with perfect equanimity.

Seated together with her mother at one of the double desks, Toby in the rear with other single young men, Lolly had turned in an unfamiliar songbook to an unheard-of hymn and heard, to her amazement, Minnie's voice soaring out with confidence and scarcely any need to glance at the words or music.

Titled "The Solid Rock" and all about One—Christ—on whom the fervent singers professed to stand, Lolly was taken up with amazement at her mother's participation and the enthusiasm of the congregation. She completely missed the words of the first verses they sang with lifted faces, shining eyes, and earnest if sometimes tuneless voices. But the words of the last verse caught her attention sharply, and her eyes sought out the page and the message. She felt it was sung to her and her alone:

> *When He shall come with trumpet sound,*
> *O may I then in Him be found!*
> *Dressed in His righteousness alone,*
> *Faultless to stand before the throne!*

Dressed—that was the word that fixed her careless, curious thoughts from absorption with her surroundings to a riveted attention on the song and its message.

"Dressed in His righteousness." Suddenly, in her finery and through her satisfaction, Lolly felt as though she were wearing a disguise and that beneath the facade was hidden the same old Lolly—shoddy, poor, exposed.

So vivid was the revelation that Lolly, shaken, found herself glancing wildly down at her person, greatly relieved to see that she was quite properly, even attractively, clothed.

And when the minister stood behind the battered desk, took his text, and began to preach, she found that church was deadly serious business, after all—not just an interesting place to go, not a social institution, and not a fashion parade.

Around her attentive faces were fixed on the man of God; Bibles were open, and callused fingers traced the words as they were read. As the message proceeded, heads nodded hearty agreement, and a few earnest amens lent encouragement.

"Where your treasure is, there will your heart be also," the preacher read, while Minnie found and followed Luke 12:34 in the family Bible as though she did it every Sunday of her life.

" 'Set your affections on things above' " the preacher read further, " 'not on things on the earth,' " and Minnie located Col. 3:2, the given scripture.

Torn between her fascination with her mother's obvious familiarity with things ecclesiastical and what the minister was saying, Lolly absorbed only phrases of the sermon. But it was enough to change forever the careless, thoughtless course of her life. At least it was the first step.

"Your Heavenly Father knows you have need of all these things for which you seek, spending your energy and thoughts and money on temporal things that pass away, and neglect those which are eternal. Seek His kingdom," the pastor said, "and these other things will be added to you in due time." This he said, with confidence and without apology to people who lived on the bare edge of starvation at times, whose energies were spent in scrabbling a living from stump-filled acres during a growing season of perhaps fewer than 100 days. He said it with collars and cuffs turned on his worn shirt and with his wife, Ellie, wearing her one Sunday dress.

He said it with conviction; he said it with a steady light in his eyes and a certainty to his voice. And his people, when the benediction was given, went back to their hard tasks with a hope they hadn't known before and a peace imparted to those who love God's law.

One heart was troubled; one heart was stirred; one heart was empty. While she smiled on the outside and even noted Kingston Plummer's absorbed study of her and obvious approval, she met people and chatted with them. But Lolly's heart had heard and would retain and struggle with the pastor's final injunction that his hearers be clothed with the garments of salvation and covered with the robe of righteousness.

Gazing almost fearfully into those kind eyes, Lolly wondered if Pastor Victor could see the nakedness of her soul and the poverty of her heart. Finally, recognizing the foolishness of this, she managed her good-byes, aware that life for her would not, could not, ever be the same again.

"Mum," she had said, on the way home, "I never knew you knew all those hymns . . . and the Bible—you turned right to the proper place. Colossians, was it? Who ever heard of that?"

"Well, me, for one," Minnie admitted. "You never quite get away from those things, once learned."

"You went to church as a child?" Toby asked, as amazed as his sister. "How come you haven't gone, all these years?" There was no condemnation in Toby's voice, just curiosity.

"It was a decision I made, I suppose, when—when I left home."

"Got married, you mean?"

Minnie was silent for a minute. The horses' hoofs thumped through the dry roadbed; the harness creaked, and so did the old wagon.

"You mustn't blame your father," said their mother finally. "It was a choice I made, you see. One has to think seriously about such things when one marries. I was young . . . very much in love . . . wanting to be independent and have my own home."

And it's been one shanty after another, Lolly thought with some bitterness. There's apparently no treasure awaiting in heaven, and there's certainly been none here.

Each deep in thought, they wended their way homeward.

"We'll go again, won't we, Mum?" Toby eventually roused himself to ask. "Will you go with us?"

"I'll go, Son."

The house-raising day was probably the happiest that Lolly had ever known. The people of the district came, laying aside their own tasks to assist a neighbor; food was abundant and tasty; fellowship was rich and meaningful.

But best of all, the Daltons would have a house—just like real people.

Hudson had completed the hole for the cellar, although, "I wonder if it should have been dug after the walls go up," he pondered dubiously. "It will be something of a trick to work all around that great, gaping hole without falling in!"

Placing boards over the hole while they worked solved this particular problem. And, of course, when the floor was laid and a trap door made with a ladder leading below, it all came right.

Hudson and Toby and Rufe had snaked the logs to the building spot by team and chain. They were fortunate, they said over and over, that Mellon had cut them and squared them and that they had dried sufficiently so there would be no shrinking.

The men of the neighborhood arrived with their own

tools—axes, planes, and saws. They knew what they were doing, and the job went ahead rapidly, one man notching the corners well ahead of the demand, others raising and putting them in place, others cutting windows and doorways. When the roof went on and the gables went in, it began to look very substantial indeed—far more substantial than the Daltons were accustomed to, Lolly thought uneasily, though Hudson was in great good humor, a gracious host.

Minnie was in perfect control of the generous spread that appeared at noon. The ladies of the district, not willing to be left out of a day of such goodwill, had outdone themselves. Fried chicken, ham, potato salad, baked beans, feathery loaves of bread, homemade butter and jams, pickles and relishes, and every dessert imaginable made the planks set up on sawhorses truly "groaning boards."

The existing tar paper shack was attached and became the kitchen area of the new house. The front window had been moved to the side, and the door became the doorway into the new living area. When one end of the new section had been divided into two small rooms and Lolly's cot had been moved into one of them, her happiness knew no bounds. Mum and Dad got the dresser, and the old trunk was delegated to Lolly for use in her room.

It was raw, it was small, but it was home. Minnie talked of curtains; Hudson promised linoleum; Rufe warned that before winter a heater would be imperative.

Toby's dog, Faithful, went quite mad with ecstasy over the heels to nip, the scraps to eat, and the children to chase. Tiger, the cat, disappeared at the approach of the first rig and didn't reappear until sundown and normalcy. Then she crept around the new house, sniffing suspiciously and leaping into the air at every unaccustomed sound or sight.

The Szarvas family had come—the women to visit and

help with the meals, the men to add their expertise to the house-raising. They had, after all, built their own home and all their own outbuildings. Toby, almost transported into realms of bliss by the strength of his own body and exhibiting every bit of it proudly before Kitty's fond eyes, performed as never before possible, and he felt no ill effects. Confidently he climbed onto the roof with the others.

The widow Fanchon came and brought Yukon. The man was a machine for work.

Marta Szarvas's old-country sweet-sour stewed cabbage made a hit, as always, as did the widow's specialty—floating island dessert topped with the bush's tiny, piquant strawberries. Celebrating their crop of green peas, Minnie produced a steaming pot of new peas and drop dumplings, to her family's surprise and pride.

At chore time everyone packed up and returned to the routine and mundane tasks. But Wildrose was subtly changed; a family had been ministered to in profoundly simple ways, and it would make them full members of the community, in their own minds and in the minds of their neighbors.

The widow Fanchon, packing up her dishes and preparing to leave, announced, "Tomorrow my niece Nannette arrives. Most of you know her, of course. You, Toby, might like to be the one to drive to Meridian to meet the train. Come over early, if you can. And," her eyes twinkled, "you might like to look your best."

Minnie stood in the middle of their new "room," so called by the entire area to designate the "front" room of any home. In her hand she displayed to her family, for the first time, the long-hidden treasure from her old life in her old home: the delicate, intriguing napkin ring.

"It's too bad we don't have a mantel," Rufe said, eyeing

the uniquely fashioned reminder of other days and better times.

"It's not a problem" his mother said softly. "If you'll put a shelf right here," and she indicated the wall directly behind the place where the heater would sit, "I'll put it there."

This was the spot where any comfortable chairs would be grouped. Here company would sit when they came. Here the family would gather after supper when chores were done to nod sleepily, faces scarlet from the blazing heat and backs a-shiver from the encroaching cold. From this spot eyes would lift to the shelf and the beautiful thing it held. Did it, in Minnie's mind, promise better days?

 **20**

There was no doubt about it—Donal agreed with what John Hager's pamphlets had said and what the first settlers to the Territories had maintained: the "fertile belt" was choice land. Until the railway pushed through, the majority of homesteaders migrated to this parkland, usually called bush.

As a result, the farmland Donal and the Smedleys now drove through was for the most part already taken and quickly coming under cultivation. The fields were small as yet, the clearings often stump-filled. But it was green, so green, and indeed fertile. It gave ground reluctantly, but once conquered burgeoned forth with the new crop as generously as with the old.

As the two wagons proceeded from Prince Albert to a place called Wildrose, women, pinning clothes to sagging lines, waved in friendly manner. Children leaned on hoes in productive gardens and waved as well. Being that season, men rode mowers as proudly as a lord of the manor surveyed his estate from a gilded carriage. Critically they watched the hay fall, assessing their need and the supply.

One man had stopped his team and had clambered down from his rake, making some inspection. Donal pulled his wagon to a halt and, behind him, Dave did likewise. With a few long steps they reached the half-mown meadow and nodded a greeting.

"Sure beats scything," Donal grinned, obviously recalling backbreaking work in earlier days. The men shook hands.

"Yep, it's some improvement," agreed the mower as he proudly touched a wheel rim.

"The dumping arrangement is so simple," he explained, "that a child could do it. It just takes the slightest movement of the lever to break the lock."

"By hand or foot?"

"That's the great part! Either one. Then, when this has been done, the operation is automatic—it's practically a self-dump rake."

"Looks simple enough."

"Very little power needed. The throw or sweep of the lever is very short, and the smallest movement breaks the lock, as I said. Then you just remove your hand, or foot, whichever, and it dumps itself."

"Steel teeth, I take it?"

"Twenty of 'em. The axle here is stiffened by a truss rod to prevent sagging." The men solemnly examined the truss rod.

"Can a person ask the price?" Dave inquired.

"Costs $13.25 with these wood wheels. Steel wheels woulda cost $14.50. Sometimes," he said regretfully, "I wish I'da paid the difference. Oh, well," he brightened, "I still make a little on it by renting it out to folks who don't have one yet. But if I do say so, there's not a lot of cash involved—usually barter of some kind—mebbe I use my neighbor's seeder or something like that."

It was a good system, his visitors agreed.

"Now if I could just come up with enough money for a hay loader—" the homesteader said longingly. "But—$41.00? It'll be a while."

After a few more comments and questions, the travelers turned back to their rigs and the patient Angie with baby Frankie and moved on.

"No telling what Uncle Willoughby's place will have in the way of equipment," Donal said. "He didn't make all that much sense when he talked to me. Seemed bound and determined to get me out here, no questions asked. I wonder sometimes if I agreed to the most foolish move of my life—"

"Could be the wisest," Dave said and climbed up into his wagon as Donal did his rig, still pulled by Dandy and Willie, the faithful team that had brought him across the prairie and into the bush.

With two wagons and two teams they would be well fixed for horsepower. Uncle Willoughby had mentioned cattle, kept for him at a nearby farm with a foreign-sounding name— it was written down in the papers the old man had given him.

Would there be a house? For Angie's sake, he hoped so. And it would simplify things a great deal, eliminating the necessity of throwing up some kind of temporary shelter and delaying the work they would need to do if they were to get any kind of grub put by for winter. That money of Uncle Willoughby's—Donal didn't feel good about it. He had touched very little of his own funds and preferred to pay his own way. But—put his time and energy and money into something that wouldn't belong to him in the long run? *I must have been crazy to listen to the old gaffer!* he sighed. *I'm not sure I can maintain this charade, pretending to be his heir—nice though that'd be.*

Yes, a cabin already up would be wonderful. Angie didn't seem to be particularly concerned, but whether from trust in Uncle Willoughby's provision or faith in the Lord's provision Donal didn't know. Her quiet, uncomplaining ways made her a joy to have around. Thanks to her presence, he and Dave wouldn't be that most pathetic of all creatures—bachelors.

Homesteading regulations stated that a claim had to be lived on for six months out of the year; men from such places as eastern Canada or up from the States usually went home during the summer months, to get work. Then they returned to their homestead for the required six months, having paid a neighbor, also in need of cash, to do their cultivating for them, and having enough money left to see them through until another work season rolled around.

But pity the poor men from overseas; they were far, far from home. Many of them were unsuited for the rigors of pioneering and would have gone home in a moment if money had been available. All of them—full-time or part-time occupants—suffered the miseries of their own cooking, often subsisting on oatmeal and tea all winter long. Many more of them would have stuck it out if they had had a wife.

Following their map and counting off the ranges and the townships, Donal and Dave were able to turn at the exact corners, with no difficulty in that regard. So precise was it that Donal appreciated wholeheartedly the "square survey system" Canada had adopted from its neighbor, the United States. The little cavalcade went directly to its destination; they had expected no problem and had none, turning into Willoughby's property eventually, quite certain of their last and final turn.

Houses, all along the way, had been built close to the road. No one, it seemed, had chosen to hide away in some secret recess where access would be difficult or impossible, whatever the weather. If one passed a place in winter and saw no smoke and no sign of travel in or out and the place was supposedly inhabited, it was cause for concern and called for an investigation. More than one homesteader had been found injured, sick, or dead. And no one knew who would be next.

Therefore it came as no surprise to find Uncle Willoughby's buildings just a stone's throw from the road. Donal pulled his wagon in and stopped; Dave pulled up beside him. For a moment they all surveyed the place that Donal, supposedly, had "inherited."

Dave shrugged. "Could be worse."

Donal pushed his hat onto the back of his head, scratched

his dark thatch, and with a short laugh acknowledged, "Serves me right. The old boy was smarter than I gave him credit for."

It was raw and it was new, obviously just a whacked-out clearing with the rudimentary beginnings for proving up. But there was a cabin and, at first glance, it appeared snug and well made.

Angie, on her perch atop the old wagon that had trundled her many weary miles and in which her baby had been born, sighed a great sigh of relief, and a tear welled up into her eyes and spilled over—and welled and spilled. But they were tears of relief. It had been a long trip for her.

"Get me down, Dave," was all she said. Handing baby Frankie to her husband, Angie was over the side, onto the wheel hub, and to the ground, the first one inside the door of the cabin.

"It'll do . . . very well," she said to the men, who followed on her heels. There was the usual large room that was kitchen, parlor, and dining room all in one, with the far end divided into two cubicles for sleeping quarters.

"We could throw up a lean-to in a hurry," Dave said thoughtfully, and Donal nodded; it would increase their living space a good deal and make for considerable comfort.

They first unloaded the household goods, which Angie began unpacking and bestowing in their proper places. Uncle Willoughby's furniture was simple but adequate and consisted of the necessary table and chairs, the required cookstove, and numerous shelves strategically placed around the stove and above the table area. When Dave had lugged in Angie's two comfortable rockers and her bed and dresser, the cabin began to take on the aspect of home.

"Curtains—later. Rugs—there are a couple in the wagon."

"I can hardly wait to see what that old gent considered his

treasures," Donal said, "especially in light of everything else he said and was mistaken about. If he ever had 'help,' it isn't obvious. There doesn't seem to be much done except this cabin and a barn."

"There's a well, of course," Dave said, "and don't make up your mind just yet about anything else. Looks like a trail to the back of the property; if we're lucky he'll have some clearing done. After all, he was here two years, you said?"

"We have to get Frankie bedded down—a box will do for now." Angie's concerns were more immediate. "And then I'll get supper."

Soon a fire was chuckling away in the range, over which Angie had oohed and aahed, as if happy to make its acquaintance after all those campfires. She was already up to her elbows in flour, making biscuits. Dave and Donal continued bringing in boxes and barrels, leaving the opening of most of them until another day. Beds were made up—Donal's on the floor, with the promise from Dave to soon have a bed frame made and a tick stuffed with straw.

With supper over and Frankie asleep, cherubic in his box-bed, Donal began opening Uncle Willoughby's boxes. His "treasures."

"How about that!" Dave muttered, perhaps disappointed. "Seems Uncle Willoughby's treasures are mostly books."

Aside from a compass, a globe of the world, silk plush glove box with no gloves, handy "self-operating mucilage bottle," bronze farm bell, sleigh bells on straps, shaft bells and saddle chimes (Uncle Willoughby must have a love of jingling transportation), and a number of boxes containing a hodgepodge of what appeared to be various and sundry household items, Uncle Willoughby's boxes were crammed with books. Books and the shelves on which to place them. Books, books, and more books:

Webster's Unabridged Dictionary, revised and enlarged by Chauncey A. Goodrich, professor at Yale College, bound in "sheep," with embossed sides and marble edges and claiming, "This dictionary contains every word that Noah Webster ever defined and 10,000 additional words, 1,708 pages [it was a *tome!*], 1,500 illustrations, and an appendix of 10,000 words."

The Unique Album Atlas of the World. "Astronomical, geographical, historical, political, statistical, chronological, financial, commercial, educational, diagrammatical, descriptive, and illustrative . . . containing over 700 pages, many of which are profusely illustrated."

"This should keep us entertained for many a long winter night," Dave offered after first whistling with unbelief.

There was *Isaac Pitman's System of Phonography* [no phonograph]; *Donovan's Science of Boxing*; *North's Book of Love-Letters*, "with directions how to write and when to use them . . . few people are able to express in words the promptings of the first dawn of love, and how to follow up a correspondence with the dearest one in the world."

"Looks like it hasn't been cracked," Donal said, turning the stiff pages.

"Waiting for you, Donal," Dave said with a wink at Angie. "Are you writing anyone back home, by the way?"

"Just my brother, Dave. No females waiting for me there."

Angie crowed with delight to find *Lee's Priceless Recipes*, with its 368 pages and its seven "departments."

"Maybe I'll find rabbit fricassee," Angie said ruefully.

"Don't get too excited," Dave said, laughing. "Look at these departments: 'recipes for the druggist, the chemist, toilet articles, the household, the farm and the dairy, all trades and professions, etc.' "

Angie's enthusiasm wilted a little. "Oh, well."

"Now we're getting somewhere! Here's a two-volume set of Emerson's works; five volumes of *The Leatherstocking Tales* by Cooper; Alexander Dumas' books, 15," he said, counting. "Fifteen of them! Jules Verne . . . Thackeray . . . Hawthorne—my estimation of Uncle Willoughby just went up a bunch!"

Box after box they opened, pile after pile of books stacked up.

At last Donal held up a book printed on fine calendared paper: *A Trip Around the World*. It was well worn, showing signs of much use.

"Uncle Willoughby seems to have traveled around the world—by means of this," he said softly. "Listen to this introduction: 'Contains a rare and elaborate collection of photographic views of the entire world of nature and art. Presenting and describing choicest treasures of Europe, Asia, Africa—' "

"His treasures."

"Can't you just see him?—hunkered down with this in the long winter evenings, taking flights of fancy to goodness-knows-where."

Silently now they laid most of the books back in their boxes; they would set up the bookshelves tomorrow and make choices concerning what to pack away and what to leave out.

As the fire was dying out and the steam from the kettle dissipated, the three adventurers leaned back, looked around, and admitted, "It's been a long trek, but it's been worth it." Tomorrow and tomorrow and tomorrow looked promising, worthy of work and plans and the investment of everything they had to give.

Just before they blew out the lamp and went to bed, Angie said, "One more thing. It seems fitting, I think, that we read something special."

" 'I will make with them a covenant of peace . . . ,' " Angie read from the little Bible she unpacked from her trunk, " 'and they shall dwell safely in the wilderness, and sleep in the woods. And I will make them and the places round about my hill a blessing; and I will cause the shower to come down in his season; there shall be showers of blessing. And the tree of the field shall yield her fruit, and the earth shall yield her increase, and they shall be safe in their land, and shall know that I am the Lord.' "

"Couldn't ask for anything better," Donal said finally in the silence that fell when Angie had closed the Book.

Bedded down on the floor, just before much-needed sleep claimed him, Donal felt again that small pang of guilt for what he saw as misrepresentation of himself to Uncle Willoughby.

"For heaven's sake!" he growled, thumping his pillow and turning restlessly on his pallet, "it's no more than he deserves!"

But what was it Angie had read? "I will make with them a covenant of peace . . . and they shall dwell safely in the wilderness." If one dwelt in the wilderness by fraud, would there be peace? Donal's conscience wrestled briefly with the troubling thought, and his first "sleep in the woods" claimed him.

21

"Good morning, Lita."

"Good morning, King."

Lolly still found it difficult to address her employer as anything but "Mr. Plummer," but "King" came particularly hard. Somehow she felt it was more his status than his name. (And she would call no man King but Victoria's dead spouse!)

As for "Lita"—spoken with the dry tones of Kingston Plummer—Lolly found herself rebelling against it even more heartily than "Lolly." When she thought of answering to it all the rest of her life, she flinched and made an involuntary moue.

How silly! If she could put up with the man himself, she could put up with whatever name he chose to call her.

"Lita." In spite of her dislike of the name, it did fit the grander lifestyle that would be hers when her scheme was realized. And if it pleased "King" Plummer, well, a wife's duty was to please her husband. Hadn't Mum abandoned certain things and ways to accommodate her husband's way of life? On the other hand, had it been the best choice for her and the children? But Mum's decision had been to step down a few rungs on the ladder of society; Lolly's was to climb up a few rungs. Surely that was a good thing.

But Pastor Victor's words about setting one's heart on things above and not on things on the earth nagged at her thoughts until she almost regretted going to church. Still, she was drawn and knew she would be there next Sunday, folded into one of those child-sized desks. "God willing," she added quickly with a new piousness.

And so she smiled at King Plummer, making her eyes linger just a little longer than was necessary on his face and hating herself for doing it. That was because he always seemed to be watching for the glance, and his own gaze held hers steadily until hers—usually in some confusion and to her shame but his approval—dropped away. At times she could feel heat gathering in her cheeks; this, too, seemed to please the intent watcher.

Rather vague about such things, Lolly had an idea that Kingston Plummer—though he was devout enough publicly and would expect from her decency and decorum—might secretly relish the wanton and suggestive. Dedicated as she was to the plan, this aspect of it made Lolly decidedly uncomfortable. She was playing a game about which she knew little or nothing and feared she was in it much deeper than she could handle. Mum would be scandalized if she knew. Rufe, who suspected that something was up, glowered at her and warned, "Watch your step, Missy!"

"Why, Rufe, whatever do you mean?" she had managed as innocently as possible in the face of the rather intimate scene he had noted when she had said her good-byes to Kingston Plummer one day. Particularly bold on that day, he had let his hand slide down her bare arm as he walked with her out onto the porch to see her off.

Now walking beside him from the yard where he had greeted her, Lolly found herself wishing her suitor—if indeed that's what he was—would come to the point, ask her to marry him, and be done with this play-acting. She had always supposed courtship was a lovely, special experience, but this was something—something distasteful.

If Kingston Plummer would just get on with it, she thought now, all the while allowing her hand to touch his tantalizingly as they walked side by side. Yet she despised herself for the game she was playing. But it would be worth it, wouldn't it, when she was mistress of this fine house and free, once and for all, of poverty, insecurity, and a nomadic lifestyle?

Upon entering the house, Kingston shut the door behind him, looked around carefully to see that Anna-Rose was not within hearing distance, and—made his move. He made his move, but Lolly found herself strangely in a panic about it.

"Lita—"

It was more than his hand on her arm and the closeness of his body; it was more than his breathing, which had quickened. It was his voice.

Kingston Plummer was a man in control. Lolly had often heard him give instructions and directions to Rufe and Arnie as well as to Anna-Rose, and there was decision and authority in his voice. Now that same determined note was heard, and Lolly, suddenly, wasn't ready for it.

"Lita—my dear," Kingston began.

"Oh, isn't that Anna-Rose? Anna-Rose . . . Anna-Rose—"
It was all she could think of to postpone the moment, the moment for which she had planned, of which she had dreamed, and for which she had . . . cheapened herself. And so she called an absent Anna-Rose.

Lolly turned quickly and blindly toward the kitchen, leaving Kingston with his mouth open, eyes angry, and face flushing as he stood on the small rug at the door.

When the door slammed and the house rang with nothing but silence and the beating of her own heart, Lolly leaned sickly against the heavy dining room table. "What have I done . . . what have I done?" But whether she seemed rude to send Kingston on his way or painfully in regret of her foolishness in encouraging him in the first place was not clear.

Even Lolly was confused about her feelings. But it had to

do, she realized dimly, with what she had heard the preacher say. Remembering his words, she could not be free to go her selfish, silly way any longer. If only she hadn't gone to church—had never heard. But a Voice other than that of the preacher was speaking to her now. Though gentle, it was insistent. Though ignored, it was persistent.

All unknowing of its happening, Lolly was face up with a phenomenon—the faithful pursuit of the One who said, "Behold [Here I am!], I stand at the door, and knock" (Rev. 3:20).

When Anna-Rose finally appeared, her arms were full of clothes.

"Papa and I were going through Mama's things," she said softly, "and he . . . we thought . . . you might like to do something with some of these."

Catching sight of Lolly's face, perhaps, and being more sensitive and understanding than Lolly had given her credit for, Anna-Rose added quickly, "Being as how you're so good with a needle, and all—"

"I'll make some of them over for you, Anna-Rose," Lolly said quietly.

Truth to tell, Lolly had already looked longingly at the full closets and mentally lengthened the gowns and taken in the waists to fit her own proportions.

"But there are plenty—for both of us—" Anna-Rose pursued, holding the scarlet twilled jacquard, the black-and-white and brown shepherd plaid, the puff-sleeved Persian percale, the changeable taffeta silk, the velvet-collared Scotch mixture, the ribbon-ruched kersey.

Lolly looked but let them go as naturally as though she had awakened from a nightmare to find reality better than she had dreamed.

At home again, her tasks for Minnie accomplished and a

few minutes to herself, Lolly went to the trunk that held most of the family belongings and lifted from it several flour sacks that had been washed and ironed after they were emptied of their contents. She looked at them critically.

She *was* good with a needle. Even though the sack material was of the simplest cotton, with a little skill she could make herself a dress entirely suitable and pretty as well. Until now she had planned to use them for, if not tea towels, those hidden personal garments that she badly needed. Now, her face flushing with shame for the foolish pride she had harbored, she looked at the dainty flowers, pink and yellow and green on a white background, and felt relief like a cool healing breeze fill her sore heart.

At least, she thought, *they will be honest garments, not bought at the cost of a good conscience!*

"Look, Mum," she said, going into the other room and holding the flour sack up to her face. "What do you think of this for an everyday dress?"

"Good idea," Minnie said placidly. "You have your new skirt and waist for best. Those will be fine for anything else."

Trust Mum! Lolly felt her throat thicken momentarily with appreciation for her mother's support. Maybe she was too uncomplaining of her husband, and maybe she went along with his weaknesses too easily. That same faithful support was available to her children. Lolly, the recipient of it now, was almost passionately grateful. Home, simple though it was and poor in many ways, was an island of safety in a harsh world. And to think that she, Lolly, had been considering trading it for *things!*

Lolly shivered. Her mother, more keen-eyed than her daughter knew, noted but kept her silence.

Lolly laid the material out on the table and studied it; it would have to be cleverly pieced together. Sleeves—could they have a puff? The skirt alone, if it was to be full enough, would require several sacks. Humming to herself, Lolly figured and schemed, finding satisfaction in making something from practically nothing. For the moment, King Plummer and his attractions, such as they were, seemed far away. Lolly knew, however, that he was a problem that was yet to be faced.

"You know, Mum," she said, finally, "I'm not going to work for Mr. Plummer very much longer."

"Oh, no?" Minnie asked quietly.

"It's—it's not really the best idea, Mum." After a short silence she added, "If you know what I mean."

"I think I do," Minnie said matter-of-factly, snipping a thread of her darning wool. "I'm wondering—"

"Wondering, Mum?"

"About Toby."

Lolly frowned, head lifted, puzzled. "Toby? What about Toby?"

"I'm wondering if Toby won't need to make the same decision."

22

"Toby, you silly boy! Help me down!"

The words were spoken by the red lips of Nannette Fanchon. Red, pouting lips. Delectable lips.

"You said you wanted up on Fancy," Toby argued, having spent a good deal of time away from his work to saddle and bridle the riding horse, as well as help the girl up onto the skittish mare.

"I changed my mind, you silly boy!"

It seemed to Toby that Nannette was always changing her mind. One minute she would be teasing and tormenting, the next playful and tender, then suddenly wide-eyed and childish. Not that she was very grown up at any time. Toby knew very little about Nannette's upbringing—just that it had been one of luxury with every need (and probably every want) fulfilled.

Still, she loved the farm, or so she said. "I've been coming ever since I was 10 years old," she had explained on that first day when he met her train and had opportunity to get acquainted on the long ride from Meridian to Wildrose.

Widow Fanchon, not feeling too well these days and always suffering to some degree from rheumatism, had declined to make the buggy trip to get her niece. Yukon, she said, had more important things to do than take a half day and more away from the homestead. Toby had been commandeered for the task.

And he didn't mind. The Fanchon horse was first rate and the rig handsome and well sprung. Toby had been entrusted with a list of supplies and was urged out of the yard early enough to get the household business done before Nannette should arrive.

"She's not known to be the most patient child," the aunt said with frankness. "But goodhearted. It's always a bright spot to have her here. I suppose she'll be quite grown up now . . . she's 16, I guess."

"Same age as Kitty Szarvas."

"Yes. But seems like they've never had too many things in common. Nannette's too given to fun. Kitty has too many responsibilities. Good girls, both of them."

"How will I know her?" Toby was nervous about meeting a strange girl.

"Know her? You can't miss her!"

How right that was! His errands completed, Toby watched the train come in. Even if there had been a dozen passengers disembarking, he could not have missed anyone by the name of Nannette—at least not *this* Nannette.

In the first place, she was small but perfectly formed—a miniature woman.

Second, she was perfection. Her attire demanded immediate admiration. Even after a tiring and dirty train ride, she was elegantly turned out with expensive traveling suit, kid boots, and elaborate hat.

She was imperious, as only the totally self-satisfied can be. "You there," she had called to Rudy Bannister, the station master. "You may remember me from last year. I'm—"

Rudy, not terribly impressed, interrupted. "And how are you, Miss Nannette?"

Frostily she had continued, as though he hadn't spoken, "I'm looking for someone from the Fanchon place—"

"Right over there, I expect." Rudy pointed out the hovering Toby. Rudy knew the Fanchon rig as well as he did his own worn turnout.

It was Toby's clue. With an effort, he discontinued his study of this rare female, took off his cap, and spoke. "Miss— Miss Fanchon? I'm Toby Dalton. Your aunt sent me to get you."

"You can put your hat back on, you silly boy," the girl said with a laugh. But Toby felt it was a laugh *at* him rather than *with* him. It was the first of many. He turned red as he jammed his shapeless cap onto his head.

"No—take it off!" her highness demanded. "Your hair— it's too beautiful to be covered up." She smiled her co-quettish smile, the first of many he was to see, and trilled with laughter when Toby snatched the cap off and stuffed it into his pocket.

At the buggy, after her things were loaded, she held her hand out imperiously for assistance to step up into the rig. Toby had blushed, holding that small hand, but had been game.

"Your blush is almost the same color as your hair," Nannette had said, watching him critically, which made Toby blush the more.

"Oh, this is going to be a good summer—I just feel it!" the girl had announced.

When the buggy was well on its way homeward, over the track and onto the Wildrose road, Toby dared another peek at this tantalizing creature. Nannette removed her hat and was running her hands through her abundant dark hair, loos-ening it from its pins and letting it stream over her shoulders and down her back. Her eyes, dark and narrow, flew every-where, taking it all in; she threw back her head and breathed deeply.

"No place smells like Wildrose," she declared. "I forget what it's like when I'm gone. The moment I'm here, I recog-nize it. Do you know if Abbie—what's-her-name—"

"Jameson, I suppose you mean. That's their place we're passing."

"Yes, Jameson, the widow who married the widower. Has she had her baby yet?"

"How would I know?"

"Caro—Carolyn Morris. You know, the girl who wouldn't marry that half-breed? Is she still single?"

"How would I know?" Toby asked again. "I've only been here a couple of months."

Nannette was filled with questions about everyone and anyone along their line of travel. Obviously she loved Wildrose and was interested in its people.

"How about the Runyon uncles?" she asked when they passed the school and the farm opposite. "Are Hubert and Harry"—she seemed reluctant to hear bad news—"still living? And don't say 'How would I know?' Anyone with a lick of curiosity would know about Hubert and Harry."

"I guess I saw them—two old men, sort of funny—"

"Hilarious, really. But dears."

"Well, I saw them at church. They tussled quite a bit, getting into their seat. One of them swatted the other with his quarterly."

"That's Hubert and Harry. I'll go over to see them first off. They might die before I get there if I'm too slow."

Toby was shocked at her cool commentary on the life expectancy of the two elderly men. Perhaps his face showed it; perhaps he frowned.

Nannette burst into laughter. "Don't be a stick-in-the-mud! I'd cry buckets if they did—kick the bucket." She giggled at her own joke.

And so it was all the way home.

Toby was both sorry and pleased when at last they reached the Fanchon homestead. The widow Fanchon, "Aunt

Fanny" to Nannette, enfolded the girl in her arms, and Yukon grinned and went to shake her hand. With a hoot of laughter, Nannette spurned the hand and flung her arms around the grizzled hired man and hugged him warmly. Yukon obviously loved it.

Toby was instructed to bring the luggage into the house. If he expected any more attention from that flighty young lady, he was disappointed. Nannette was flying around, reacquainting herself with remembered and loved treasures.

The day being far gone, Toby took himself off home. As he passed the Szarvas gate, he waved to Kitty who was at the eternal task of caring for the garden. Kitty laid aside her hoe and walked toward him, the late-afternoon sun bright on her yellow hair and touching with an added patina the already sun-darkened skin.

She's the only person I know, Toby thought, *whose skin is darker than her hair.*

"Do you ever think of putting on a sunbonnet?" he said now, frowning.

"It's hanging over there," Kitty said, pointing to a fence post to which the bonnet dangled by its straps. "It's got a family of the tiniest mice you ever saw in it."

"Kitty," Toby scolded, but mildly, "you know mice are dreadful pests here. Whatever will you do with them? Feed them to the cat?"

Kitty was silent for a moment, her eyes fixed on his face. Then, "She's come, hasn't she?" she asked.

"She?" Toby countered.

"Nannette Fanchon."

"Well, yes, but what's that got to do with mice?"

"Nothing to do with mice. It's just that you sound like her."

"Why, Kitty Szarvas—what a thing to say! I've hardly met her!"

"That's all right, Toby. Even *I* take on some of her ways when I'm around her. I become quite—giddy, I guess is the word. Can you imagine it?"

Toby couldn't. And he wasn't sure he wanted to. Kitty was Kitty, down-to-earth, honest, steady, sturdy Kitty. Nannette was—Toby couldn't put words to it yet, but he knew that in every way Nannette Fanchon was the exact opposite of Kitty Szarvas.

"Go look after your mice," he said gruffly at last. "Hanging there in the heat won't do them any good." Too late he remembered that his own rescue by Kitty had been during the heat of the day.

He watched her progression across the field silently. She walked with a natural grace, her braid moving with the fluid motion of her well-rounded arms and legs. He saw her remove the sunbonnet from the post, saw her peer inside at its contents, saw her lips move in what he supposed was a soothing sound, and knew he was not wrong—Kitty was predictable. For some reason he wasn't sure if that was as admirable a trait as he had thought previously.

Shrugging, he went on home to be greeted by Faithful— and to wonder why in the world he had ever called the dog that—and Tiger, remembering exactly when Kitty had named the golden, striped kitten.

At the supper table Toby kept the family regaled with an account of his day's activities with the oh-so-unpredictable Miss Nannette Fanchon.

"I need you to stay home for a day or two," Hudson said. "If we don't get some water to the corn, we won't have any. It will mean a lot of hauling with a barrel and the stone-boat."

Toby agreed, but with such an ill grace that it made him wonder why in the world it mattered so much whether he worked here or for Widow Fanchon.

The Mellon homestead was flourishing. Hudson had showed unusual ambition, for Hudson. Perhaps it was Minnie's unflagging approval; perhaps he, too, was a little tired of the continual pulling up and leaving, to start the whole go-around all over again. Or perhaps he took delight in watching an almost day-by-day growth in whatever he planted. The season might be short, but the plants seemed to know it and responded to sun and rain with an urgency to reproduce before cold weather stopped their cycle for another long hibernation.

"Where in the world have you been, you silly boy?" Nannette said in greeting Toby.

"I have other things to do, you know," Toby said with a frown. The attempt to be serious with her didn't last.

"Growing Mellons?" Nannette asked wickedly.

"I see your aunt has caught you up on all the local news," Toby said stiffly. But it didn't last either.

"All the local folks. And then there's you."

Toby looked at her quickly to see if she was laughing at him. She was sparkling with fun, so finally he smiled.

"There—that's better," she said. "And now, what are you going to be doing today?"

"Cleaning out the barn, Yukon said."

Nannette made a face. "Oh, go ahead. I'll come along and get acquainted again with Fancy."

It wasn't long until she was pestering him to saddle the mare and put her up to ride. When Yukon gave him the nod, Toby laid aside his pitchfork and did the girl's bidding. When she found she couldn't persuade him to saddle another horse and ride with her, she looked petulant, rode out to the road by herself, and turned around and came back.

Toby was hard at work. "Put me down, you silly boy,"

Nannette commanded, seeming to enjoy calling his work to a halt.

Toby suspicioned that Nannette was well able to dismount by herself. But obligingly he held up his arms, and she slid down into them. Stepping back quickly, letting his arms fall, Toby found Nannette stepping with him so that she remained in close contact with him, except that now it was she who clasped him. Looking down on that impish face, Toby was momentarily frozen. Then he made an abortive attempt to free himself; her hold tightened. Looking down into her upturned, laughing countenance, Toby decided it wasn't funny.

Doesn't she know anything about men? he wondered, desperately needing to back off from her ravishments.

Nannette knew, all right; she didn't let go. Toby's face grew scarlet.

"You aren't a silly boy, after all," she decided, smiling. "But you *are* a silly goose."

Nannette dropped her arms from around him and danced away. Soberly, with knees somewhat atremble, Toby led Fancy to the barn.

What would she have done, was his first coherent thought, *if I'd have had one of my turns?*

Probably laughed me out of it, was his next thought.

And so akilter were Toby's thoughts by this time that the "silly goose" supposed she might have worked a cure.

23

For Donal Cardigan the days slipped by in a whirl of activity. As Dave had suspected, a cleared field was found. Someone—the unknown "helper," perhaps—had planted wheat, and it was greening nicely. They would have a crop.

No garden had been planted. Late though it was, Angie worked diligently to get one started, confident she would reap enough to make it worthwhile. With Frankie in a box nearby, she thrust the precious seed into soil that had lain waiting, black and rich and willing, ever since the world began. Her harvest would go into the cellar, one way or another: boxes of potatoes, carrots, onions; crocks of pickles and sauerkraut; sealers of beans and peas; wax-topped jars of jellies and jams.

Since she was new to the area, the wild fruit and their time of ripening were unknown to Angie. So she watched the bush, picking, in season, pin cherry, chokecherry, and the delicious but tiny jeweled strawberries. She was thankful she had insisted on bringing jars with her to the wilderness; sugar and rubber rings were available at the general store in Meridian. Soon the high-bush cranberries along the river would yield an abundant harvest; the orange-blush sauce they made, served in a sauce dish with thick cream, would make a dessert fit for a gourmet's table.

Hazelnuts were filling out their prickly cases; Angie planned to gather sacks and sacks of them. Their sweet nuttiness would make her Christmas baking something special. Yes, the bush was bountiful as well as beautiful.

There was no doubt about it: as their sown seed sent out

tendrils and growths that moored them in place, even so Angie, Dave, and Donal put down roots in the fertile parkland soil.

"If only this were our own place," Angie mourned, well aware of "Uncle" Willoughby's quirky arrangement. If only she and Dave could have one quarter and make it their permanent home, with Donal taking the other quarter.

Donal struggled with the same mix of satisfaction and dissatisfaction. He loved Wildrose and would indeed make it his home. But ever and always, in spite of his grim insistence that Willoughby Ames had flat-out given the homestead to him, uncertainties about the moral rightness of it nibbled away at him.

The more he questioned, the more savagely he worked, grubbing stumps, clearing land, haying the farm's natural meadows, and helping Dave, the builder, add a lean-to onto the existing cabin.

It was the lean-to that brought about their first contact with a neighbor. A wagon paused, and the driver studied the situation for a few moments, then turned in and pulled his team to a halt at the cabin door.

Donal and Dave walked over, reached up, shook hands, and introduced themselves. Angie, with Frankie in her arms, watched from the doorway and nodded shyly.

"I'm new here, myself," Rufe Dalton said. "We live just down the road. When we put up our house, folks helped out. I'd like to do the same for you. How about if my brother and I come on over this evening and give a hand?"

And so while Hudson did the milking and feeding of the animals that evening, Rufe and Toby came to help. The job was a comparatively simple one—just a 12-by-10 three-sided addition attached to the cabin. Some work had already been done, and before the long Canadian evening was over, the task was completed.

"We'll move the cookstove tomorrow before we light the fire for the day," Dave said. "First trip we make to town we'll get linoleum for the floor."

"And before winter," Rufe added, "just like us, you'll need a good heater.

"You'll have to come on over and meet my mother and my sis," he continued as he saw Angie move a few things from the cabin into the lean-to.

"I'd love to," she said. "Is everyone as busy as we are?"

"It's that time of the year, I guess. It seems like winter is blowing down the back of everyone's neck." Rufe's words were sober, though he was smiling.

Back home Rufe told the family, "The farm seems to belong to Donal Cardigan."

"You'd like that Angie," Toby told Lolly. "She can't be much older than you."

"I'll try and get over," Lolly said absently.

"Hey, wake up! You living in a dream world or something?"

Lolly flushed.

"Kingston Plummer just left," Hudson explained.

"Ah, then—she *is* in a dream world," Toby teased, but his sister didn't smile as he had thought she would.

Instead, she looked at her younger brother sharply and said, "You'd know about that, wouldn't you, Toby?"

Toby's mouth fell open. "Dream . . . me . . . wha . . . ?"

"Think about it," his sister said crisply and went to her room and shut the door.

"What's bothering her?" Toby looked blankly at his mother, who quietly continued her mending.

Scratching his head, muttering, frowning, Toby pulled off his boots and socks, flexing his tired feet. Holding up one sock in which gaped a hole, he grinned at his mother. "*This* is no dream—that's for sure."

"That's real enough," his mother agreed. "Throw it in the wash. I'll mend it when it's clean."

Toby went off to do as she suggested, once again muttering, "Dream world—who, me? She's crazy like a loon!"

Tossing and turning on her narrow bed, Lolly went over in her mind the just-concluded visit of Kingston Plummer.

She had been sitting on the stoop in the evening's early shadows when she heard the rig approaching; it was Kingston. Pulling up before the house, he greeted her.

"Good evening," he said as he doffed his hat.

Slowly Lolly had gotten to her feet, straightened her floursack dress, and walked over to the side of the buggy. Kingston Plummer looked down on her, his face showing lively interest.

Kingston's lips seemed dry and his voice hoarse. "Lita," he managed, his face flushing even in the dim light, "I'd like for you to take a little ride with me. It's a nice evening—"

Lolly hesitated. But why? It was the perfect opportunity, away from her position as hired girl, away from her simple and poor surroundings, away from Anna-Rose, away from her family. Then she hesitated no longer. "Why, I'd like that! Just let me tell Mum."

Slim and graceful, she stepped up into the buggy, aware that the narrow seat brought her closer to Kingston than she might have liked. If she was repelled by the man's physical presence, his expensive clothes did much to further stiffen her wavering purpose.

Conversation was stilted and strained until, at last, Kingston pulled the rig to a halt at the side of the road, under the spread of a willow. He let the reins drop and turned to face the girl at his side as he spoke firmly. Enough shilly-shallying!

"You must know, Lita, that I find you, ah, attractive. And I have reason to think you haven't found my attentions in any way distasteful. I've been alone now for 10 months or so. It's time I did something about that. I find you a suitable woman in many ways. I believe we might have a, ah, future together, and I've been led to believe you might be thinking along the same lines.

"I know you're an innocent young lady—that's all to the good. I've had opportunity to see that you are also a capable cook and housekeeper. All in all, it seems a mutually profitable, ah, arrangement. Each meeting the other's needs, eh? Now, what do you say?"

Her own needs Lolly knew very well, having enumerated them to herself many times; they were at the heart and center of her entire plan. Why else would she have been motivated to try to capture the most eligible bachelor around?

But as for Kingston Plummer's needs, she was vague. A housekeeper, certainly, as he had mentioned; a companion for Anna-Rose, which he hadn't mentioned. These she could fulfill; why then did she experience this hesitation?

Somewhere in the back of her mind the pastor's words concerning treasures and the heart lingered and troubled her. Her heart, in all honesty, was not where her expected treasure was.

But the pastor's words could be hushed by the greater clamor of her current, present needs. He spoke, after all, of pie-in-the-sky-by-and-by! Pie and good old bread-and-butter on her plate in the here-and-now—that was the appeal and temptation.

In the rush of thoughts that tumbled through her mind, Lolly seemed to have missed some of Kingston's less-than-impassioned speech. His heart, perhaps, was no more in his treasure-seeking than was hers.

Kingston's arms, attempting to go around her shoulders, brought Lolly back to the present and its importance. Resisting his pull and avoiding his seeking lips, in a panic and not understanding why, Lolly did the only thing she knew to do at the moment: hedge . . . delay . . .

"Kingston . . . King . . . what you've said, I do appreciate it—"

"That's good," Kingston spoke with relief. "I was sure you would. After all—"

"I know you'll give me time to think over what you've said."

"Well, if you really need to. I thought, like me, you had been giving this idea quite a bit of consideration."

"I guess, after all," and Lolly, at last, was honest, "I'm just not sure."

"Not sure?" The man's face, in the dimming light, had a touch of grimness.

All those times she had met him glance for glance, displayed her charms to the best of her advantage, brushed against him so innocently but so enticingly—Lolly now saw her part in it clearly.

But she would make it up to him! Once his wife, he would find no reason to regret his—her?—decision.

Now, as kindly as she could, after breathing deeply a few times, Lolly said, "We haven't known each other very long."

When Kingston looked impatient, she went on hurriedly, "It would look better, to the district—all your friends—if we gave it a little more time."

"Ah, I see." She had touched on an important place in King Plummer's thinking—his reputation.

Still he was in a ferment, not one to suffer frustration

calmly. "How long?" he asked, with urgency. "Two weeks?—that should be plenty of time."

"Two weeks," Lolly agreed.

At her door, about to alight from the buggy, Lolly turned to him and said, "I think it might be well if I didn't come over any more to work."

"Not come?" Kingston's face, in the near night, was filled with surprise. "But that's the, ah, point—to have you there."

"But how does it look?"

"You're right, of course."

Lolly tossed and turned, unable to go to sleep.

Treasures. An overflowing pantry. A closet full of clothes. A rococo mantel clock. Nottingham lace curtains.

These things and others no more worthy were what she had set her desires upon. But her heart—her heart was not involved. "Set your affection on things above, not on things on the earth," the preacher had quoted from the Bible. And she had set her affections on earthly things, Kingston Plummer's things. But not her heart—Kingston Plummer did not have her heart.

Somehow Lolly would have felt better if she could feel some affection for the man as well as his treasures. Not feeling it, she felt dishonest—cheap.

Wicked. That's what it was. Wicked, and she didn't know what to do about it.

Apologizing to Kingston might help—would it wash away the feeling of being soiled? Lolly groaned the night away and never thought to pray.

 24

Toby's night of rest hadn't been any better than Lolly's. At breakfast, preparing to go off to the Fanchon place, he looked sourly at the pale face of his sister.

What in the world had she meant? Dreaming—him? Toby scoffed at the very thought. Why, nobody was more down-to-earth than he—unless it was Kitty.

Kitty. Now there was a practical, sensible, amiable girl. No foolishness about Kitty. No flightiness. No deviousness. And, in all probability, no imagination, no originality, no flights of fancy, no poetry. No teasing, no tempting, no—

Toby brought his thoughts to a halt, only dimly aware that in describing Kitty's lack he was describing Nannette's characteristics, and, it seemed, to Kitty's detriment. Such predictability—wasn't it apt to be boring, if, well, if an association were lifelong?

Just one thing bothered Toby: why had Kitty named that sick kitten Nightingale? Why not Runt, or Limpy, or Tiny? There were any number of unimaginative names that came to mind. Why Nightingale?

As long as Nightingale remained a mystery, the matter of Kitty's predictability was in question.

"Perhaps you should stay here and work at home tomorrow, Toby," Rufe suggested. "I'm going to make a trip to P.A."

"Oh, yeah? What for?" Toby asked, interested.

"I've got most of my pay for the summer," Rufe answered, "and there are any number of things we need for winter. I'll take the wagon and the team. Won't get home, of course, until the following day. Have you got that list ready, Mum?"

"I'm working on it."

"What about you, Sis? You've probably got some cash burning a hole in your pocket. Anything I can get for you?"

"I'll think about it," Lolly said so wanly that the entire family looked at her.

"What can we do here without the team?" Toby asked.

"You and Pop can work away on the cordwood. Or you can cut ties for the railway, and that will give us some cash. Our crop is going to be little or nothing this year, of course. But next year—"

Rufe went on to elaborate on plans for next year, and they all left the table with zest and enthusiasm. What fun it was to actually be doing things on your own place, for your own betterment.

"We're going berrying," Nannette said to Toby when he arrived at the Fanchon homestead. "Cherrying, that is. Chokecherrying."

"Not me," Toby said.

"Of course, you. It won't be any fun without you."

"Your aunt doesn't pay me to pick berries."

"Well, today she is! She needs chokecherries for jelly and sauce. I happen to love both madly. So there!"

Toby looked doubtful.

"Listen to me, Toby," Nannette said in a conspiratorial tone, a half-whisper. "Aunt Fanny has heaps of money—let her spend it on whatever she wants. You know, don't you, that this is all going to be mine anyway? So if I say let's spend some of it on a little fun today, we'll spend it on fun! Tomorrow you can get back to heaving slops around if you wish."

"I can't come tomorrow; Rufe is going to Prince Albert,

and Dad needs me at home."

"Oh, bother! I'll be bored for sure."

Toby couldn't help but feel a little flattered. He hadn't known he was such a fun person.

"Guess what? I've asked Kitty Szarvas to come with us. I wanted Billy to come too, but you know Szarvas! Work, work, work, kids and all. I guess if old Marta didn't need jelly, Kitty wouldn't get to come."

"That's not fair," Toby objected. "They aren't slave drivers! They're industrious—that's what."

Nannette made a face, as if "industrious" was a dirty word. And to her, butterfly that she was, it probably was. And to think this entire homestead would be in her hands! Toby had known it, of course, in the back of his mind.

Soon Kitty came swinging through the gate, her brown legs flashing below a blue gingham dress that had seen better days. Standing beside the fashionable Nannette with her full-skirted foulard percale of brilliant mixed colors, high collared and puff sleeved and eminently unsuited for berry picking, Kitty looked like a wren beside an exotic flamingo. Nevertheless, the wren was golden-topped, healthy, vigorous, and entirely at ease with her city friend. Kitty, Toby realized with some surprise, looked completely at home, but Nannette seemed like a vivid transplant.

Transplant or not, Nannette knew her way around the bush. And she needed to; her future was bound up in Wildrose with the advent of her inheritance a probability before too long; Aunt Fanny seemed frailer every day. The place needed someone with Nannette's vigor and imagination.

Carrying their pails, the trio trudged down the road. The heaviest stand of chokecherry bushes was along the roadside not far away; chokecherries had a way of growing well on cleared land if given a chance. The roadside was perfect. A berry-picker could stand more or less in the open and literally strip handfuls into the pail hung from a belt cinched around the waist, leaving both hands free—one to hold down the branch, the other to strip off the tart, somewhat astringent fruit. Chokecherries made excellent jelly.

"My hands will be purple tomorrow," Kitty offered, thinking of the work ahead and already busy picking.

"Your mouth is purple now," Toby reminded her.

"And so is yours, silly goose," Nannette injected, laughing. "Here, goosey!" Nannette took a snowy, lace-edged handkerchief from her pocket, said "Stick out your tongue," wet the cloth, and began scrubbing Toby's purple lips.

For just a moment Toby thought he discerned a gleam of something—laughter, perhaps—in Kitty's ordinarily calm eyes. At any rate, he jerked away from the ridiculous effort and stuffed another handful of chokecherries into his mouth.

Nannette looked at him reproachfully, and Toby relented. "I'll only get all purple again, anyway," he muttered, and stood stoically unmoving while Nannette, with a gust of wild laughter, pushed a ripe cherry onto his chin with her thumb, squirting juice not only on his face but also onto his shirt.

"Oops! But you look so good in purple! You should be a king, Toby. How would you like to have your own kingdom, your own realm, to rule? Ever think about that?"

"No, of course not," Toby muttered, wiping the juice and wondering about the stain.

"It needs to be soaked right away," Kitty said. "Your shirt, I mean."

"Sew a frill over it—right there!" Nannette put a purple fingertip on the stain, managing to make the touch a caress. When Toby's face flamed, she leaned toward his ear and whispered a carrying "Goose!"

Nannette subsided and the picking proceeded without further incident. Kitty picked the bushes clean and had a pail comparatively free of stems and with no leaves. Nannette's pail was as full of leaves as berries.

"Toby," Nannette said, drawing his attention to a thick growth of bush off to the right, "do you think that should be cleared? Make another wheat field, perhaps?"

"That's one of your aunt's last stands of virgin growth," Kitty said quickly. "She's been here a long time and done a lot of clearing. Those are beautiful woods—"

"Toby?" Nannette was imperious.

"It should be studied," Toby said, seriously. "Find out how many acres are under cultivation now, how much land there is in pasture, and so on. Too, there's the need for fuel every year from now on out."

"Pooh! Why not import coal? The train comes now, regularly—"

"Except in winter," Kitty warned.

"I'll have lots of money—from my aunt, my grandmother, and . . . Oh, there'll be heaps, to do what I want. Coal wouldn't be out of the question. What do you think of that idea, Toby?"

"I'd have to give it some thought," said Toby, who never saw coal and believed his own conclusion to be a wise one.

By noon their pails were full. Back at the Fanchon homestead, Aunt Fanny (looking indeed frail, Toby thought, studying her more critically than before) invited Kitty to eat with them.

"Thanks, Miz Fanchon," Kitty said politely, "but Mum and I will want to do these berries up yet today. I better get on home with them."

Kitty said her good-byes and turned to go. For a moment

Toby thought how clean and pure she looked with her golden hair and golden-brown skin, her eyes clear and blue, and her teeth straight and—purple from the berries!

But her lips were pink and firm and parted in a cheerful smile when Nannette—perhaps catching Toby's appreciative glance on Kitty's rounded person and erectly held head—said gaily, "What a little milkmaid you look, Kitty, with your skirt hiked up like that and a pail in your hands."

Why didn't she respond, Toby thought in Kitty's defense, with *"And you, my dear Nannette, look like the queen of the castle—a log castle."* But Kitty was Kitty; she'd be kind to a polecat.

"She does look quaint," Widow Fanchon said. "Quaintly beautiful and perfectly right for Wildrose." Kitty was walking steadily away.

"Indeed she does," Nannette agreed, with her generous turnaround. "She's perfect for Wildrose; that's why I'm so jealous of her. With a little help and a little patience," she said to Toby as they made their way into the house and dinner, "I'd make a true farmer's wife. Or"—she said with a toss of her head and a glance at Toby—"my husband could go east with me and live like a king. But he'd have to look good in purple."

With a gust of laughter, Nannette sped ahead, scattering chokecherries and leaves along the way.

 25

Donal straightened his back, wiped his brow, and leaned on his grub hoe. The satisfaction a man should feel when clearing his land was missing. All the tasks that moved the homestead toward a functioning farm and that should have filled a land-owner's heart with pride were sapped of their sense of fulfill-ment. And all because the land, after all, was not Donal's "portion."

Donal could remember Margot, his mother, quoting some remote Bible passage when his father came in from a hard day's work: "It is good and comely for one to eat and drink, and to enjoy the good of all his labour that he taketh under the sun all the days of his life, which God giveth him: for it is his portion." Moreover, she said, encouragingly, a man should "rejoice in his labour; this is the gift of God."

It had seemed so right, so true, coming from his mother. And his father, and later his brother and he, would sit up to the table, bow their heads, and thank God for His provision, rejoicing in it and the fact that their own hands had wrenched and dug and sowed and harvested the fare set out before them: butter from their own cows; bread from their own wheat; corn from their fields, fields from which their own hands had wrestled the stones and plowed and planted their crop; fruit from trees they had set out as young saplings and nurtured through hot sun and bitter winter to maturity. What a good and satisfied feeling it had been!

Now again Donal sat up to a table largely provided by his own hard work. But where was the rejoicing? Where was the satisfaction? It was hollow, all hollow.

Yesterday he had made a trip to Meridian for supplies and to check for mail. There was no letter this time from Moody and Esther, and he was about to turn from the small post office, which occupied a corner of the general store, when it occurred to him to ask if there was something for Jenner Coy. There was.

My dear boy, you'll be glad to hear that I'm doing much better. But still not well enough, sorry to say, to take on any of the work needed on the homestead. I know you have it all in hand, however. I hope you found things there in good shape and that you are feeling at home. Remember that it all belongs to you, my boy. Mrs. Janeway and Mrs. Prine send greetings.

Willoughby

As he had read it to Angie and Dave, they sat in silence for a few moments. Then Dave cleared his throat and said, "The old gent seems to be making more sense than when you talked to him. Like he's feeling better, for sure."

"Sounds like it," Donal said absently, deep in thought, and most of it not restful.

"He still seems set on the place being yours."

"Jenner's."

More silence.

Angie sat in her small rocking chair with Frankie snuggled down in her arms. She rocked and said nothing. It made Donal more restive than ever.

"Angie?" he said.

"I think, Donal," Angie said slowly, her blue-gray eyes looking straight ahead, "you'll do the right thing."

"What is that, Angie?"

"You'll know. Somehow you'll know."

With a sigh Donal had folded the letter, risen to his feet, and gone to his room. Kneeling at the small trunk that held the items he had brought with him, packed for him by Esther, he opened it now to lay the letter inside. Shoving some garments aside and rearranging his few possessions, his hand touched something firm among the softer clothing. Curious, he pulled it out.

It was a handkerchief, but it was wrapped around something of some substance. Donal unwrapped it, wondering what Esther had secretly enclosed for his use or pleasure far from home.

It was small. It was black. It was well used. It was worn. And it was very familiar. It was his mother's Bible.

With something very like a sob, Donal brought the Book to his breast, bowing his head over it, breathing out his deep emotions of both pleasure and pain.

How many times he had seen his mother sit beside the table, the Book before her, studying! How many times he had seen her in her rocking chair, the Book in her lap, her eyes closed, her lips moving in prayer!

There was nothing else to do: Donal closed the trunk, rose from his knees, sat down on the edge of his bed, pulled the lamp close, and opened the Book.

Proverbs . . . it was full of wise things. Donal's eyes moved over the words, to pause and read, and read again the eighth verse of the first chapter.

"Mama, Mama," he half laughed, half groaned. "Are you trying to tell me something?"

Not Mama. Not his earthly mother, but his Heavenly Father—his Father reminding him of his heritage.

But it was at the moment almost as if Margot stood there, shaking her finger in his face: "Forsake not the law of thy mother"!

For a long time Donal lay on his bed, his head on his pillow, his feet crossed, one arm behind his head, the other hand holding the Book on his chest—thinking, thinking, wrestling with the God-given (or was it?) opportunity to have land of his own.

The problem still unsettled, he had finally gone to sleep.

Now, under the wide, blue Canadian sky, the bounty of the bush spread around him, a grub hoe in his hand and a field slowly taking shape beneath his feet, Donal could find no satisfaction, and certainly no peace, in the place or the task.

Finally, in a surrender that had its roots in sheer need and desperation, and with a lifetime of his mother's prayers behind him, Donal knelt in the good parkland soil, his altar a stump of his own hewing.

There, as it always has been and always will be when hungry hearts cry out to God, whether in soaring cathedral, gilded temple, simple chapel, or at a quiet bedside, a miracle of rebirth took place.

One man long ago, as needy as Donal and more ignorant, had heard Jesus say, "Ye must be born again." Not understanding, he had asked, "How can a man be born when he is old? can he enter the second time into his mother's womb, and be born?" Jesus had explained spiritual birth—not of the flesh, but of the Spirit.

Donal remembered his mother's instruction well; how simple it was!—an earnest repenting, a simple faith, a loving Father.

The sun seemed a benediction; the birds poured forth a litany of praise; the fragrances of the bush were as a sweet incense, and the small, bush-wrapped sanctuary became a hallowed place as Donal prayed. When he rose to his feet, it was as a son of God, and all His grace and peace and joy unspeakable were Donal's.

Back at the cabin for the noon meal, Donal's face had a glow that was not a reflection of the Canadian sun. Passing his chair, Angie pressed a hand to his shoulder in a recognition beyond words. "Turn us again, O God of hosts, and cause thy face to shine; and we shall be saved," she murmured to herself and felt she had never plumbed the depths of the psalm before.

"I'm going to Prince Albert," Donal said. Angie nodded, and Dave looked at him soberly.

"I hear Rufe Dalton is going tomorrow," Dave said.

"I'll see if I can hitch a ride with him."

Mrs. Janeway herself opened the boardinghouse door.

"Why, come on in! The old gentleman will be happy to see you. You'll find him much improved."

And so he did. Entering the large, sunny front room, Donal walked directly to the chair beside the window. Uncle Willoughby sat reading, with his knees covered by a blanket and a pair of spectacles perched on his long nose.

Keen old eyes watched Donal cross the floor—much keener, Donal thought, than his previous contact. He looked around; Mrs. Prine was nowhere in evidence.

"She's gone," Willoughby Ames said in greeting. "Thankfully."

"You are feeling better, sir?"

"Considerably. Although I don't think I was ever as bad as that old harridan made out."

Donal hadn't seen the timid Mrs. Prine as anything like a harridan.

"Just wanted to keep me sick, she did," the old man continued, "to get her pay each week. How come you're here?" Willoughby's voice was suspicious. "Run out of money?"

"No, sir. In fact, here's your money. All of it."

Donal produced the metal box that had on actual count contained no more than five hundred dollars—much less than the amount the pamphlets had said was needed to prove up, or put a homestead into working order.

The old man disdained to take it, much less count it. "What's the meaning of this?" he asked gruffly. "Not backing out on the deal, are you?"

"There really was no deal, Mr. Ames. If you can recall what went on here that day, you did most of the talking, more or less pushing me on out to that homestead—"

"But it's what you came here for, my boy—a homestead!"

"I'm sorry, Mr. Ames, but I'm not your boy. I mean, I'm not the boy you expected. And I feel very bad about that . . . deceiving you, going out there and taking over, under false pretenses. You see, I'm not Jenner Coy."

"Knew that the first time I set eyes on you."

Donal was silenced for a moment. "You—you knew?"

"Of course! All the Coy family are flaming redheads . . . every last one of 'em. There was no way, no way at all, you could have been Jenner. Besides that, if I needed any proof, I got a letter from his sister. Seems the family got the letter you wrote 'em, telling of Jenner's death out there on the prairie. No, young man, I wasn't fooled for one minute. Fact is, if anyone owes the other an apology, it's I who owe you.

"You see, the minute I knew you weren't Jenner, I got desperate. My plan may not have been a sensible one, but it was the best I could come up with on the spur of the moment. If I sounded irrational, it wasn't all from the fever."

"You were very demanding," Donal said in agreement. "Wouldn't listen to anything I had to say. But I shouldn't have agreed to the masquerade. It was a purely selfish thing to do. I just made a snap decision when I saw you weren't going to listen to me."

"Sorry," the old man mumbled, although he didn't look repentant.

"Now," Donal said, "let me tell you what all we've done out there—"

"We? Are you married?"

"No. Nothing like that. I have a friend and his wife who agreed to go along, and they have worked right along with me. You do remember that you have a half section?"

"I'm not insane yet, my boy! Of course I remember. And if I don't get it proved up, I'll lose it all. You haven't got any funny ideas"—Willoughby Ames's eyes narrowed—"of backing out on me, have you?"

"It isn't right," Donal said patiently, "to you, to me, to Dave and his family. We're all wasting our time. There's enough good weather left for me to locate another homestead and try to build a shanty or shack or something to get me through the winter. I'll cut cordwood or some such work to get by until spring. I rather think Dave Smedley, my friend, will want to do the same. I'm sorry, Mr. Ames. I feel that my going out there in the first place has delayed your plans too."

"Foolishness! My place is much better off. But I'll never get back out to the place—I'm sure of that. So you see—"

Willoughby opened the drawer of a small table at his elbow and withdrew some papers. "I wasn't kidding when I said the place was yours. You got my letter? Well, my boy, I've got it all set up here—the Wildrose place, which I can't do anything more about, is yours."

Donal was speechless. "I can't let you do that, sir."

"Foolishness!" the old man said strongly again. "What am I to do with it, then? Tell me that!"

"Surely you have some other relative—"

"No. There's no one. Shall I just let it go back to bush? Would you like that, huh?"

"No, of course not." Donal thought of the delightful clearing, the comfortable, picturesque cabin, the developing fields, and had to admit he felt a pang.

"I can't take it, Mr. Ames," he said now, firmly. "Perhaps if I had talked it over with you honestly in the first place, and we'd come to these arrangements then, I'd feel all right about it."

"But," Willoughby Ames almost exploded, "it was my own fault! I wouldn't listen—I deliberately overran anything you tried to say. I remember it all! And I was ever so relieved when you walked out of here—"

"Pretending that I was Jenner Coy."

"Will you listen to reason?" the grim-faced older man snapped. "You were so all-fired upset at me that other time that you went ahead and did what I wanted out of spite. Now that I'm trying to talk reason to you, you won't listen! What's a man to do?"

In spite of himself, Donal smiled. It wasn't easy, he supposed, to be incapacitated and have to rely on others.

"I'd still feel like a cheat if I go back with those papers," Donal said, shaking his head with a finality that left the old man collapsed back in his chair, rage and disappointment written on his face.

"Please—," he managed, spluttering.

"Look," Donal said, "I've brought you an old friend."

Reaching down, Donal picked up the package he had set on the floor beside his chair. Holding it out, he placed it in the blue-veined old hands.

Willoughby untied the string, loosened the brown paper, and lifted out the battered and well-thumbed *A Trip Around the World.*

The grim lips softened. The faded eyes lit up. The unsteady hands fondled the book as though it were indeed a priceless treasure. Once again, it seemed, Willoughby Ames would travel the world—even if it was from the limits of his boardinghouse chair by the fireside and the comfortable cushions of his favorite chair.

With the old man caught up in the pleasures of his new-old book, Donal turned toward the door to leave.

"You need to tell me," he looked back to say, "what you would like me to do with the rest of your belongings. Leave them there for someone to enjoy, or bring them here to you?"

"I told you," the old man said, looking up and raising his voice with each syllable and finally shouting, *"They're yours! I don't want 'em!"*

With a sigh, Donal turned to the door to take his departure from this irritating, stubborn old man.

"Idiot!" Willoughby was shouting furiously, helplessly. "Dunderhead! Stubborn nincompoop!"

26

Lolly's second church attendance was no more restful than the first. There was the same hearty singing, a pastoral prayer, the passing of the offering plates (no wonder the pastor's suit looked so shiny—the plate was scantly supplied indeed), and a few announcements. And it was all to the sound of feet shuffling on the oiled floor, two old men wrangling joyously over their hymn book, friendly smiles and warm handshakes, and a few curious glances.

Lolly was beginning to feel comfortable until the pastor took his Bible and read what he called the parable of the rich fool.

The ground of a certain rich man, he explained, had produced a bumper crop. "What shall I do," he thought to himself, "because I have no room where to bestow my fruits?" (Luke 12:17).

So he decided what seemed right and natural to Lolly: "I will pull down my barns, and build greater . . . and I will say to my soul, Soul . . . take thine ease, eat, drink, and be merry" (Luke 12:18-19).

So far so good. The trouble was that God required his soul of him *that very night*. Lolly shivered. Mum, at least, had faithfully prayed, "If I die before the day, angels, bear my soul away."

Now God asked the rich man, "Whose shall those things be, which thou hast provided?" (Luke 12:20). *Things* meant nothing now.

"There's nothing wrong with money!" the preacher said. "We would all benefit from a little more of it."

There were smiles and hearty "amens" at this point.

"However," the pastor went on, "a man's life doesn't consist in the abundance of things he possesses."

In spite of deprivation where material things are concerned, they all could be, the man of God explained, richly blessed in the things that matter most.

This was a great consolation to his congregation, who murmured another round of "amens."

As for Lolly, she felt poverty-stricken indeed. She neither had worldly possessions nor was she rich in the things of God.

But it seemed the pastor knew her problem and was offering the solution. It was to be found at a place called the mercy seat. The congregation stood and sang about it:

> *From ev'ry stormy wind that blows,*
> *From ev'ry swelling tide of woes,*
> *There is a calm, a sure retreat—*
> *'Tis found beneath the mercy seat.*

This mercy seat, the pastor said, was represented by the bench placed at the front of the room. Just a crude, unpainted board, it was called the "mourner's bench," and here the heavyhearted and heavy-burdened could bring their load of sin and spirit of heaviness and exchange them for "the garment of praise."

In confirmation the congregation sang,

> *There is a place where Jesus sheds*
> *The oil of gladness on our heads,*
> *A place than all besides more sweet—*
> *It is the blood-bought mercy seat.*

Mercy seat. It seemed the most precious place to be in the

entire world. And still—perhaps from backwardness, perhaps because of the inner battle that, to her surprise, waged to keep her from it—Lolly hesitated.

At her side, her mother whispered in a tender voice, "I'll go with you. I need to."

Together mother and daughter stepped forward to be met by the outstretched hand of the pastor and to be surrounded, soon, by loving, caring, praying people.

And when they had been guided through what the pastor termed "the sinner's prayer," when the praying was done, the burden lifted and the promised peace imparted, tears were mingled with joy as the congregation sang one final verse:

Ah! there on eagle wings we soar,
And sin and sense molest no more;
And heav'n comes down our souls to greet,
While glory crowns the mercy seat.

All Lolly's newfound peace and grace were needed the day she turned her feet toward the Plummer place to give Kingston her answer. The one and only possible answer had been known to her at the time he asked, but she had been reluctant to give it, since it meant turning her back forever on the comfort and stability she so sorely wanted. Now her course of action was clear, but that didn't make it any easier.

Because she no longer worked there, Lolly felt she should not just walk in, and so she knocked, her heart pounding as loudly as her fist.

Kingston Plummer opened the door. "Lita. Ah, of course. Come in—come in." Kingston was rubbing his hands together in anticipatory glee over the expected victory.

Seated on the plush parlor sofa with Kingston at her side, attempting to take her hand in his, Lolly began badly by putting her hands behind her back. Kingston assumed a patient look. The prize would be his soon enough, and then there would be no more of this silly prudishness. Playing hard-to-get made the final capitulation all the sweeter.

"Ah, my dear Lita—let me have the good news!"

"Kingston," Lolly swallowed, rather loudly, she realized, and flushed, not helping her need for a sense of dignity about the entire matter.

"King," he reminded a little pettishly. When would she learn to call him *King?*

"King—Mr. Plummer—" In view of the little game she had played all along and the subtle signals she had tried to send, even in her actual ignorance of things relating to men, she found it difficult now to reverse her position. What an impostor she had been! Remembering, Lolly shrank into herself, and only the knowledge that she was a new creature in Christ Jesus gave her courage.

Kingston Plummer was trying to be tolerant. *The little minx! What a pleasure it would be to have her submission.*

"I'm appreciative of your offer—" Lolly began.

"Of course, my dear, of course," Kingston Plummer purred as he reached his arm across the back of the sofa and leaned his face toward Lolly expectantly.

"But—"

But? Was it possible the chit had certain conditions to lay down, demands to make?

"But . . ." she was continuing bravely in spite of the flash of irritation she glimpsed in Kingston Plummer's eyes.

"My dear Lita," the man began, with an attempt to control his impatience. These amenities were so meaningless, so ridiculous when they each knew what they wanted!

"What I'm trying to say, Mr. Plummer, is that, though I thank you and appreciate the offer you have made, I really can't accept your proposal of marriage."

Into the dead silence that fell between them, Lolly saw a frightening coldness come into the eyes of the man sitting at her side, his arm withdrawing itself from back of her shoulders, his face slowly whitening, his jaw tightening, his nostrils flaring.

Whether Kingston's response was in fact the truth or actually a cruel backlash in an attempt to preserve his pride and deal her a blow, Lolly never knew.

"Marriage?" he spat out, his voice like a whiplash for fury. "Don't get above yourself! Do you honestly think I'd offer my name to the likes of you? Marriage! Did I ever mention the word?"

Lolly felt the blood drain from her face; she sensed the squeeze around her heart; she felt her head spinning.

"What . . . what then?" she whispered, hardly able to even imagine the intentions of Kingston Plummer.

"Certainly not *marriage!* Me marry someone from a family of ne'er-do-well transients? Me marry someone with a gadfly of a father and a mayfly of a mother? Ha!"

Not entirely certain of the meaning of the terms, Lolly knew they were as uncomplimentary as the man could manage and were, in fact, terribly derogatory. But it got her on her feet in a twinkling, her mouth opening to respond as he deserved.

And then a strange thing happened; could it be the faithful ministry of the One who had come to abide with her forever, the One who promised to bring all things to her remembrance?

For in that moment the scripture she had read that very morning came back to her. Titus—that was the book: "We ourselves were sometimes foolish, disobedient, deceived, serving divers lusts and pleasures, living in malice and envy. . . . But according to his mercy he saved us."

With a light in her eyes that baffled her previous suitor and a lift to her shoulders that infuriated him, Lolly managed to say, "I'm sorry, Mr. Plummer. I truly am. I'm sure you'll find . . . happiness with someone else."

Arms crossed, eyes narrowed, jaw muscles working, Kingston Plummer watched Lolly walk across the floor to the door.

Being such a new follower of the One who urged His disciples to turn the other cheek and whose Word teaches that a soft answer turns away wrath, perhaps Lolly could be excused the final sentence she flung over her shoulder just before she closed the door behind her: "And don't call me 'Lita'! It's almost as silly as—as 'King'!"

27

Donal explained soberly to Angie and Dave his decision to make a clean breast of things to Willoughby Ames and make a new start on his own.

"How did the old boy take it?" Dave asked. Though he had never met Uncle Willoughby, he and Angie felt they knew him.

"Not well. I don't know if his concern was for himself—"

"Well, he had put a lot of himself into the place."

"Sure he did, and he can be excused his distress now that he can't carry through with what seemed to be a labor of love. I can't think he needed any income this place might bring him; the returns will be so small and so long in coming, he'll be long gone, I'd say. No, I believe he really wanted me— Jenner, that is—to have the place. And," Donal continued with some regret, "it *is* a great place. I don't suppose I'll find another I like so well."

Dave nodded, and Donal thought his eyes looked around the comfortable, homelike cabin wistfully.

"I'm more sorry for your sake, yours and Angie's and Frankie's, than I am for myself," Donal said regretfully.

"Don't worry about us," Dave answered staunchly. "If it was right for you, it'll be right for us."

"The Lord will have a place for us," Angie said with conviction.

"You're right, of course. And for me too. I guess we better start looking around. I'd like to stay in the Wildrose district if possible."

"Me too. I love it here," Angie said softly.

Ruth Glover

"We'll need to carry on the same as usual until we know what we'll do. No need in letting the garden and corn and stuff go to waste. We can sell the grain, I guess, and send the money to Uncle Willoughby."

"I suppose there's no hurry?" Dave thought to ask.

"None, insofar as I can figure out. Willoughby can't get out here himself—that's for sure. If someone else shows up and declares themselves the new owners or hired help, we'll have to handle that when it happens. We'll stay the winter probably. Nobody plans to begin on a place when it's six feet under snow."

"Six feet—more or less," Dave said. "Likely a lot more."

They parted for the day, faithfully carrying out tasks that they wished wholeheartedly were for themselves. Moving on would be painful.

Early in the afternoon Angie took a pail and started down the road to pick chokecherries. Frankie nodded sleepily on her shoulder, and she held a galvanized pail in her other hand.

Locating a thick stand of bushes hanging heavy and purple with the fruit, she cleared a place of twigs and stones, spread a small quilt, and put the sleeping Frankie down.

Angie fastened the pail in the belt at her waist, settled a wide-brimmed hat on her head, and began picking. Moments later she paused, listening. Nearby berries continued their *thunk-thunk* into a container.

Parting the bushes, Angie peered through. Not far away a young woman, about her own age, she thought, was also picking chokecherries. Masses of red-gold hair, curly and stubbornly resisting any confining pins, curled around the girl's face, tumbled onto the shoulders of a dress far too small for her, and glinted brightly in the sun as it fell spottily through the leaves of the surrounding, taller trees.

214

"Hello there!" Angie called, not too loudly for fear of waking the sleeping baby.

The girl turned, and Angie saw a face dewy with perspiration, fresh-faced and quite lovely; the unusual hair, Angie was to try to describe to Dave later, was a "blaze of glory when the sun touched it—a magnificent mane."

"Why, hello," the girl said and made a futile effort to gather her outgrown bodice together. It made perfect sense, to Angie, to wear one's oldest and most worn clothes on a berry-picking outing.

"I have my baby—back here, asleep," Angie explained.

At this the girl with the flame-touched hair stepped toward Angie and held out her berry-stained hand. Angie's equally purple-tinged hand met hers in a friendly grip.

"You must be Rufe Dalton's sister," Angie said. "He's been by a couple of times. Donal went to Prince Albert with him."

"Well, then, you're Angie. And I'm Lolly Dalton."

"Lolly—what a pretty name! Descriptive somehow." Angie was never to explain to herself the quick look, perhaps of pain, that flitted across the sensitive face of the girl. To compensate, she supposed, or simply because the Word of God dwelt in her richly, she said quickly, " 'A good name is rather to be chosen than great riches.' "

Lolly looked at Angie sharply. "Who said that?" she asked.

"A very wise man, Solomon, said it. It's one of his proverbs."

"Tell it to me again," Lolly said intensely, "and tell me where it's found."

Angie repeated the scripture and added, "Proverbs 22:1."

The girl Lolly muttered the reference to herself several times. Then, with a lightening of her eyes, said, "You don't know what that means to me. Thank you for quoting it to me.

One's name can be good, can't it, even if it's Hephzibah . . . or Amoretta—"

"Or Angelina," Angie added, catching the spirit of Lolly's new revelation.

"Angelina?" Lolly repeated.

"Yes," Angie admitted. "Awful, isn't it? Angela, at least, would have been some improvement. But Angelina!"

"Almost as bad," Lolly said happily, "as Lolita."

"When my baby came along," Angie confided, "I made up my mind I'd give him the prettiest name I could find. So I chose Franklin Elvin. Elvin—that's my brother's name. Oh," she finished anxiously, "do you think he'll hate it when he grows up?"

"He'll love it—I'm sure," Lolly consoled, and went back to stripping the berries into her pail. *Thunk . . . thunk . . .*

"That proverb," she said finally, "is it possible, do you think, to have a good name *and* riches?"

"Of course. But if it comes to a choice, the good name would be better, I believe."

"You're right. One isn't very likely to have to worry about getting rich here in the bush anyway. Right?"

"Right. At least not money-wise. But you know, Lolly"— here Angie's voice became even more gentle—"I wouldn't trade what I have—my husband and baby, and our life here in Wildrose—for any amount of money."

Lolly looked at her new acquaintance wonderingly. This must be what it is to be in love, she thought, and felt a pang of envy. Would it ever happen to her? And could she give up her own dreams and plans for it? Suddenly she longed passionately to love something—someone—so much that she would put them, their welfare, their hopes and dreams, before her own.

Frankie gave a wail, having awakened and found himself alone.

Angie flew to her son's side, Lolly at her heels, and gathered him into her arms. "There . . . there," she crooned. "Mama's here, little pet."

Of course her pail was in the way, and Lolly helped unfasten it and set it aside.

"I suppose I'd better go," Angie said, looking ruefully at her half-filled pail. She stood to her feet, Frankie in her arms. She then managed to pick up the quilt he had been napping on. After considerable juggling and rearranging, she reached for her pail.

"You can't manage him and the berries," Lolly said.

Angie agreed. "I'll have to come back for them."

"Tell you what," Lolly said, "I'll carry the berries, and you can carry the baby. What's more—" Lolly dumped her half pail into Angie's pail—"I'll come back by here and get me another pailful before the day is done."

"Oh, thank you," Angie said gratefully. "I hadn't thought of this problem when I started out."

So, talking and laughing, the new friends made their way down the road, under the fence, and across the yard to the cabin.

"There's Donal," Angie said, waving at the man who stepped out of the shadows of the barn. "I want you to meet Donal. Hey, Donal! Come here a minute!"

Lolly watched with fascination as the long legs, slim hips, and wide shoulders swung easily across the yard. What a— manly man!

Donal halted in front of the women, his booted feet planted solidly, his upper arms thrusting against the thin material of his shirt, his neck brown and strong exposed to the sun and damp with his exertions. He pushed his hat back and a dark thatch of hair spilled out and over his forehead.

"This is Lolly, Donal," Angie said. "You and her brother

went to Prince Albert together."

His dark blue eyes twinkled at Lolly charmingly as he wiped his hand on his trousers leg and shook the hand she offered, having first wiped it on her skirt in teasing imitation. The three of them laughed, and small Frankie grinned, his few teeth showing and a dribble of saliva running down his chin.

"Hey, fella," Donal said, and took the baby and swung him up into his arms. *What a waste of muscle,* Lolly couldn't help thinking, then reproached herself. The baby and man obviously adored each other. *No wonder Angie is so contented,* she thought.

The house, not much larger than the Dalton house, was neat and attractive, even comfortable. *Love lives here,* Lolly felt without surprise.

"I'm going to make us a cup of tea," Angie said. "They say something hot helps you cool off. I don't have anything cold to offer, except for well water. It's wonderfully cold."

"Tea would be fine," Lolly assured her, knowing she should turn around and head back to the berry patch, but drawn to the easy, pleasant atmosphere of the small home.

There was an open Bible on a small table at the side of a rocking chair and another on top of a bookshelf, the five shelves below it crammed with books.

"That's Angie's Bible; that one's mine," Donal explained. "Mine came with me all the way from Ontario, though I didn't know it." With Angie busy in the lean-to kitchen, Donal rocked Frankie and told Lolly about his decision to leave the home farm in the east and head west. In the telling, his dreams lay open and obvious for anyone with a heart to hear.

Lolly, accustomed to the shiftless moving of her father with no rhyme or reason, was captivated by the account. Yet the man had given up everything—security, family, a known future—to pursue his dream.

Angie bustled about in a lean-to no better than the Daltons' own in a dress not much better than Lolly's. She hummed as she poured tea into three cups that didn't match. This woman apparently had just as willingly left all to follow her man.

When Lolly, with reluctance, turned back to her berrying and home, it was with an insight into a life that was worthy of all one could put into it. A life that would pay rich dividends—true riches.

Why her heart should ache so, she didn't know. Anyway, these new neighbors would be gone before long, possibly. They were looking for another homestead. Perhaps, Lolly admitted with an honest heart, it was just as well.

28

It was heady stuff, this availability to money and what it would do. For a young man like Toby, raised without it, it was almost intoxicating.

He had been assigned the responsibility of driving Nannette across the district to investigate a new disc harrow recently purchased by someone and which the Fanchons were considering buying. Toby felt Yukon would have been a much better choice for the job, but since Nannette insisted, he would accompany her and be what help he could.

"Actually, Toby," Nannette said as the horse trotted briskly down a road on which the dust had settled during a night's rain, "it will be a wonderful opportunity for you to learn—well, me too." Nannette didn't know much about farming, she admitted. But she was old enough now to begin to take on some of the load Aunt Fanny had carried alone for years. "After all," Nannette said, "it will all be mine one day, and by the looks of it, sooner than I had thought."

The Widow Fanchon seemed much in control of things. But it was good, wasn't it, that the niece who would one day have the full load on her begin to learn how to go about it? If Toby could help and learn in the bargain, all the better.

The farmer, Mr. Busch, pointed out the disc harrow's advantages while Toby and Nannette looked and nodded and made notes:

Points of superiority:

1. The discs being in one gang and turning the earth in one direction, there is no ditch left in the middle or any ridge made where the earth laps or comes together.

(Comment by Mr. Busch: "All farmers who have used the old style discs will see the advantage of this.")

2. Being carried on wheels, the depth can be perfectly controlled, as the discs will run at full angle without running so deep the team cannot pull it.

(Comment by Nannette: "The horses will appreciate this!")

3. It can be raised off the ground to move about the farm or turn around at the end of the land.

4. The disc box is oiled through the top of the standards . . . (Find out what standards are!) the oil going just where needed and the oil holes being where no dirt can get in them.

5. If it is necessary to move the discs over rocky ground, the flanges or knives can be easily taken off by removing four bolts.

(Easily for whom? Mr. Busch got red in the face and muttered questionable words as he wrestled with the bolts!)

Thanking the struggling but determined Mr. Busch, Toby and Nannette got into the buggy and headed for home. They were barely out of sight around the corner of the barn before Nannette burst into laughter. It was so loud on the still air that Toby wondered uncomfortably if the unfortunate Mr. Busch had heard. He had, after all, been gracious enough to take his time away from his work to unveil to them the secrets of the "perfect cultivator and weed killer and the best machine for cultivating summer fallow."

"I'm not sure of the advisability of that disc harrow," Toby said doubtfully, hurrying the horse into a trot.

"Now that's why you'll be good for the place," Nannette said. "You're cautious, and you think."

"I am . . . I do?" Toby was surprised, then pleased.

"Yukon is getting old, and he's set in his ways. Mostly he

just smiles when I make suggestions. Now you, Toby—"

"Now me?" Toby asked, half afraid to follow up the thought that popped into his head and which, he was honest enough to admit, he had been toying with ever since meeting Nannette—an incredible thought.

But Nannette was pursuing the idea of his replacing Yukon.

"Maybe not right away," she said, "but I think you should just keep working yourself in until both Yukon and Aunt Fanny see how important you are. I already see it," she said softly.

Then, with one of her mercurial mood swings, Nannette cried out, "Stop! Stop the buggy!"

"Whoa! What's the trouble?"

"No trouble, you silly goose!"

Toby noticed he was back to "goose" from "boy," a step up, he gathered, from previous comments on his status.

"Well, what then?" he asked.

"I want a bouquet. Get out and pick some of those yellow things—goldenrod, I think they are."

Handing Nannette the reins, Toby slid out of the rig, walked into the growth at the side of the road—once cut back but growing again—and gathered an armful of the brushy-topped plant, actually a mass of tiny yellow flowers. Toby had never thought goldenrod was particularly pretty, so he gathered several brilliant stalks of fireweed that had been swaying nearby; he found them to be eye-catchingly colorful and so graceful.

Handing the bouquet to Nannette and climbing back into the buggy, he took up the reins and clucked to the horse.

"Ugh!" Nannette was saying as she sorted through the mass on her lap, pulling out the fireweed and tossing it to the road.

"I think they're pretty," Toby said. "What's wrong with them?"

"Weeds!"

"But beautiful."

"Weeds! You really need to cultivate an appreciation for quality, Toby! It's like the difference between a princess, say, and a . . . a milkmaid!"

Toby was silent the rest of the trip while Nannette cleared her bouquet of the beautiful fireweed and kept the gold-topped flower of her choice. To Toby's way of thinking, she had it all backward.

It occurred to Toby on his way home that he hadn't spent much time at the Szarvas place or with the Szarvas family. It lacked an hour or so to suppertime, so he turned his feet from the road to the Szarvas yard. Neat, so neat. The house gleamed with whitewash, the fence posts were straight and firm, the barn doors hung straight, the haystacks were regular, and the garden was free of weeds.

Kitty was at the well. The water she pulled up and poured into her pail was coldly delicious. Toby took a dipper from the side of the well and drank deeply and satisfyingly.

Everything here had that effect on him, he decided. The peace of the place—where order, good sense, and thrift reigned—was completely felt.

"Come on in," Kitty invited, as if she had seen him an hour ago rather than several days.

Toby bent toward the girl to pick up the pail of water: earth, sun, and soap—Kitty's trademark. Predictable Kitty.

I could find her in the dark, Toby thought fleetingly with a small inward smile, and he breathed deeply of earth, sun, and soap before he turned with the pail toward the house, Kitty's sturdy form leading the way and her flaxen braid swinging.

"Iss it our Toby?" Marta greeted him, and he sank comfortably into a chair at the side of the table. Marta pushed a plate of doughnuts toward him. With perfect comfort, he took a doughnut and the cold glass of milk Kitty set before him. *The "milkmaid," I suppose,* Toby thought as he relished the drink above a monarch's richest negus or wassail or whatever it was a potentate might drink. When he said good-bye and headed home, he shut the door on everything that seemed blessed and secure and permanent.

And he was seriously thinking of trading it all in for the comfort that money brings—a comfort he had never known and which had a powerful appeal. Money—and the princess who went with it.

29

While the family was gathered around the supper table, Hudson Dalton chose to explode his bomb.

Minnie had barely passed the chicken (two of their own small pullets), served up the new potatoes from their own garden, and mentioned there would be rhubarb tart for dessert when Hudson said, "I think we'll just pull up stakes and go on back to Prince Albert. Come to think of it, some of those jobs there look mighty tempting."

Silence. Absolute silence reigned. Forks were suspended and bowls were held in midair. Jaws stopped chewing.

"Think you could be packed up and ready to move out by, say, next Monday?" Hud asked brightly, helping himself to small green peas from his own garden.

Lolly was literally too sick to swallow. In spite of her aborted relationship with Kingston Plummer, she felt her future and her happiness were in Wildrose.

Toby paled and felt momentarily as if one of his turns might be coming upon him. Here in Wildrose he had found health and purpose and had become a man. Here—he secretly thought—he might step into a life the likes of which he had only dreamed, a life built around Nannette Fanchon—and her wealth. What an opportunity! But now Dad was casually and thoughtlessly suggesting they chuck it all and move again? Toby breathed deeply and felt the room whirl sickeningly.

Minnie sat as solid as a rock—and as speechless. Her mind was already so full of canning and weeding and sewing much-needed clothing and building her flocks of chickens and ducks and geese and . . . Minnie might as well have been pole-axed for all the response she was able to give. She was dazed; she was dumb; she was stricken.

As for Rufe, he heard his father out silently. Then, calmly, as if having prepared himself for this very situation, he rose from the table, went to the drawer by his bedside, withdrew a paper, and returned. The eyes of the entire family, his father included, were fixed on him.

"This here," Rufe said, "is the deed from the Lands Office in Prince Albert. I got it when I went in a couple of weeks ago."

"The Lands Office?" Toby half-croaked. "You mean you have another place? Are you going to head out on your own, Rufe?"

"This is the deed to the Mellon place," Rufe said quietly.

All eyes swung to Hudson, who had the grace to look uncomfortable.

"What?" he asked innocently. "Why are you all looking at me like that?"

Minnie had no need to explain her look—and no heart to do so.

Rufe, paper in hand, had clearly spoken.

Toby, a man in some ways but a boy in the home of his father, choked back the wild response with which he wanted to burst forth.

It was up to Lolly—so sick and tired of moving and so fulfilled in Wildrose—to put into words the accusation that was in their hearts and eyes.

"You never got any legal right to the Mellon place."

"Well, no," Hudson admitted. "The place was here . . . we needed a place . . . nobody's complained about it, have they? It's time to move on, before we get too attached to this Wildrose country."

Too late, Hudson, too late.

"This deed, Rufe? What are you saying?" Lolly asked, turning her thoughts and her eyes in the direction of her older brother.

"I mean it's mine. I did what Dad should have done."

Although he didn't say it, it was clear that Rufe had known his father well enough to be suspicious of him. And, like the others, he was sick to death of being transient. He had noticed the happiness in his mother's eyes; he had approved of Lolly's decent clothes—a lady at last! He had seen his dearly loved brother strengthen and stand tall both outwardly and inwardly. He had done what he had to do and made a trip to Prince Albert to settle their future.

"I'm not moving on, as you can see," Rufe said, and flourished the paper that made the Mellon place his.

"Mellon abandoned this place. Anyone who wanted to badly enough," Rufe said as he glanced at his father, "could have taken steps to have it."

Rufe looked at his sister, who seemed to have shrunk since he last looked at her; even her hair, which was usually so full of life and vibrant, seemed to have lost its sheen for the moment. There was no glory about his sister now.

"Lolly, I can't keep house; you know that. How about, for the time being"—his half-grin seemed to hint at serious changes for his sister in the future—"you stay here with me?"

The glory returned to Lolly's pinched face. "Oh, Rufe!"

"Toby—"

Toby turned tortured eyes on his brother, but eyes in which hope was beginning to dawn.

"There's a lot of work to be done here, Toby. Are you game to stay on and help me?"

Toby's face, flooding with color and relief, gave him his answer.

"Someday, if you want, we'll look around for a place for you. But there's no hurry," Rufe said. "I need you . . . I want you."

"And I need to be here," Toby said in a burst of confidentiality most unlike him. Toby felt like adding a heartfelt "God bless you!" but settled for "Thanks, Rufe!"

Rufe turned his eyes on his mother. "Mum?" he said softly. Minnie rolled the edge of the red-checked tablecloth in her hands—hands that were work-worn, hands that had labored unstintingly for all of them for years, hands that looked pathetically empty for all her labor and toil.

"Your father and I need to talk," she said finally, and her children rose and silently left the room and the house. Toby milked a cow that he patted with a fiercely proprietary air, Lolly fed chickens whose cackles tonight sounded like a paean of praise, and Rufe chopped *his* wood cut from *his* land to burn in his stove before ever he closed his eyes in his own bed for the first time in his life.

There was silence in the house. Minnie continued rolling the tortured edge of the tablecloth.

"Well," Hudson said, "it seems we got us a homeowner for a son. I say good for him. You'll go with me to Prince Albert, old girl. We'll make our way, like always, eh, old girl?"

Still Minnie rolled the tablecloth. Hudson watched, perplexed, as the minutes ticked by. Perhaps the time was necessary for him to entertain the tiniest, the smallest question.

With more consideration than his children would have given him credit for, Hudson reached across the table and took Minnie's hand in his.

"What is it, old girl?" he asked finally, knowing her well. "Something on your mind?"

"Hudson," Minnie said, turning her eyes on her husband with such a depth of longing and pleading in them that it quite took his breath away, "you know I love you."

"Of course . . . never had cause to doubt it."

"Would it matter to you if I said I was happy here in Wild-rose—happier than I've been in, oh, years?"

Hudson was silent for a long minute. Then with a sigh he asked, "Are you saying you want to stay—not go with me?"

"I'll go, Hudson—you know I'll go—if you ask it of me. But once, just once, will you ask me what *I'd* like to do?"

"I always thought—" Hudson floundered, truly surprised.

"I know you did. I spent my life letting you think that. Maybe I was wrong, from the beginning."

"Has it been so bad, old girl?"

"No. Not too bad, Hudson. But it's time . . . it's time . . . it's time—" Minnie couldn't finish.

But Hudson knew. "It's funny," he said, "but I thought you were always ready to move on. Why didn't you say, long ago?"

"I should have. I thought you would be happier—"

Hudson squeezed Minnie's hand, and they fell silent, each aware that they had wanted the happiness of the other and had pleased no one, in the long run—certainly not their children. Just one glance out of the window told them that: Lolly was now happily gathering eggs, Toby healthily and strongly milking the cow, and Rufe chopping wood when the wood box was already overflowing.

"I want to stay, Hud." It was as simple as that.

"Then we'll stay."

"For sure? I won't have to wonder if you're going to want to move on next year or the year after that or—"

"You have my word on it. Unless we find a place of our own—" Hudson felt the beginning of a convulsion in the hand he was holding and added hastily "Here in Wildrose, of course."

"Oh, Hudson, are you sure?"

"Let's just say 'Barkis is willin',' " Hudson quoted with his old spirit.

Still Minnie toyed with the tablecloth with her other hand. She was still too silent for Hudson's peace of mind.

"Anything else?" he asked, giving her hand a tweak.

"Hudson—you're 51. But I'm only 46. Would you stop calling me 'old girl'?"

Now Hudson was really shaken. "I'll try," he gulped, knowing that at times the old habit would creep up on him.

"That's all I ask. And, Hudson—"

"Something else, old, uh . . . Minnie?"

"Could you . . . would you . . . call me Minerva?"

And so it was their children entered the house to find their parents hand in hand, Hudson looking shaken, but game, and Minerva, their mother, ensconced on her rickety kitchen chair as proudly and contentedly as though she were a queen on her regal throne. It was a new day for the Daltons.

 30

"We're going to stay!" Lolly caroled immediately upon stepping into her friend Angie's house.

"Was it in question?" Angie asked, motioning Lolly to a chair by the fire. The day was overcast with a hint of autumn in the air.

"More than we knew," Lolly said seriously. "You see, we all thought our father had the Mellon place all signed up right and proper."

"And he didn't?"

"No. We were squatters, I guess you'd say. But my brother—"

"Rufe?"

"Rufe—bless him! Rufe went to town and—well, it was that day your husband went with him—"

"You mean Donal."

"Yes, your husband, Donal, went with him."

"Donal isn't my husband, Lolly."

Perhaps Lolly's shock and dismay showed on her face, for certainly Angie's insinuation shook her terribly.

Angie laughed merrily. "You don't need to look like that! It isn't anything wrong at all!"

"It isn't?" Lolly managed weakly.

Angie sobered. "My husband is Dave, Lolly. Haven't you met Dave? Is it possible you didn't know?"

But Lolly found herself unable to answer. The day she had first met Donal Cardigan and every time she had seen him since, she had recognized the admiring glances he gave her and had felt like weeping.

"Not another Kingston Plummer!" her heart had cried, though Donal's glances had held none of the rapaciousness of the older man. His interest, coming from a single man, would have made any girl pleased, even responsive. Thinking him married, Lolly had ached but didn't know why and had taken the wiser, saner path—she avoided Donal whenever she could. True, he had looked a little puzzled, and his friendliness had turned to simple politeness.

Lolly had taken to visiting Angie and Frankie when she knew they were alone, if at all possible. Whenever she had met Donal she had nodded and hurried past. But her heart, she had to admit now, had pounded, and her eyes had once or twice filled with tears for what she did not have, could not have, and for which her wayward heart longed.

Even now her heart was pounding, and her eyes threatened to fill with foolish tears. Angie, seeing and perhaps understanding, went into the story of how she and Dave had met Donal on the prairie and how their lives had been intertwined since that momentous day.

"So," Angie said finally, when she felt she had caught Lolly's attention again, "you're going to stay in Wildrose. I can imagine how happy you must be. I only wish we were as settled in our plans."

"There's some question—about this place?"

"Yes. Or no, I guess. Donal has told old Mr. Willoughby Ames that he can't accept the homestead, mostly because he felt he was underhanded about taking it in the first place. Of course, he didn't fool Uncle Willoughby; he knew from the minute he saw him that Donal wasn't a redheaded Coy."

"So you and Dave and Donal are looking for another place?"

"We'll look for our own, Donal for his. It may be far from Wildrose, I'm afraid." Angie's face was regretful.

"Uncle Willoughby wrote Donal just last week," she went on, "just begging him to take over the place, insisting that Donal was his chosen heir. But Donal wrote him right back and sent back the papers the old man had given him concerning all that. No, Donal won't take it. It isn't right, he says."

Angie and Lolly had a cup of tea and a gingersnap together. Lolly played with baby Frankie for a while and then took her departure.

Stepping across the yard with the lightest heart she could imagine, Lolly came face-to-face with Donal Cardigan. She knew how she had dismissed him, probably hurt him, for he bowed slightly, tipped his hat, and kept going.

But he made the mistake of taking one last glance at the girl he had found so lovely but who had treated him so coldly. It was a glance that was to change his life forever.

The face of the girl Lolly was lit by a brilliant smile. And her eyes were as luminous as eyes can be and not be stars. The smile was followed by a flood of color to her cheeks—more than the rosy blush whipped into them by the rising wind. It was a flood of color that almost rivaled her hair that tumbled in the wind. And then she was gone.

Entering the cabin, Donal leaned against the door. "What went on in here?" he asked, figuring he had glimpsed some kind of miracle.

"Do you know," Angie said, giving Donal's bemused face a keen glance, "that girl—"

"You mean Lolly Dalton, the icicle?"

"I mean Lolly. She's thought all this time, Donal, that you were my husband."

"So *that* was it!" Donal's face was thoughtful at first, then lit by a grin. Whirling Frankie up into his arms, he did a wild jig around the room until Frankie screeched and Angie begged him to stop his mad capering.

★ ★ ★ ★ ★

With his brother's words still ringing in his heart if not his ears, Toby walked—or rather floated—to the Fanchon homestead. He was free! Toby Dalton was free; he need not be any man's slave—or any woman's either.

Only now did Toby admit the desperation that had haunted him and the measures he had been willing to consider to allay that desperation.

Until now, now that he was well and strong, Toby had been so deprived of plans that a normal young man would make for his life that he had unwittingly grasped at an opportunity to make his own way in life. But would it have been his own way? As a bondsman (hired help or husband, he hadn't figured out—he supposed it was whether he remained a boy or became a "goose" full time), Toby would not have been his own man, ever.

Rufe had given him his freedom. Rufe had said the words that acknowledged him, Toby, as a man in his own right. Toby felt like skipping (but he was much too grown up for that).

"Help me," Rufe had said. But still he gave him the option of getting his own place someday. Never were kinder, more life-changing words spoken to any youth's heart. Though not skipping, Toby strode out down the road, relishing the strength in his long legs, the clean Canadian air in his expanding chest, and the tightness of his old shirt around arms that were bunching with never-before-developed muscles.

His business was with the widow Fanchon. She had given a scared, green boy a chance. Seeking her out at her fireside, he explained in simple, honest terms his search for security, for a future for himself in a world that seemed to have no place for weaklings. Widow Fanchon listened quietly, perhaps having known it all along, and stretched out her hand to him to wish him well.

"But you probably should tell Nannette," she said. "I'll send her in."

A few minutes later Nannette tripped in, roguish as ever. "What is it, silly? What is it to be today—boy or goose?"

"Not boy," he said strongly and so strangely that Nannette studied him with interest.

"No? Can you prove it?" She stood enticingly near, her head tilted, her eyes inviting.

"I've come to say I won't be working here anymore. You see, I'll be helping my brother run his own place." This he said with such pride and satisfaction that Nannette's lips, so ready to be kissed one moment, curled disdainfully.

And to think he had ever found this chameleon-like personality to be appealing! This changeable on-again, off-again quicksilver manner—how dull and predictable it had become!

"The Mellon place?" Nannette almost spat out, and it sounded like a dirty word. "That place over this one? Ha! I suppose," she went on spitefully, "you prefer a milkmaid to gentility, also."

"If the milkmaid," he said with more confidence than he had ever before been able to muster around Nanette, "was as good to her cows as she had been to me."

"Good luck to all the cows—and all the geese," Nannette said with a toss of her head. "I shan't be around to see it."

With feet that seemed to fly, Toby turned his steps toward the Szarvas farm. He was sure of his welcome, sure of his place, and quite certain of his future. How could it be otherwise, with Kitty being the dependable, predictable person that she was?

Knowing that predictability, Toby paused long enough to gather a big bouquet of fireweed. Weed or no, Kitty would love it—of that he was sure.

As he turned in at the gate and waved to the girl, who lifted her flaxen head from her vegetable-picking task to watch him with steady eyes just before he began to run, he took a moment to wonder why Kitty Szarvas had named that puny cat Nightingale.

If she were wise, and she was wonderfully so, she never told him. It didn't hurt, she knew, for a woman to have a touch of mystery about her.

31

After Donal came face-to-face with Lolly that cloudy day, it was only natural that he would follow up the sparkle of those eyes and the warmth of that smile. The surprise of this unexpected greeting had made him, for the moment, speechless. He had let her go her way, almost a-reel with surprise. Expecting from her a cool, distant nod, he was unprepared for what almost seemed like a glimmer of sheer delight on her face, a face that had been closed to him when they had met previously but was now open, wholesomely inviting. The barrier, whatever it had been, was gone.

And, of course, Angie had immediately explained to him that Lolly had thought he was a married man.

It was the most natural reaction for him and undoubtedly an expected one for her when Donal turned up one evening shortly thereafter on the Dalton doorstep.

Lolly's face was the only one in the household not to show surprise when at Rufe's invitation Donal stepped over the sill into the room. Lolly's face was the only one to bend over the work in her hand with an effort to hide an impish grin when Donal offered, lamely, his reason for coming. It was given lamely, perhaps, but it was a masterful stroke.

"I thought you might need something to read, now that the evenings are lengthening and the weather is getting colder." And Donal extended a sack containing several books.

"Look here," Toby exclaimed delightedly, coming out of the reverie that had him dreaming comfortably by the heater. He was certain his neighbor had him in mind. "This is perfect, just perfect! *Conquering the Wilderness*," he read, "And *Heroes and Heroines of Pioneer Life and Adventure*, by Colonel Frank Triplett. And listen to this." Toby turned to the fly leaf and read, with no one in particular listening, "'An interesting account of the romantic deeds, lofty achievements, and marvelous adventures of Daniel Boone, Davy Crockett, Sam Houston, Kit Carson, Buffalo Bill.'" If these men could win, so could Toby Dalton!

The sack also contained Sir Walter Scott's *Rob Roy* and *Ivanhoe*, Mary J. Holmes's *Tempest and Sunshine*, and Thomas Hardy's *Jude the Obscure*.

"Something for each of us!" Minnie exclaimed, already beginning to feel the emptiness of long evenings and being shut in with each family member knowing not only any news but also almost the inner thoughts of every other family member.

"There are plenty more where these came from," Donal assured them as he took the seat offered to him after he unbuttoned his coat and handed it and his cap to Rufe.

"That old gentleman—Willoughby, was it?—must have been some collector," Hudson said. "I understand he isn't coming back, can't come back, due to his health. I haven't been over, sorry to say"—Hud was apologetic about his lack of neighborliness—"but I hear you have a good place. Like my son here, the Dalton place." And Hudson's face shone with pride in Rufe's home ownership.

"I'm not staying," Donal said regretfully, to everyone's surprise except Lolly's. Donal tried to explain carefully but honestly. "The old gentleman presumed I was his relative at first and really wasn't in possession of all his faculties when he urged me out here to take it over. I don't feel right about having it on those terms. So I'll be moving on, probably by spring. It's pointless to waste any more time on land that isn't mine. But until then, you are more than welcome to any of the books in his extensive library. Just come and look them over and get a fresh one whenever you're ready. Someone's always home."

And that was the only invitation Lolly needed, the only excuse.

A few days later, Donal opened the door to her as she stepped into the cabin, a demure look on her face with one of the books held out to him.

"You said—"

"I did indeed. Give me your coat . . . Lolly." First-name terms had been settled upon before he had left the Dalton home.

"Lolly." Did Donal's tone give the name a soft caress or was it her imagination? "Lolly"—never had it sounded so good, so right.

Angie filled the teakettle, stoked the stove, and bustled around setting out cups and serviettes and cutting fruitcake while Donal and Lolly settled themselves on the floor before a bookcase.

Donal sat cross-legged; Lolly was at his side with her skirts spread around her on the rag rug. They happily debated the superiority of Cooper's *Leather Stocking Tales* over his *Sea Tales*, of Nathaniel Hawthorne's work over George Eliot's. They mutually scorned the gravely solemn works of one Samuel Smile: *Duty*; *Thrift*; *Character*; *Self-Help*.

"Can you take seriously anything a man named Smile might have to say?" Donal asked, and they laughed.

"Who is this Bertha M. Clay, anyway?" Lolly wanted to know, pointing to that author's books: *Lover or Friend*, *Love's Broken Chain*, and *Foiled by Love*.

"I don't know, but it gives me a new insight into Uncle Willoughby—that's for sure. Those books may have turned him from love and marriage forever."

"Ah, the Alcott works," Lolly said with pleasure, choosing one and one only. Being a quick reader and without much to do now that she was almost completely confined to the house and its limited amount of work for two women, a trip for books would be a perfect solution on two scores: it would indeed get her out of the house and, blessed secret reason, make it possible to see Donal.

After the tea and a visit with Angie, a romp with Frankie, and her first meeting with Dave, who came in at that moment red-nosed and cheery to give Angie a hug and the baby a toss in the air and to meet Lolly delightedly, Lolly put on her coat, hugged *Under the Lilacs* to her in her gloved hands, and turned to go.

She wasn't even yet across the yard when Donal bounded down the steps and called, "Hey, wait!"

Lolly turned, smiling, to walk backward until Donal reached her side. Then, companionably, they walked down the road together, as naturally as if they belonged together. *As if they belonged together!*

Almost to the Dalton home, Donal turned back. But first he turned Lolly toward him, his hands on her elbows, and looked down into her rosy face raised so naturally to his. "Hurry through the book," he said with a smile, and she dimpled up at him.

"I think I'm about to become a scholar," she said. "If you decide there are subjects I need to study, feel free to bring them on over."

It would have been such a perfect moment for a kiss. The silence of the woods called for it; the secrecy of winter's first snowflakes falling around them in an enveloping shroud invited it; late afternoon's dusk awaited it. In that breathless, beautiful, special moment—Faithful, Toby's dog, rushed upon them with wild, joyous capering.

Donal loosed his grip on Lolly's arms, stepped back, and drew a deep breath. Or was it a sigh?

Leaving her, he walked backward until, lost in the curtain of snow, he turned and walked briskly home.

"Umm—some girl!" Dave said with a wink when Donal came in. Angie, of course, had told him all about her new friend Lolly, and Donal's interest was plain to be seen. Neither Dave nor Angie blamed him!

Donal took his coat off and sat for a few minutes by the fire. He looked at the flame that flickered behind the mica window and put his damp shoes up on the foot rail of the Merry Sunshine Heater with its "full nickel top, improved duplex grate and shaking rings."

Donal's earlier happiness had fled, leaving his face downcast.

"Hey, man, what's wrong?" Dave asked, "Lolly turn you down—already?"

Donal shook his head. "Nothing like that. I just don't know if I have the right to pursue anything—that way—with her. It's this place—or rather the leaving of it—and that miserable old man's miserable way of getting me involved uselessly!"

"I can see it's made you miserable, all right," Dave said, and got the expected smile. But it was a brief one.

"I have nothing, absolutely nothing to offer her! What sort of a girl would go along with a fella like that?"

"Angie, for one," Dave offered, and Donal murmured "Sorry. Maybe Angie's one of a kind."

"A girl who loves you—that's who would go along with a fella like that," Angie said. "You know, 'Whither thou goest, I go,' and all that." Donal was silent.

"That old gaffer," he half groaned eventually, angry at

Willoughby Ames again. "He sure didn't do me any favors, for all his big talk. I should have had a place by now, with a house—"

"But it wouldn't have been in Wildrose, more than likely," Dave reminded him. "And you'd never even so much as set eyes on Lolly Dalton."

"That's right," Angie confirmed. " 'In all thy ways acknowledge him'—remember?"

"You're right, of course. I haven't prayed enough about it."

"What's more," Angie encouraged, "Lolly will be praying about it too—you may be sure."

"How can we go wrong?" Donal concluded with a smile, albeit a wry one.

And so Donal prayed and tried to plan. Lolly prayed and kept her heart in peace. Angie and Dave prayed and trusted.

Can that much prayer escape the ear of the Father who invited, "Call unto me," and who promised, "I will answer thee, and show thee great and mighty things, which thou knowest not"? (Jer. 33:3).

The answer came in due time and according to His will one snowy afternoon. It was followed almost immediately by great and mighty things.

Lolly had agreed to "sit" with Frankie while Dave and Angie had a few hours to themselves. True, it was only to drive to Meridian in the cutter for supplies and mail, but privacy of any kind was hard to come by in a small home in the middle of a winter with its smothering snows.

Off they set, with a wave and a smile, leaving Lolly rocking Frankie, who was soon to go down for his afternoon nap.

"He'll be in soon—wanna bet?" Dave said as he and Angie sped off, confident that Donal was even now making his way from the barnyard to the house.

When Lolly returned from putting Frankie down, Donal had swept his boots free of snow, removed his coat and ear-flapped cap, and was warming his hands at the heater. It was their first-ever time alone, except for their drives and walks through the winter landscape.

Was it surprising, then, that she paused as she entered the room until Donal raised his head and looked at her, his eyes steady and unwavering, and, needing no other invitation, flew across the room and into the arms that were spread to receive her?

It was heaven on earth. It was bliss. It was all dreams fulfilled.

Finally, "Sit, my love," he said huskily, and she did, but very near to her beloved and never letting go of his hand except for a futile attempt to tidy her tumbled hair.

"We have to talk," Donal finally managed, soberly, and Lolly looked at him with starry eyes and agreed.

"I don't know when we can marry—," he began, on a groan that was part longing and part despair.

"I'll wait."

"This place, Lolly, isn't mine—"

"I know."

"I have no prospects, absolutely none at the moment. And when I do locate another homestead, it may not be in Wildrose."

"It doesn't matter."

"It may mean hard-scrabble times. Not a lot of cash, a small cabin, at first, a great deal of work—"

"I'm ready."

So prompt were her answers, so steady her voice, so firm her commitment, that Donal, with now a full-fledged groan, took her in his arms again. "Oh, Lolly . . ."

"See, Donal," she said tenderly and never for a moment

considered it a strange thing to believe, "things don't matter. We'll have everything that counts most."

Even the sandman was on their side, for Frankie slept on. The fire burned low, was replenished, burned low again, and was stirred into life again before time had any meaning to Donal and Lolly.

They were waiting at the door, warm-lipped and smiling, when Dave and Angie reached home. Explanations were unnecessary. Laughter and hugs sealed the bargain, it seemed, and a cup of tea further confirmed it while the four talked and planned and finally brought Frankie out to join the general air of festivity.

"Say—I forgot for the moment," Dave said, going to his coat and extracting an envelope from his pocket, "but there's a letter for you."

Letters were always something special, and this one looked official. Donal tore it open, read it, read it again, and looked up to meet the waiting glances of the other three.

"He beat me," he said with an unbelieving shake of the head. "The old rascal. He's beat me for sure."

"He?"

"Uncle Willoughby. I might just as well have given in from the first. This letter"—Donal indicated the paper in his hand—"is from the Lands Office. They're writing," he read, " 'at the request of Willoughby Ames.'

"Uncle Willoughby," Donal finished with a burst of pure laughter, "has abandoned his homestead!"

About the Author

A Place to Call Home is Ruth Glover's sixth book in the Wildrose Series, and she is a contributor to numerous Christian periodicals. Mrs. Glover was raised in the Saskatchewan bush country where she experienced firsthand the dangerous beauty that she describes so richly in her books.

The author and her husband, Hal, currently live in The Dalles, Oregon, where he is a retired pastor. The couple have three children and several grandchildren.